STEALING PROPELLER HATS FROM THE DEAD

DAVID JAMES KEATON

PMMP

Perpetual Motion Machine Publishing
Cibolo, Texas

Stealing Propeller Hats from the Dead
Copyright © David James Keaton 2015

www.PerpetualPublishing.com

Cover Art by George Cotronis www.ravenkult.com
Jacket Design by Dyer Wilk www.aseasonofdusk.com
Interior Art by Luke Spooner www.carrionhouse.com

ADVANCE PRAISE

"The collection's ironic B-movie sensibility taps into the ongoing obsession with zombies and what they represent: the thin line between the human and the monstrous, and our desire to be scared, to 'always keep our radio between stations.' The author's joy in his subject matter is obvious, often expressed with a sly wink and wicked smile. Decay, both existential and physical, has never looked so good."

—Publishers Weekly [Starred Review]

"It is impossible to have more fun reading than this. Z-fic that is steeped in the gonzo tradition on pages that flap when you turn 'em. I dig it."

—Tony Burgess—*Pontypool Changes Everything* and
People Live Still in Cashtown Corners

"Keaton combines smart, subversive high-mindedness with flat-out genre thrills like no one working today, and *Zee Bee & Bee* pulls off that balance about as well as you could hope for. It works just as well as an odd, slightly silly, weirdly romantic horror comedy, a heartfelt love letter to the width and breadth of zombie culture, and a wild and witty deconstruction of everything that 's come before it."

—David Tallerman—*Writing On The Moon*

"Take warning before you crack the cover. Plan. I mean, figure that three, four, five hours after you read sentence one, you will stagger to your feet and hurry for the bathroom because you've been holding off the urgent need to pee for at least an hour. You'll need a *big* glug of water because you're dehydrated from mouth breathing *fast* for hours. You'll need a quart of Visine because your eyes will be burning. Yes. It moves just that fast . . . "

—A.J. Hayes

"Unfortunately, I just couldn't get into the writing style . . . "
—Sarah Jahier—*Fatally Yours*

"The writing here is sharp as a six thousand dollar suit. Tailor made. Keaton's voice rings out with an air of genuine American authenticity that is surprisingly lacking in a lot of contemporary commercial fiction. The plots function perfectly, but it's Keaton's style, voice, and artful wording that keep me reading sentence after sentence. A great man once said, in regard to writing well: Write every sentence. Keaton does just that."

—Jason Stuart—Author of *Raise A Holler*

" . . . there is some pretty clever dialogue that horror fans will appreciate though."

—Sarah Jahier—*Fatally Yours*

" . . . it's pretty much every damn zombie (don't use that word I said!) story and movie and history and reference and Theodore Sturgeon's *Some of Your Blood* and Dead Kurt V's *Harrison Bergeron, Welcome To The Monkey House* and *Catch-22* and *Frankenstein*—Doctor and Monster, both—and, oh, gee, about a billion other references that will suddenly tumble into your mind an hour or a day or, hell, for all I know, a lifetime later. And . . . oh, for gosh sake, buy it and read it. I'm running out of space and time and body parts."

—A.J. Hayes

"David James Keaton gnaws his tongue-in-cheek to a bloody stump in *Zee Bee & Bee,* a slick stream-of-consciousness (consciousness? zombies?) tale. On its surface, the snarky narrative seems almost too clever, but read beyond the obvious genre affection and surprisingly heartfelt details of everyday life and you come away with a strange nostalgia and fear for a self-absorbed culture's obsession with their next slice of entertainment."

—Walt Hicks—*Page Horrific*

"Calling all zombiephiles! (is that a word? who better to ask?) This is one zombie experience you don't want to wait until you're dead to have. Get your 'Z' Love on. D.J.K. is the Zombie Man."

—Randy Chandler—Author of *Daemon of the Dark Wood* and
Dime Detective

"A few of the finest zombie tales of recent years . . . [*Zee Bee & Bee*] is the zombie story against which all should be judged going forward . . . a crown jewel to this collection of stellar fiction."

—Tim Potter—*The Horror Review*

"B-B-B-Bollocks!"

—King George VI

TABLE OF CONTENTS

RESURRECTED FICTIONS FOUND WITHIN THESE PAGES WERE ORIGINALLY ENTOMBED IN THE FOLLOWING PUBLICATIONS:

"Greenhorns," *Tony Baloney's Pan Galactic Shit Show*

"Do the Münster Mash," *Fish Bites Cop! Stories to Bash Authorities* (Comet Press)

"What's Worst?" *Cavalcade of Terror* (Undead Press)

"Zee Bee & Bee (a.k.a. Propeller Hats for the Dead)" *Deadcore: 4 Hardcore Zombie Novellas* (Comet Press)

"The World's Second Shortest Zombie Story," *Horror d'oeuvres* (Dark Fuse)

"The Ball Pit (or Children Under 5 Eat Free!)," *Spiders* (May December Publications)

"Doppelgänger Radar," *Fish Bites Cop! Stories to Bash Authorities* (Comet Press)

"Three Ways Without Water (or The Day Roadkill, Drunk Driving, and the Electric Chair Were Invented)," *Pulp Modern II* (Uncle B. Publications)

FOR GEORGE ROMERO, WHO STARTED
AND ENDED IT ALL

LOOK BUSY!

Foreword by David Tallerman

DAVID JAMES KEATON is going to be famous as hell. I mean, as much as he's been carving himself a more-than-respectable niche in the small press over the last couple of years, it's tough to imagine that those achievements are more than the lighting of the touchpaper on his rise to stratospheric fame. After all, the wider publishing world can only stay blind to what this guy's up to for so long. Maybe history is full of tales of talent going unnoticed until it was too late to do said talent any good, but this is the 21st century, damn it, news travels fast. Surely it can only be a matter of time before the right editor gets fried with a thousand volts of Keatonesque pulp-literary goodness?

So depending on when you read this, me saying, "David James Keaton is going to be famous" might not be much of a prediction. Maybe you're skimming through this and his first novel is already out and winning awards and getting all sorts of praise from all sorts of people and you just finished watching him talk up a storm with Letterman (post-retirement) or shaking hands with the President and you found yourself wondering what else this David James Keaton dude had done. Maybe the thought that there was a time when he labored in obscurity was just so damn tough to wrap your head around that you

I

figured you'd better hunt up some of his early work. In which case . . . welcome, visitor from the future! Take care to strap that Steelers helmet on tight before the bodily fluids starts flying.

Then again, maybe this here book has just come out and you're one of the faithful who've been following Keaton all along. In that case, I'd like to think you read that potentially brash statement above and thought, "No shit, Sherlock!" After all, this is just another date in your love affair with his peculiar body of work, right? Probably you came across one of his early stories and realized that here was something special, something new, something you'd need to see through until its end, however much of your life that happened to eat up. I hope so. I know I did.

I first came across Keaton's fiction in an anthology we both had stories in, a collection of crime and horror fiction named *The Death Panel*. It was a great book, all told, with nary a bad story within its pages. But one piece stuck out like a sore and badly mangled thumb. Keaton's "Nine Cops Killed for a Goldfish Cracker" was something else altogether. Not only was it great, it was unique. I'd literally never read a thing like it.

Which was pretty amazing, first because I read a fair bit and second because, although the small press often throws up excellent work, the one thing you never really expect to find there is the unique. You don't expect to have your mind crowbarred wide open and its contents smeared across the ceiling. You don't expect to have your perspective on the world kicked over like a tower of puppies. Yet there it was, larger than life and at least five times as ugly—a true original.

"Nine Cops" was funny as all fuck. It was sharp, weird and vicious, and it was clever, too. Word-clever, sure, in the way it toyed with language like a cat with a dying bird, but also genuinely-smart-clever, in how it shouldered its way through the usual rules of narrative to make its own path, one more digressive and yet unexpectedly, impossibly, straighter and more true.

But more than all of those things, it was humane. I think Keaton might just hate me for saying this, but it's that quality that makes me love his work, more than the wit and the cleverness and the sly melding of pop and highbrow culture. It's superb writing about flawed people. Because however much he might want you to think otherwise, Keaton cares about this people stuff. He writes characters you can believe in and even fall in love with for a little while, even when it's clear they don't entirely deserve it. His work never lacks for a heart, even when said heart is black as the blackest pitch. The perfect example is his novella "Zee Bee & Bee"—a.k.a., in case you hadn't noticed, "Propeller Hats for the Dead," the black heart at the center of this collection.

You might think at first glance that in this case, that heart isn't only black, it's stopped beating altogether. But put your ear a little closer and really listen. Somewhere amidst that barrage of pop culture references and sharp verbiage, head-spinning wordplay, and bone-crunching violence, you'll hear the unmistakable throb of a pulse. For in the midst of death we are in life, and the best zombie fiction has nothing whatever to do with the deceased. Who are these characters who shamble through the darkness spouting movie quotes and tearing strips—both literal and metaphorical—off of each other? Who are these losers, these crazies, these no-hopers who can no longer tell life from death, game from reality, sex from violence?

As the spiritual godfather of this novella would no doubt point out—and as Sour Towel Zombie would be the first to reiterate—"They're us."

DAVID JAMES KEATON

The first time I read it, as much as I was thrilled and fascinated by it, I didn't fully understand "Zee Bee & Bee." I don't immediately understand a lot of what Keaton does. I'm okay admitting that. I don't understand gravity, but I'm glad as hell it's there and that I get to enjoy its benefits. Anything that stops my plummeting into space is all right by me. Likewise for anything that pops my brain out and dropkicks it far past my comfort zone.

In this case, though, I'm glad I got the opportunity to come back—to reread these Frankenstein's Monsters crafted from four decades of zombie culture and Keaton's own strange headspace. They deserve it. Like great albums, they let up their deepest revelations only under close attention. Like a great lover that intrigues you and scares you the more you get to know it. Like a great zombie movie that suckers you in before it starts painting the walls with intestinal tract.

So if you're reading this in the future, you should have gathered by now that you're in for something special. And if you're a Keaton regular coming back for another dose then, hey, good call. Either way—welcome to the Z B & B. This is where the world ends every weekend.

Look busy.

INTRODUCTION
SCARE QUOTES AND COFFIN RIDES

SO . . . **AMY'S FRIEND** Jen was flying in from Memphis that day, and she wanted to hit all the Pittsburgh landmarks like the Duquesne Incline (insert picture of the worst ride at any theme park), that crazy church they turned into a bar (insert picture of weeping Jesus and Church Brew Works), the overrated Primanti Brothers (insert picture of inspired truck driver jamming an entire meal into a sandwich so he can deliver that Coors), the site of that motherfucking rapist Roethlisberger's near decapitation (insert picture of headless stone statue), etc., etc. Also, despite being like two foot two, Jen apparently thinks of herself as some sort of competitive eater because she engulfed an omelet bigger than a hubcap and then wanted to hit up the "Atomic Hot Wings Challenge" at Quaker Steak and Lube (most deceptive restaurant title ever) before I was barely out of bed.

But it was already a big day. That morning, I'd just gotten word that my zombie story, "Zee Bee & Bee," a tale that had gotten out of hand and expanded way past the point of publishability and had been chopped up into more anthology-friendly pieces, was finally being published in its entirety (as you'll see it's even longer now, as well as both more and less fucked up). So to celebrate we decided to check out "Monroeville Zombies" a.k.a. "The Mysterious New Zombie Museum at the Monroeville Mall I Kept Hearing About At Work," the not-so-hidden shrine for George Romero's original masterpiece *Dawn of the Dead*.

"Maybe Jen could add this to her Pac-Man tour?" I begged. "We'll still eat something weird, I promise! Pleeeeease?"

This was easier said than done. First off, it was getting late in the day, and we were still dealing with Chicken Wing Hiroshima, or The Day We Do Not Speak Of.

See, Jen had signed a waiver before she started eating those nuclear wings, in case of an untimely death, but where was my waiver? Because the boneless wings with the "mild" sauce that I ordered (translation "for pussies") were barely friggin' edible at all. Amy was filming Jen's valiant, red-faced attempt to get down that last wing *Cool Hand Luke* style (more like *Burning Hand Luke* style if you made the mistake of touching the suckers, and God help you if you tried to piss afterwards), but I kept trying to point her camera phone at my desperate attempts to penetrate a boneless wing with a plastic fork. "Wing," my ass. Try "flipper." It was impossible. This was the true challenge they did not dare advertise. Luckily, there were wrenches and screwdrivers glued to the walls because, hey, it's a theme joint. But I have to assume those are sneakily stuck up there in case of a rubber-chicken-penetration emergency and not really for the kitsch factor at all.

So, while I was still whining about my meal, Jen ate that last toxic fin, er, wing, grabbed her awesome "trophy" (a.k.a. "crappy bumper sticker") and we ran out the door to meet my friend Nate at the mall before the exhibit closed. See, Nate's kind of a zombie connoisseur and the type of guy who takes his apocalyptic scenarios more seriously than most, so I figured he'd dig this "museum" we'd somehow missed.

(By the way, there will be more scare quotes than usual in this adventure. You know, the ones they used in newspaper headlines to be sly and/or indicate insincerity? The ones they put around "doctors" in those books about Nazi medical experiments? Apologies for that. I mean, "sorry.")

Okay, so there we were. It's like 5:15, and the internet was telling us the Zombie Museum closed at 6:00. So we come flying in the Barnes & Noble side of the mall at Mach 2, and we (me) immediately get distracted by zombie anthologies and DVDs on an endcap. So by the time we get into the mall itself to claw at the directory, it's 5:30. And, of course, there's no listing for anything containing the word "zombie" or "museum."

Amy tries asking some employees at a jewelry store and gets back an audible scoff in return. Nope, no idea what she's talking about. So Amy and Jen wander off to get some ice cream, sort of giving up (and Jen needs ice cream to wash the delicious atomic chemicals out of her mouth), but Nate and I are still hopeful. We notice a GameStop out of the corner of our eyes, ("Gotta be movie geeks in there, right, right?!"), and we run inside.

There are two employees working. One is a very athletic-looking young man who's not doing much of anything. The other is the expected slovenly, disheveled, basement-dweller type who is furiously helping some screeching family buy games for their Wii. Do they still make a Wii? Or is it now Wii III? Either way, I choose poorly. The sporty kid doesn't seem to understand anything I'm saying, let alone where this mysterious "museum" is. But then, like a chorus of angels, Mr. Disheveled tips his head towards us, never even looking up from his transaction, to explain within the duration of his weary sigh:

"Take a right out of the store, take a left by the escalators, a left where they used to sell snowmobiles, a right where Old Man Witherspoon's barn used to be, a right near the creek, a left near the Hurricane Booth, and there you'll find a toy store. It's in the back of the toy store."

Holy shit, we're back in business. 5:53 and counting. As Nate and I run out and grab Jen and Amy like a couple of footballs, I swear I see Disheveled mutter into his watch just like those creepy skeletal secret alien overlords in *They Live*:

"I'm sending down four more."

But there it is! Buried in the back, a converted storeroom entrance in the shadows of this toy store reads, "Zombie Museum." And it apparently doesn't close any time soon. None of this "Open till 6:00" bullshit like it warned us on the website. But there's no one in here at all. Just some punk on his laptop messing with Facebook who doesn't even stop Jen and Amy from bringing in drippy ice creams.

But for a museum, hell, it's not bad! Small but heartfelt. Sad but earnest. Among the attractions: full-size replicas of the Nazi Zombie from *Shockwave*, poor, doomed Flyboy and pint-sized Roger from the original *Dawn of the Dead* (Flyboy is in his tragic limp-necked final state, of course), the barrel with the Army stamp and emergency phone number from *Return of the Living Dead* (yeah, don't "dial down the center," dude, unless you want a mushroom cloud for breakfast), authentic severed-limb props from the original trilogy with blood bladders and tubes still attached, a TV running the special features off the '78 *Dawn of the Dead* DVD, an actual framed newspaper headline from *Day of the Dead* screaming, "The Dead Walk!" but, thank Christ, with none of those insincere quotation marks around "dead" to ruin it, and, last but not least . . .

The coffin ride.

Wh-What? Well, there's this full-size coffin being guarded by a replica of the graveyard zombie from *Night of the Living Dead*. Unfortunately, he's holding up a sign that reads:

"Sorry! Coffin Ride Out Of Order."

But there's nothing at all to indicate that this is a "ride." It's really just a coffin. With a small milk crate step to climb up and flop on into the coffin. No electrical cords, no lights, no controls of any kind. Just the coffin. So we start to suspect that this "coffin ride" might be, uh, death? So if it wasn't out of order, maybe you would pay your dollar and . . . get shot in the face? It raises all sorts of questions. At first, we think, okay, maybe it sort of vibrates like those lame vehicles outside a K-Mart, but the more we talk about it, the more we're sure it means that, yes, you will be killed. We don't dare ask the punk at the counter 'cause I learned my lesson earlier when I foolishly tried to get an extra large T-shirt with the "Monroeville Zombies" hockey logo on it and I only saw small and mediums hanging. But Captain Spacebook mumbled, "No, those are the most popular, so we never have 'em." Which was very Yogi Berra. Like saying, "Yeah, no one goes to that restaurant anymore because it's too crowded."

So, anyway, that's about it, I think. What else did we do? What else could we do? We watched the TV cycling the special features off the *Day of the Dead* so I could point out that all the zombie extras were also munching on hot wings during those movies, just like Jen (apparently because it most resembled delicious human flesh), and we got some cool snapshots of the scale-model dollhouse replica of a Monroeville Mall of the '70s (ice rink included?!), and I even snuck some bubble-gum machine Homies onto the teeny dollhouse escalators to pose for some pics with all the toys (security was quite lax, remember? "No Shirt, No Shoes, Bad Service"), and then, when other people started to wander on in, we wandered on out.

But at the door, there was this one hyperactive brat who seemed to be making fun of the meager attractions, as we'd been tempted to do before our communion, and Nate surprised us all by cornering this snarky little fuck away from his parents and hissing:

"Listen, kid, when I was your age, zombies were real!"

And get this, remember that "Hurricane Booth" that the other clerk mentioned earlier on our adventure? It actually existed, too. But, sadly, it was just as busted as the coffin ride. A sign on it promised "200 mile per hour winds!" so we quickly bullied Amy inside (the only one of us wearing a skirt), and I desperately tried to get it to take my dollar. Nothing. Well, not exactly nothing. The second the glass door closed her inside, a crowd magically appeared, expectant looks on their faces, as if that's what the dollar paid for, rubberneckers. I'm not kidding. It was like *bam!* Suddenly, out of the hazy fog of mall odors, there was now a crowd watching me fumble with my soggy dollar and Amy scratch at the glass like she was in a microwave set on "broil." I swear some of these bystanders must have rappelled out of the ceiling at the prospect of seeing some nudity. But much to their disappointment, we let Amy and her skirt back out of the booth, never knowing what the booth really did at all, if anything (had to be a microwave, seriously). But now that I'm typing this, I wonder if its function all along was to authentically imitate the experience of a hurricane's devastation by just taking all your money and then spitting out a small piece of paper that states:

"Now you're homeless."

Oh, yeah, there really was a "creek," too. No joke. Sure, it was more like a stagnant little pond, right outside the store with a tiny bridge going across it, but, still, there was a river in this mall. Just like that clerk said. A stern sign nearby warned, "Don't feed the fish!" and, sure enough, it was packed full of those bloated, sluggish mutant koi (koys?) that you see in septic pools at your local zoo. Remember those squirming abominations and those black, horrific ponds? Talk about an aquarium of the undead.

And this creek was full of money, too. So, apparently, you couldn't "feed" the beasts because that's cruel, but you could whip coins (koins?) at their heavy, bulbous heads. One of the big ones even had this big, nasty black hole in its side, right near the gills. Clearly the result of a child's wish gone wrong. What did the little cherub say before those lethal pennies were launched side-arm into the creek? "I hope these fishies are happy!" Smack. "I wuv you!" Thud.

As we were leaving, we did consider trying to "rescue" the injured one for a good minute or so. Translation: "Grab the struggling, diseased, foot-long monster and bumble out the door, chased by security the whole way, so it can likely die in my car."

Coffin ride indeed.

Anyway, to make a long story longer, and to celebrate the release of my first collection of zombie fiction that you now hold in your fins, our intrepid crew will be heading back to Pittsburgh tonight to tackle that ride again! I mean, tonight! Or . . . tonight, depending on when exactly you threw dropped your dollar into the hurricane to ride this thing.

And you know what? It's no accident that coffin rides,

hurricane booths, and zombie collections are all a buck in this brave, new, digital world. Is that devaluing "literature"? Maybe. But maybe a buck is all you need for anything. Also, in an attempt to entice readers who may be familiar with these stories' early incarnations, besides the re-insertion of more disturbing elements and a reckless indulgence of some narrative dead-ends, I've attempted to add even more Bang For Your Buck than this endless introduction. So if you flip to the end of this godforsaken thing (you may need to use a button if we're digital, but, fuck it, it's still your thumb sorta flipping, right?), you will find, finally compiled in its glorious entirety, *Send More Paramedics: The Zombie Movie Drinking Game.* I would have put it up here before you started reading the story so you could drink and play along, but we tried that with some volunteers just last night. And, yeah, it was fatal.

Don't be like them.

Okay, hit the book or the buttons with every thumb you got, even the thumbs you were saving for hitchhiking to the Monroeville Mall, or that special thumb you were saving for lunch. And thank you sincerely for reading my stuff.

David James Keaton

5:30 p.m. Eastern Daylight Time
July 3rd, 2015
Louisville, Kentucky

GREENHORNS

THE SIX NEW recruits stagger up the ramp, heads down, feet dragging, gear slung over slumped shoulders, mouths pulsing in exhaustion. The job hasn't started yet, but they are already sluggish from the night before, an informal orientation at the bar where the captains selected new crew for the beginning of King Crab season. Jake had competed for a spot on a crab boat before, playing violent party games like Mumblety-Peg, Knifey-Spoony, or the dreaded Record Races, where you supposedly ran relays with vinyl LPs in the crack of your ass or whatever the hell else a deckboss thought up to make you dance for your dinner. But he had never auditioned so hard before.

All night long, the captains had them bounce from table to table to enlist in every possible drinking and eating competition known to man, stuffing bellies with vast amounts of burger, bear, beer, cod, beer, some Australia import called a "Bogan Burger," which was a sandwich apparently crammed with kangaroo, beef, egg, bacon, ham, elk, emu, reindeer, tofu, squirrel, rabbit, ostrich, platypus, shrimp, turducken, and rumor had it, man (but more likely just a ton of bear pressed into different shapes). And more beer, of course. Jake vaguely remembers passing out after some arm-wrestling turned thumb-wresting tournament, where the girth of the victor's biceps were logged and recorded for posterity. They weren't his.

There sure was a lot measuring going on that night, he realizes as he sizes up his new shipmates. All the rulers reminded Jake of his first day of kindergarten, when his mom drew a crayon outline of him on the wall to show him how much he would grow. The outline never got much bigger. And eventually his brother traced it with masking tape and X'd out his eyes to call it a crime scene.

"Hurry the fuck up, greenhorns," comes a voice from the deck. It's weary, disengaged, seemingly uninterested in whether the crew heard it or not, kind of like someone telling their dog about a particularly long workday.

Jake squints through his headache and the rest of his shanghaied brothers to scan the imposing girth of his new home, and he can't help but smile when he spots the nuclear-waste logo on the bow.

It's the *Gone Fission*, the biggest ship in the fishing fleet. It took its name from a baseless rumor that it was actually a converted World War II mine-sweeper. He remembers the boat from the show *Crab Masters*, at its peak the most popular television program on the planet. His brother even had their original logo stitched onto a baseball cap, a crab flipping the bird, a combination that made even less sense than the one they painted on the bow with their Hollywood money.

Greenhorns.

Jake always hated all those labels. "Swabby," "nugget," "squid," "wog," "pollywog," "fumblefuck." They all meant the same thing to him, "half pay."

"Naw, 'greenhorn' is the *worst,* man," a deckhand told him once. "You know what that shit came from? It means a freshly slaughtered calf, so young the horns pop off in your hands like cucumbers."

***

Once aboard and one lap around the stern, the six of them

are divided into pairs. The deckboss, Randy (just coffee breath and a beard peeking out of a rubber orange hood like the rest of them, but a lot more smiley), he says they'll be working shifts two at a time to prove themselves. Competition apparently didn't end at the bar.

"Two by two!" he barks. "And we'll pick the best two. Just like Noah's ark!"

"How is that like Noah's ark?" Jake can't help but ask. "They took two of *everything*."

The grinning beard twitches, happy that someone took the bait.

"Not everything, boy! Read your fuckin' Bible. Unicorns didn't cut it. And guess what color that horn was?"

Before anyone can answer, another hooded beard is pulling them along and explaining they'll be on bait duty. He says it so quiet they barely hear him.

Then all six of them spend the rest of the night hacking up crabs. King Crabs. Jake can't believe it. As he pops the legs and cores the meat out of a Red Alaskan the size of a medium pizza, he looks around for another orange slicker to ask more questions. When a crewman finally scurries by to drop off a hammer for chopping ice off the crane, Jake taps him on the shoulder with a broken crab claw.

"Hey, man. You don't use crabs to catch crabs, do you? This fucker's probably worth fifty bucks."

He doesn't answer. No one does, not even his fellow recruits. Jake looks around at the other five hangovers, all dutifully cracking shells. He's amazed at the number of greenhorns they've gathered for one trip, confused how a crab boat, even one as big as the *Gone Fission,* could ever sustain this kind of crew. What will the final numbers be? Half of a half of a half of a share? The math almost makes his nose bleed.

After a while, a bigger man with an even bigger beard shows them their bunks, then peels off two of the recruits to drag back out into the night to tie down the pots. Jake climbs into his bed and peeks out of a portal, watching them throw the ropes off the dock and head out.

"I can't believe we're leaving on a Friday," the greenhorn below Jake sighs, pulling a cowboy hat over his face. "I thought that shit was bad luck."

"Bad luck for someone is good luck for someone else," Jake offers, and closes his eyes.

He lies there, listening to everyone's stomachs bubbling as they work to process the new situation along with all the food and drink from the night before in Dutch Harbor. He waits for the first stomach to empty, and sure enough it splashes against the wall about an hour later.

Jake has been hungover before, but he's never been seasick. Ever. That night, he sleeps like a baby and dreams of his brother drawing lines around his body over and over as he's shrinking.

***

The next morning, one team of greenhorns is gone, and they're down to four.

In the galley, as they carb-load piles of eggs and doughnuts and fight to chug all the coffee they can, someone finally asks what happened to so-and-so, this guy and that guy. But crew members are already suiting up and moving through too fast to throw anything back at them but stock responses.

"Couldn't hack it."

"Weak."

"No heart."

"Pussies."

"We dropped them off."

"You dropped them *off*," Jake asks, without the question mark. "Where exactly?"

"Dogtooth Island," someone mutters.

Jake can't believe it. For one thing, he's never heard of any "Dogtooth Island" before, and, more importantly, one of the two newbies who's missing is Bobby "Stack" Hillstack. Stack was the biggest kid in Dutch, biggest kid by far at the bar the night before. Looked strong as hell, a little dumb, but tough as shit. Jake remembers at least five separate captains fighting to measure the monster's legs.

"What does that even mean, 'No heart'?" Jake scoffs, but scoffing real quiet.

Later out on deck, Jake helps shuffle the swaying metropolis of massive cages, or "pots" as they called them, into a more manageable pyramid. The pots are a wall of iron, pushing the ass end of their boat so low that the waves hit their faces as often as the hull. Jake notices the pots themselves have changed a bit since he's worked on a crab boat. As he steers the crane over to the stack, he kicks up something like a dog door on the end of one pot and then lets it drop back down.

It only swings one way. More like a raccoon trap than a dog door, he decides.

But "dog door" sounds better.

"Is this even necessary?" Jake asks. "They ain't *that* smart, are they? You just need a hole, don't ya?"

"You're about five questions past your limit today, kid, but I'll tell you this," Randy the deckboss says. "There's been a lot of debate about that very same inquiry lately. How smart they're getting. Shit, to save metal, we considered just making pots totally open-ended, like a tube."

"No joke?"

Randy pulls back his hood a bit to let in the sun,

almost let out a smile, then he screws his new cowboy hat tighter on his head.

"No joke."

Jake ponders this as he kicks at a pile of fish against the base of the crane. Looking closer, he notices teeth marks in a tuna, small half-circles with the uncanny resemblance of a football mouth guard running along its scales. Jake stares at the deep, pitted impressions, subconsciously flinching at the memory of a high-school bully dropping a steaming bowel movement into his football helmet one time after practice. For some reason, this kid, a Bobby Something, pulled this prank at least once a year on the smallest of the JV squad. Glancing around, Jake half-expects Bobby's shit-eating grin to pop out from under an orange hood at any moment. Back in high school, Jake never got the taste out of his own mouth guard and couldn't afford to buy a new one, but he'd be making real money now.

"Did they come up with those bites like that?" Jake asks. "What kinda fish has a mouth like that? Wait, how the hell . . ."

There's a squelch of static on the intercom, and Randy flinches and looks around, beard twitching guiltily. He Frisbees the cowboy hat away, and his hood comes back up fast, smile erased.

"Skipper wants to see you, boy. Go on up."

Jake shudders. When a captain wants to see you, up always feels like down.

But when he gets to the wheelhouse, the Captain doesn't let him come all the way up. He makes Jake stand on the stairs like he's in time-out while he lectures him about asking stupid questions, tucking in his gloves, talking when he should be listening, the usual crap Jake has heard all his life from all three of his dads.

But even though he's sequestered on the stairs, Jake

can still read the radar over the Captain's shoulder. On the screen is a thermal outline of a huge, red biomass. Excited, Jake points at it.

"Sir, aren't we steaming right over a ton of crab?"

The Captain smiles, and Jake braces for an ass-chewing. The Captain's a big Kenny Rogers-looking motherfucker, and Jake figures this lulls his crew into a false sense of comfort. But the smile doesn't slip. He does shake his head sadly though, clearly worried that nothing he's said has impressed Jake in the slightest.

Even growing up in harbor towns, Jake was never comfortable around captains, or any authority really. Captains' attitudes always reminded him of dirty cops. If there was only one dirty cop in the world and the world was only as big as the boat in your bathtub.

Then the Captain reaches back and flips a switch. Suddenly, the red blob turns blue and the blue one turns red.

"*That's* where we're going." A smile so big the hinge almost slips.

"Isn't it too warm for King Crab there? I thought we were headed for . . ."

"We'll be on them all tomorrow. Get some sleep, boy." The Captain is positively giddy now.

Don't say it, Jake thinks. *Don't say it . . .*

But of course the Captain says it.

"You'll need it."

***

That night in his cabin, Jake hears the crabs scuttling around in the hold. Tapping, tapping, tapping. But the echoes sound big, heavy. Too heavy. He figures there must be a pile of them tangled up, moving as one.

They don't act normal when their claws are tied shut, he tells himself. *I've seen it before. That's all it is.*

Jake tries rolling on his side in the rotting bunk to get

comfortable, using his tried-and-true tactic of focusing on a broken nail to keep the spins at bay. A couple of seasons back, he used to stare at a dog-eared Polaroid of his ex, Jennifer, until he lost it. Lost her, too. She didn't have a picture of him, but she did own a prized collection of cigarette lighters adorned with the deceased captains' faces from the cancelled show. Fuck her. Goddamn groupie.

Then he sits up, for the first time noticing the slew of abandoned electronics all around him. There's a camera mounted in each corner of the room, plastic bags over half of them, wires hanging from everything, even colonies of corroded batteries rolling across the floor with the dip of each wave.

Remnants of the show, he realizes, a bit awestruck. *Crab Masters.*

A much-revered, reality-based program that turned out to be the last of its kind, it dominated television right up until the final season, when every boat except this one suspiciously capsized in the finale.

In a way, that turned out to be the final season for everything, now that Jake thinks about it. Reality TV suddenly became a poor substitute for the sorry state of the world outside everyone's window.

He kicks over a bag hanging by his feet and hears his bunkmate grunt as it spills an intestinal coil of cable and rolls of masking tape across the metal floor. Someone had stenciled "gaffer" across the side, a word that makes Jake smile. The gaffer on a TV show and a fishing vessel were two very different creatures, but Jake thinks they would probably complement each other quite well. The gaff could stab a beast and haul it on board, while the gaffer taped up an outline of where it landed. Just like his brother.

Jake reaches behind his head to discover his lumpy

pillow is actually a backpack with official *Crab Masters* stickers slapped all over it. He dumps it out and finds a tightly-wound stack of pastel-colored index cards detailing the scripted reality of the show. He pulls three cards from the bottom of the pile and reads the final episode titles:

"Last Boat Standing," "Gone Fishing," and "Apocalypse Not!"

Jake smirks and puts the bag back behind his head to get comfortable for his flashback. He remembers the theme song of the original crab show where it all started, a similar show and the granddaddy of them all, belting out some dated, hair-metal power ballad given a new lease on life by pairing it with slow-motion shots of frosty breath and manual labor. Jake remembers waiting for their promo as a kid, right before the final Crab Count of each episode. His brother always tried to scare Jack by convincing him the announcer was saying, "Next time, Un*deadliest Catch!*" But it didn't work. Of course, he also mistook the show *Cops* for *"Cocks"* sometimes, but that wasn't as surprising.

Always bad at math, Jake loved that Crab Count. To him it sounded like more crabs than all the oceans could hold.

Later, as the waves and the heavy thumps and scratches deep in the hold rock him to sleep, a red link winks on the top of the camera at the foot of their bunks, and a tiny motor hums as the electronic eye bounces back and forth between the remaining faces.

***

The next day, Jake is pulled off bait, and he finally has the opportunity to haul real gear with the veterans. He's so excited to prove his worth that he doesn't notice they're down to just two greenhorns, including himself. It's just

Jake and Josh now. Josh being this lanky punk that Jake watched earn his golden ticket at the bar back in Dutch by keeping up pound for pound with the Captain's Salted Cod Chowdown. And, amazingly, *not* puking after the infamous Milk Gallon Challenge. Jake made the mistake of trying that challenge once. Once.

Josh is assigned to the bailer, coiling the rope that's coming out of the ocean boil, and Jake is put on the rail, ready to swing the cage once it comes up. There are hooded beards everywhere now, movements suddenly sharp in the flurry of activity, the cowboy hat riding different heads every few minutes like a beach ball at a rock concert. Jake notices they all carry huge Bowie knives on their hips and wonders when he'll get his.

"You'll get yours," Randy promises.

Then an air horn shrieks, and everyone freezes.

A pot is coming up.

Jake can hear by the strain of the line that it's full. He can tell by the creak of the cage that it's packed with squirming cash money, a massive, wriggling rich reward. He can't quite see through the crowd and spray, but the practiced eyes of a crew member to his right quickly assesses the bounty it holds, and he turns to silently signal the wheelhouse. He holds his arms high, then opens and closes both fists over and over:

Five, five, five, five, five.

There's a rousing cheer from the crew, and Jake frowns. Twenty King Crab? That's it? Doesn't seem like much to get excited about. He's still struggling with the math when the cage finally swings over the boat and bangs into the rail.

Then he sees what they've been hauling out of the Bering Sea, and his eyes go wide and burn in the salty mist. The yellow sea of slickers parts to reveal the cage, and Jake forgets all the math he ever learned, which wasn't much.

Flopping, fighting, squirming and elbowing for the door are dozens of mewling human beings. Black water empties from cracked noses and mouths, foam trickles from pitted holes picked to the bone by sea life, and deviled-egg eyeballs squint at a sun they've long forgotten. Jake recognizes them from comic books, horror movies, and reality shows alike, of course. It doesn't matter whether they're choking and coughing up water or just moaning like their famous fictional representations.

They are the dead, and that's what they've been fishing for all along.

***

In shock, Josh stops coiling and looks to Jake for help. Jake gives him a "let's get to work" shrug and grabs a corner of the cage to steer it to a sorting table the size of a festival stage. Josh gets ready to pop the dog door, and the crew is suddenly all around them and all business, heels of their hands on the butts of their knives, their long, hooked gaffs thrust out like gladiators.

The gaffs, Jake laughs to himself, thinking about the roll of masking tape in his cabin. He remembers his brother taping his outline on the wall, and, at that moment, he wishes he could climb inside.

Then the door is open and Jake isn't thinking about anything except how to steer the slippery, snapping abominations to the swirling drain in the floor.

The crew herds them to the open manhole with the skills of Animal Control, popping the grey skin of their necks with the tips of their hooks, stabbing and scruffing them like puppies. First up and away from the mob, then stuffing them down, down, down the hole, leaving just a bit of meat and scalp behind. One gaff hooks in too deep behind a lolling head, and a vertebrae pops out dangling like a busted gas cap. The corpse loses motor control and starts a breakdance seizure at their feet, hands squeaking for a desperate grip on any rubber raincoat.

"Fuck! That's a thousand bucks you just flushed, asshole!" the Randy deckboss yells.

Whoa, whoa, whoa. A thousand bucks?

Jake tries calculating again, while Randy pulls his Bowie knife and starts sawing under the dead man's chin. Tiny crabs and crustaceans ride the flood of pink water out of the corpse's throat as its moans turn to hisses, then gargles.

"Snuggle . . . nnnnn . . . guggle. Snort," it seems to sing.

That's when Jake sees Josh slip on the deck.

Sliding with the roll of the boat, he tumbles into the writhing gauntlet of bodies the crew has corralled with their hooks, and suddenly every dead eye rolls toward him like marbles. The hooded beards pull back and offer no help at all, one of them wringing the water from the cowboy hat. Randy actually stands up straight, sheathing his knife and snapping it secure with a yawn.

Jake starts to move in to help, and a crewman slaps him in the chest with a huge gloved hand.

"Don't move, boy."

Before Jake can protest, ten or so corpses fall on Josh to disassemble him like a piñata that's just hit the floor at a birthday. Purple hands scratch until they find a tiny hole in Josh's raincoat, then they make it bigger. Then they find his mouth and make that bigger, too. They stretch it so wide that Jake is convinced they're going to turn his head inside out, lips and jaw first, before any bones ever snap. Josh screams protests through it all, tongue rolling back into the deep crater that used to be his face as his struggles start to waver. That's when they find the ripe melon of his stomach, and punch and pull and dig until volcanoes of beer foam and gore surf meaty chunks of salted cod out into the sun.

Jake watches in silence as Josh is painted like a Jackson Pollock onto the deck next to everything else that gets gutted for bait. A cub of cod bounces off Jake's boot.

Jesus Christ, Jake realizes. *No wonder he won that contest. He was barely chewing.*

Jake stays quiet, up until one claw punches real deep and he gags at the white bomb of milk exploding from Josh's innards, bleaching the deck with proof of his ultimate victory at the Gallon Challenge. At the time, Jake couldn't believe he kept all that milk down, even accused him of cheating. He'd read somewhere that consuming a gallon of milk was impossible.

And they were right, he thinks wildly. *You just adjust the time limit to the next day and everything comes back.*

He watches dead men with milk moustaches angling for a drink, and imagines a billboard above it all reading, "Got Dead?" Then he laughs and pukes at the same time.

It's the first time he's ever done that at sea.

Then Josh's tongue is pulled free, and the screaming stops completely. Jake can't believe tongues have always been that long, buried so far inside people's heads. The boat pitches, and two crewmen slip on the blood.

Gaff indeed, Jake snickers, sanity slipping. He remembers half a conversation he had with a recruit two days prior. *Now there's a third definition for that word. Meaning "fuck up."*

Once they've eaten, the howling, waterlogged mob is considerably slower, and Jake stands back to watch the crew run them into the hold like cattle. When they're all below, Jake carefully creeps over the hole and looks down, watching them mill around underwater, making no attempt to surface. Sluggish with their loaded bellies and the weight of the hazy stew agitated around them, they bump the walls, hands probing for seams and bolts, lazily feeling for exits, pinballing around in drunken circles like old people doing water aerobics. The dead move slow enough without being submerged, and Jake finds that watching them down there is as soothing as those fish tanks in Chinese restaurants.

He finally snaps out of it when the crew pushes him aside and upends what's left of Josh into the hole. The black water swirls blacker as the underwater dance speeds up along with Jake's brain.

He grabs Randy the deckboss by the collar, but doesn't even get his question out.

"It's worth it, kid," Randy says, sympathetic smile. "It's hard work, but it's fuckin' worth it."

"There ain't nothing worth this," Jake snarls.

"Bullshit. If we didn't do it, someone else would."

"But how did they get down there? I mean, how are they . . ."

"You remember when all that shit went down? Back when they were, you know, everywhere?"

"No," Jake laughs. "I missed that when I was living under a rock. Why don't you tell me all about it."

"Well, we were fucked. Then suddenly we weren't fucked. Didn't you ever wonder why?"

"No, I mean I was seriously living under some rocks. I wasn't kidding. I missed a lot of it. But, yeah, it was the Army, right? They took care of it."

"Are you fucking kidding, boy? There ain't enough bullets in the world for everyone. Haven't you ever heard the story of the Marching Chinese?"

"No, but . . ."

"But nothing. They're all down there now. Down too

far for anyone to cash in except us professionals. To a military lab, they're worth ten times as much as the biggest King Crab. Sometimes more."

"Shit, that's almost worth as much as a real person," Jake says, even more sarcastic.

"Almost," the Captain's voice comes from behind him.

"They walk. It's as simple as that," the Captain explains. "That's the one thing they do. All day, even when it rains. And if you walk long enough on this planet, you're gonna hit fuckin' water. So that's where they all went. They cover the ocean floors like a living carpet. Thicker than Tanners, thicker than Opies in the off-season . . ."

"And they follow warm currents, don't they?"

"Yep. Which is good for them, and better for us. Keeps them away from the crab, mostly. But you can see by their faces that the critters down there will eventually pick 'em away to nothing. But they'll just keep walking until there's nothing left, walking where it's warm."

Suddenly, Randy the randy deckboss is grinning on Jake's other shoulder with a heavy hand rubbing his back.

"If you want to make good money, boy, consider joining this crew."

Jake considers it so hard his nose is really bleeding this time, and his stomach flips again.

Everything comes back up, he thinks. But they were making sense.

"Full share?"

They nod.

Then someone slaps a Viking helmet on his head with two horns painted bright green.

"I know it ain't easy, but you made it, kid!" the Captain says. "We needed one bait boy, just one. And you're it, goddamnit. You are *it*."

While he's thinking about hide-and-seek with his

brother and how it was punishment to be "it," they yank the Viking helmet and replace it with a baseball cap. Jake pulls it off to get a good look. Across the brim it reads, "Don't Worry, Mom! *Gone Fission!*"

He shakes his head, almost sniffling at the gravity of the ceremony. He's always wanted one. He can't lie.

"I always wanted one," he says, not lying.

Pats on the back, affectionate squeezes from Randy, suddenly less creepy.

"I'll do it," Jake announces, even with those horrible sounds under his feet.

He sleeps well that night, like all men do after hard work for good money.

***

The next day, Jake drinks black coffee with the crew and can't believe he didn't dream of his brother. He looks around. He's the last of the greenhorns. Five young men gone. He doesn't need to dwell on this. Jake was never good at math, but subtraction wasn't usually a problem.

But today, they treat him different. Not cruel, like at the bar, but with a crushing indifference that somehow feels worse. He's watched every episode of that crab show, both crab shows, all crab shows, long before the world turned to shit, so he assumes this is just the typical shunning of a new crew member. A little more hazing out of habit.

"Come on, boy," someone claps him on the back. "Get the fuck out there. You're on bait."

Out in the blast of sunlight and brutal wind, Jake checks the bin but only sees a couple strips of scales in the pile of snow and ice.

"What bait?" he asks, but there's suddenly no one around to answer.

He walks around the deck to find the deckboss alone, standing near a cage primed to go over the rail.

"Are we out of crab already . . ." Randy asks kind of without asking. Without looking at Jake either. He doesn't wait for an answer. ". . . then check the hook in this pot. There might still be enough meat for one more soak."

Jake opens the dog door and leans in to check the hook. There's a chunk of something red hanging, and he tugs to gauge if it's enough to set the trap. His nostrils flare in alarm, and he takes a closer look. It's certainly not crab, or fish. He thinks it could be a piece of skate, but "hopes" is more like it. Whatever it is still grips the hook, even without its body.

He's still hoping right up until he sees the fingers.

Then there's a work boot kicking him hard in his spine, and the door slams shut, dumping him facedown in the cage. Three of the crew stomp on the bottom of the dog door to trap him inside. Then, as a final insult, a gloved hand reaches in to snatch the baseball cap back off his head.

"Motherfucker," Jake hisses, teeth clenched so hard a molar fractures.

The crane starts to whine, and Jake grips the bars to get ready for his ride.

The beards watch emotionless as he goes over the rail, though one of the men seems to hold a cowboy hat over his heart. And down he goes. Down to the bottom.

At first, his hatred keeps him warm. Jake's brother once told him that you could only live three minutes in water this close to the North Pole, that you would never touch bottom. But Jake discovers it's more like nine when you're angry.

He makes it all the way.

It's dark, but he can see. And he sees more of them down there than he ever suspected. Thousands, maybe millions, a lurching idiot parade of green skin, grasping hands and teeth, all eyes locking on, tattered arms spiraling in toward his cell like the first tiny hurricane of hot soup around a spoon. Crowding through the door, they surge into the cage with him, find him fast where he's hanging onto the hook, cracking his bones as easy as green vegetables, biting, biting, finding all the existing holes in his body where the soup is the warmest.

Then they start making their own holes. Their fingers and tongues worm into these new spaces like the slick, hairless heads of buzzards.

And right before the red water turns black forever, Jake sees one of them lift the dog door and hold it high above its head to let the rest of them march in as efficient as any crew. They know what to do. They know where they're going. They know the drill.

Everything comes back . . .

With the last of his strength, Jake tries to protect his mouth and lets them ruin the rest.

He hopes he still has some teeth when his crew hauls him back up.

...AND I'LL SCRATCH YOURS
(OR THE ONE WHO HAD NONE)

*"Let's get up off the floor and use our feet for hands.
I see double, I see double yellow lines."*
—Everything Everything, "Feet for Hands"

WHEN SHE WAS just a kid, for a few glorious years, Flora had the perfect backscratcher. It was a busted bat, the result of a baseball hit all wrong and visibly throwing a ripple of pain down the player's arms, then hurled away in disgust so hard it whipped over the dugout and into the crowd, catching Flora's dad in the shoulder with the blunt handle. Which was damn lucky, as the cracked end was a jagged wooden stump of splinters and shards, a memento that her dad saved to hang over their fireplace for a few years, until nobody in the world cared about baseball anymore, and for good reason. She'd take it down when no one was watching, running the sharpest edges along the soft skin of her forearms, sometimes slipping it down the back collar of her shirt to find that perfect spot she could never reach. Then one day, the broken bat vanished, and she searched the fireplace for the shadow of the Louisville Slugger emblem in ashes, remembering from her tour of the Slugger Museum that all the bats started out as "ash," Northern Whites to be exact. But she found nothing, not even the disclaimer her father had scratched near the sticky tape of the handle: "Avoid Alcoholic Beverages While Operating This Machine."

But her dad hadn't burned it, despite the bad memories baseball couldn't help but conjure up in the collective consciousness, and when Flora was 13, she found it discarded in the corner of their garage. She rescued it from behind a stack of cobweb-marbled *National Geographics* and discovered that those sharp edges, even after years of childhood had worn them down to nubs, could still scratch the uncharted territory between her shoulder blades more effectively than any human being.

When she turned 16, her dad disappeared, and he must have taken the broken bat with him. But she always missed it, because one thing Flora loved was to have her back scratched. Traps, delts, the whole posterior landscape where nerves hummed so close to the surface, and where she would always be amazed to find that spines were so easily visible to the naked eye. Her mom swore she was half cat by the way she'd flex that backbone when anyone's fingers dug in, before she was even old enough to realize she couldn't do this for herself, before she was old enough to walk without using her hands.

***

Christmas morning, years later, when things were getting back to normal, at least normal enough to try national holidays again, Flora snuck down early to shake one of her presents. She'd dropped enough hints in the preceding months, but she never knew with him lately, glued to the TV, glued to those screaming newspapers, glued to his work, which, as an insurance adjuster, consisted of literally gluing people's lives back together, one smashed family photo at a time. Hard to blame him really, the way things had been out of control for so long. Her own five-year plan had been put on hold until recently, too, with a wrong turn into "massage therapy" when her university was converted to a temporary triage. But now grad school was up and running again, and she found it easier to forgive his absent-mindedness when it came to their marriage. Besides, judging by the sounds coming from inside the box, Flora thought he might have gotten this one right.

Her husband heard all the rustling around the tree, and he came down yawning and nodding to go ahead and open it, but she was already tearing into the newspaper. They'd always wrapped everything in the funny papers to save money. Never the front pages, of course, as there hadn't been a headline without a picture of something horrible or an exclamation point for at least a decade.

Her present was long, like a flower box, or more like a newborn's coffin, and as she tore open a duct-taped corner, she saw one inquisitive finger poking out of the hole it had dug out from the inside, and smiled as her gift helped meet her halfway. Her husband laughed nervously and took a step back, sloshing his coffee a bit on his knuckle, and she blew him a kiss. He had trouble with that cup sometimes, but it was his favorite, despite the cracked handle. Hers, too. It read "Big Shrug Mug" in big orange letters down the side.

She held her breath and gave the box a final fast rip to open a hole big enough for the whole hand to worm its way out. The full arm wriggled free of the box, flopping on the floor with a thud, then started to creep forward on its fingers towards her bare foot. Her husband spilled the rest of his coffee, but she calmly retrieved it and brought it to her lap for closer study. The finger movements slowed once it was cradled, projecting the vibe of a contented pet. She rolled it over and checked the end of the arm where it had been severed from its body, just above the elbow, rubbing her thumbs over the seal of smooth, cauterized flesh. It reminded her of plastic, or tallow, and she thought back to when she was little, when Flora and a neighbor boy used to steal his mother's oldest candles, the ones with the deepest hollows, and light the wicks until the tall edges became soft. Then they would work each side of the candle together, collapsing the edges until the soft wax sealed itself completely to snuff out the flame, forever trapping the smoke inside. The neighbor boy could never leave well enough alone, and loved poking holes in the sealed candles to let the smoke pull out the sides, but Flora's favorite part was simply securing the top, smoothing the hot wax of those corners with her thumbs until the scars were healed, long after the neighbor boy couldn't bear to touch it anymore without crying.

"Well, is that the one you wanted?" her husband asked.

"It's perfect," Flora said, hugging her new arm against her chest, where it dutifully climbed her clavicle and started to give her shoulders a gentle pinch. It felt good, strong but not unpleasant, like someone you trust reminding you they had your back.

"Make sure you use the sealant," her husband said, tipping his coffee cup to point at the spray can still in the box. A warning near the stain where he'd scraped off the price sticker shouted, "Keep away from fire or open flame."

"You have to give it a shot of that stuff once a day or it'll fester," he said.

Flora leaned down and grabbed the can, letting pages of paperwork, warranties, and rebate postcards flutter to the ground. She shook it and heard the ball-bearing rattling inside, then saw another warning wrapped around the bottom of the can, "Apply every day! Not responsible for any damages direct, incidental, consequential or otherwise."

I didn't say you were, she thought.

The hand increased its motion with the rattle of the aerosol can, going from a gentle scratch, then back to a deeper rub. Spraying it with anything once a day seemed like overkill at first, but she knew it was probably less about decomposition and more about the little-known fact that any dead body, if left to its own devices, particularly if left outdoors, would eventually begin to glow in the dark. She knew this bit of trivia, even before the headline with the exclamation point. Postmortem luminescence of corpses due to various fungi and bacterium was very common. And as much as it sounded like a good opportunity to get these products to work double-duty as back-scratchers and as night lights, the glow of the recently deceased was just too unsettling for most people. The sealant must inhibit this, she figured. But only if you gave it a new coat every single day. Because judging by the font size and bold type on the bottom of that spray can, these arms really, really wanted to glow in the dark.

She wasn't sure if she believed it though. She'd heard it was just a myth. In fact, her cousin Rudy had gone off to seek fame and fortune on a reality show being filmed on a crab boat in the Bering Sea, where they hauled up thousands of pounds of squirming bodies every week, for millions of viewers, and she asked Rudy himself about this mythical bioluminescence.

"Scientific name Aliivibrio fischeri you mean," Rudy corrected her. "It's a bacterium lurking in the deepest oceans that finds a home on decaying flesh. Supposedly it's 'crowd-sensing,' too, so a biomass shouldn't even need our sonar to light it right up! Right?"

"So you've seen this?" she asked him.

"Nope. Oh, I've heard for years about these famous glowing, subaqueous corpses, even seen it myself in a gaggle of bobtail squid. But as far as them dog-paddlin' deceased glowing like a buncha nightlights? Nah, that part's just an ol' dead-wive's tale."

But none of this first-hand color commentary impressed her husband. Rudy always rubbed him the wrong way, ever since he and his crew played hockey with that legless crab during the end credits of their season finale. Flora explained that crabs automatically jettisoned their legs when the conditions demanded it, but her husband didn't buy it and secretly wished his show would get cancelled again.

"Seriously," her husband said with his stack of heavily highlighted think pieces he'd printed from the web. "Who knows what these things do? Read everything. Over and over. That thing was ridiculously expensive. We don't want to risk it going bad."

She frowned, not because of the crassness of reminding her of the cost of the gift, but at the idea that she was suddenly so trendy. Helping Hands were all the rage lately, mostly due to their meditative qualities in a society that certainly needed some relaxation, outselling even those office chew toys, even those rubber tension blocks, even those celebrated Burmese Ben Wa balls that Captain Queeg rotated in his hand to calm himself after mutinies. Flora had considered getting one of the cheaper, star-shaped head-scratchers that flowered open to massage your scalp. They were rubber and looked and felt a little like fingers, but she couldn't get past the idea of everyone scratching their heads with them in the stores to try them out. So nasty.

The hand seemed to be flicking at itself in frustration, and she rolled it back over to find more directions on a small tag wrapped around its pinkie. Its motions turned dutifully limp as she carefully untied it.

"Any resemblance to real persons, living or dead, is likely coincidental. Safe and effective when used as directed. Choking hazard." Smiley face.

The warnings seemed to be getting cheekier, and she appreciated this, seeing how there were apparently so many. Her Helping Hand went back to kneading her shoulder, finding itself a parrot-like perch, and her husband touched her arm to get her attention, as she'd missed something else he just said. She flinched at his touch before she could stop herself, then saw him holding the breakfast-in-bed he'd made for her. She felt guilty and reached out to scoop a spoonful of grapefruit as the hand tumbled from the unexpected flex of her shoulder and crashed into the TV tray. Rolling and splashing her corn flakes, its fingers grasped blindly, feeling for the sensation of any skin, until it settled on the fruit instead. It squeezed it until it burst, the juice catching her husband in the eye. Now it was her turn to laugh.

"Don't look so scared, honey. That thing was almost rotten, anyway. A child could have ruptured it."

***

The instruction booklet was called *The Care and Keeping of Your Helping Hand*, and the tone and colorful illustrations reminded her of a book on puberty her mother had once given her. In the upper right-hand corner was a flip cartoon of a hand touching each finger to the tip of its thumb in turn, and this additional flourish to the instruction guide encouraged her to flip through all the rules a little too rapid fire. But she was pretty sure she caught the important stuff.

Spray it with the sealant once a day so it doesn't glow, yeah, yeah, she already got that. Put mittens on it during the winter, not to protect from the cold, but to protect from any particularly tenacious insect infestations? Crazy.

Never, ever, put it in your mouth. She knew all of this already, as she'd researched the limbs for months before she considered getting one. And who would do something like that? Now she wanted to. During all of Flora's internet research, she read how morticians and embalmers would often spin tales of intimate, low-impact exercises with the mortal remains they'd been entrusted, routinely extending and bending the limbs like they were preparing for a marathon, sometimes listening to the *Vision Quest* soundtrack at top volume. But there was no need to flex the fingers or twist the wrist of her new arm, even if this had always been the tried-and-true method of keeping away rigor mortis. Those days were over because, due to any severed limb's unique condition these days, the fingers would already be moving non-stop, before or after the arm's amputation. Also, in the old days, a body was normally drained of blood and filled with formaldehyde/methanol cocktails to slow decomposition, or luminescence, and obviously an arm had no organs or cavities that would necessitate the "hydroaspirator" or "Hoover vacuum" or any other fancy suctioning device. But even if it *was* a whole body she wanted for Christmas, the problems with intact reanimated corpses ran in other directions, simply because the outdated practice of embalming the limbs of the dead stopped their movement, and no amount of stretching would get them to move again. And who wanted that? Maybe people who dealt with the original Incident, as it meant the mythical bullet-to-the-brain solution was no longer necessary. Of course, the newspapers with all the exclamation points showed nonstop defensive firepower, barrages of haphazard ammunition, blasting open the bodies of the Shufflers, causing them to bleed out and stop shuffling fairly efficiently. This was also a potent strategy for the

Shamblers, too. Not so much the Scufflers though, and certainly not on any run-of-the-mill Stumbler, specimens which, for whatever reason, pressed on with little or no blood in their veins. But like anything in the world when it's perforated by gunfire, they all moved less and less effectively regardless.

But they never really stopped moving. And sometimes they still squeezed their dead hands with a surprising amount of vigor. Some people called them Overachievers, and they sported the best limbs for harvest.

Flora flipped through the instructions one more time, trying not to stare at the cartoon in the corner so much, making sure she didn't miss everything.

"At night, give it a dog toy!" the booklet recommended. "But not one that squeaks! If it squeaks, besides the annoyance factor, it might also encourage your Helping Hand to squeeze faster and harder. But don't worry, the grip *should* never become dangerous. However, any noisemaker might result in a hand that speeds up in a futile attempt to silence it. Again, don't worry. This is completely normal!"

She scratched a thumbnail on the page, double-checking the word "should" to see if it was really in italics.

"And don't let it get the mail!" the booklet pleaded with a wink. "You may remember *The Addams Family,* that popular television show from a century ago with its own handy, disembodied hand much like your own. Well, that 'Thing' did all sorts of household tasks for its masters, and you may be encouraged to try something similar. But *do not* leave anything in your hand overnight that you value. Keep in mind, the makers of Helping Hand are not responsible for direct, indirect, incidental or consequential damages of personal property resulting from any defect, error or failure to perform based on willful dismissal of these warnings. But speaking of *The Addams Family*, don't let it "fester" . . ."

Smiley face.

"Do not submerge in fluids . . . slippery when wet . . . do not put in eyes . . . do not leave near genitals . . . do not swallow . . . recommended for ages 18 and up . . . avoid alcoholic beverages while using . . . avoid prolonged contact with sun-damaged skin . . . use only in well-ventilated area . . . no animals were harmed within reason during testing . . . one size fits all . . . this is not a marital aid . . ."

That's what you think, she smiled to herself.

". . . remember to lock up your new arm . . . get into the habit of storing it in drawers, closets . . . muscles will move slower in lower temperatures . . . as well as in dark places . . . use only as directed . . . no assembly required . . . if left unattended, not responsible for loss or damage . . . may cause excitability, especially in children . . ."

No kidding, she thought. She'd heard of overzealous pubescent boys buying them for masturbatory purposes, then discovering they were just as likely to get ripped off monetarily as organ-wise.

". . . and whatever you do, no matter how much it wiggles, no matter how much it twitches, always leave your Helping Hand on its 'back,' never on its fingers."

She quickly flipped it back over.

***

Christmas dinner at her mother and stepfather's was as tense as ever. It started with an argument with Tim, her stepbrother and nemesis, who wouldn't leave the arm alone. Flora's husband gave her a shrug to remind her that he'd recommended leaving it at home for this very reason. But it was a long drive to her mom's, and he never played with the hair on the back of her neck anymore on these road trips, and she thought it would probably come in handy.

But as soon as they got through the door and she laid it on the floor to tangle its fingers in her shoestrings to keep itself occupied, Tim had to grab it. He ran around, making it flip the bird, tried unsuccessfully to get it to hold a fist and punch himself in the face, then chased Flora's mother around the kitchen, slapping it at her behind. Flora and Tim were close in age, but he acted the fool, probably always would, even though he had two sons of his own. Eventually Tim calmed down a bit, but he still wouldn't give it up. He sat on the couch, trying to crack its knuckles, so Flora waited for her mother's back to be turned, then finally snatched it back and hooked its thumb in her belt loop, like her husband used to do when they walked the local art fair with matching designer blue jeans.

"Oooh, someone needs watered," Tim laughed.

It was an old joke that she hated. People mistook her name for meaning "flower," but it was actually an Anglicized form of "Fionnaghal," a Scottish Gaelic word meaning "white shoulder," her favorite part of the body actually. Her real dad had named her this, as he was big into Scotts. And shoulders apparently. But this entomology was way too much for poor Tim to remember, of course, sporting the immaturity of either an idiot teen or an extremely successful adult. Tim would unlikely ever be the latter, having been unemployed since his delayed high-school graduation.

But, in fact, everyone in her new family loved the "flower" jokes, stepsisters and step-nephews alike, and she continued to get bombarded with all sorts of seed-bearing gags, ever since her mother married into this new guy's excitable brood a decade ago.

Her stepdad came up from his basement to gave her a half-hearted hug, pretending there wasn't a severed arm hanging from the back of her pants, swinging by its forefinger and pinky from loop to loop like a tiny Tarzan. Then he peeled her husband away from her to show him the new bar he'd built downstairs, and her mom sent her to get fireworks. Ironically, fireworks had become a weird ceasefire around that house. It gave her stepdad something to do and also made him the center of attention. But they didn't sell fireworks in Kentucky, which meant they had to get them in Indiana, a trip her stepbrother loved to make at every opportunity, on the off chance he could sneak in a little blackjack.

Besides the ban on fireworks, there was no gambling allowed in Kentucky either. Dancing had recently come back. The new bi-racial union formed by her mother and Tim's father still turned a few heads though.

Tim grabbed the arm off her pants on their way out the door, its finger and thumb snagged on her zipper and struggling in vain to hang on.

"Sorry, sorry, I won't break it," he pleaded, pulling its fingers back dangerously far again. She glanced at it flopping around Tim's lap as she pulled out of the driveway. It seemed restless away from her, and its first three fingers were all scissoring so quickly that they almost disappeared. It was the fastest she'd seen it move yet, and she imagined those fingers as cartoon legs, running so hard they'd hover in the air before they could hit the ground and escape.

***

In the months leading up to the holidays, there weren't nearly as many warnings in the newspapers as there were coming out of her husband's mouth.

"Are you *sure* you want one?" he asked her one night in bed as she pretended to read the ceiling and not hear the stretch in his "sure."

"Yes, please."

"Deformities and black market limbs are cheap, routinely abused, used in pornography, used to abuse. Chilling stuff."

"Petrifying!" she joked. "You can do all of those things with any household item, by the way."

"Joe at work told me that he caught his son . . ."

"Did you know that, a couple years back, there was a bit of a movement to treat these arms with respect," she interrupted, rolling over to look at him. She stared at his mouth a lot these days, something she heard was less intimate than staring at someone's eyes, but she could tell when he was lying by how many times he nibbled his lip.

"I did not know that," he lied.

"Yep, it wasn't quite a civil rights march or anything, but there was a conscious effort to shame people into using them for good, not evil. On Twitter, this movement trended for six solid months, calling itself "Hashtag Notallbackscratchers."

"What's Twitter?" he asked. Then, "Using it for *good*, huh?"

"Well, if not 'good,' at least a good scratch," she laughed.

"Just as long as you're not trying to replace me," he joked, face betraying the seriousness of his question. He sat up and began to rub her shoulders, even resorting to running his fingernails down her spine. She tried to remain still out of politeness.

"Of course not," she assured him. "Mostly I want it for the car. Everything in Kentucky is an hour from everything else. And you know how long my work commute is. Car seats are terrible on my back."

"I don't know if you remember," her husband said as he scratched a little harder, not acknowledging her flinching. "But *I* remember some marching in the streets actually, and some initial controversies regarding the color of these appendages. White arms outselling black arms, then vice versa."

"I guess I don't read the paper."

"Well, I do."

But Flora remembered it clearly. There were some initial tribal skirmishes involving companies promoting the arms of certain ethnicities over others, but people quickly learned that after regular treatments with the anti-decomposition sealants and the inevitable epidermal changes these limbs underwent, they all ended up the same color, a dull gray. And after that, everyone stopped demanding their favorites or fetishes. And although these wriggling gray backscratchers weren't quite the United Color of Benetton, Flora liked to think that they were, in their own small way, much like the traumatic epidemic that spawned them, an incidental victory for solidarity and an almost imperceptible move toward a post-racial society.

Once, she saw a man in overalls selling them in a basket at the bar. They were holding roses, but not really moving at all. But in spite of the sketchiness of his operation, he still succumbed to the urge to officialize by writing along their forearms:

"Colors may, in time, fade." Then, under that, "Skin tags or moles may not be removed under penalty of law." Frowny face.

One time on the cross-town bus, she saw a T-shirt that read "I Believe in a Gray America," and couldn't be sure if it was serious, but that was a long time ago.

Flora hissed at her husband's backrub before she could stop herself, and he jerked his hands back.

"What did I do? Please don't do that."

"I'm sorry. Just tense."

"You know, Joe from work said that the normal 50% divorce rate in this country climbs to 57% when one of these things is introduced into a household."

"Nonsense," Flora scoffed. "Besides, this was your idea, remember?"

He didn't remember that detail actually, but had no way to deny it. This was something she could usually count on to help her win most arguments.

"Joe from work said that a couple years back someone bought about twenty of these arms and put them in a big ol' cake to surprise a loved one returning home from the war."

"Sounds like a great idea," she said, waiting for the twist. "Those party planners organizing soldiers-coming-home surprises are still big business. They make more money than those dance instructors that help wedding parties learn 'surprise' choreography for the reception. And there's always a new war."

"Yeah, maybe not, because this surprise ended with a man dead."

"How did he die?" she asked, shaking the ad section of the newspaper. It said right there in the fine print: 'Approved for Veterans.'

"Peanut allergy. Something in the cake. Joe said that . . ."

"'Joe from work,' 'Joe from work,'" she sighed. "So what does that have to do with . . ."

"The point is, no one knows the possible dangers here."

He tried to sound confident, but he felt foolish, and he pulled the covers up over half his head. She sighed, doubting the validity of his fear-mongering. The biggest P.R. disaster they faced was at the beginning, maybe a decade ago, when teens tried to use the disembodied arms to take extended "selfies" but were surprised by the dead hands' lackluster grip, resulting in hundreds of camera phones, camera watches, or just plain cameras plummeting over Niagara Falls or tumbling off the observation deck of the Empire State Building.

"Listen," he finally said. "If I get you one, just remember to lock it up at night, okay?"

She would have no problem remembering this, since it was something the instructions would also remind her many times over, but without his petulant tone.

He turned out the lights, and unseen in the dark, she took turns gently stroking the lifelines of her palms with each fingertip. She was still doing this as she began to dream.

***

Flora and her stepbrother drove on, not talking. The sign said thirty miles to the Indiana state line, where they had fireworks on every corner, and Tim turned to her with an impatient look she instantly recognized from his dad. The last time she saw this scowl was creasing her stepfather's head, arms crossed in his captain's chair at their last Christmas dinner. Her nephews, technically step-nephews, were desperately try to suppress giggles as Tim demonstrated with salt and pepper the proper way for his boys to shake hands after their next baseball game. She'd asked the bigger step-nephew, the one a lot like the real brother she used to have, if they still made Little League players say "good game . . . good game . . . good game . . ." as they shuffled through the line clapping hands after it was over. The little step-nephew answered instead, the one who was a lot like her, back when she still had a real brother.

"Yep, they still make us do it. And I hate it!"

Flora said next time he should stop at each opponent's hand and instead say, "Hello, fine game you played today, aggressive yet sensible, victory was well earned . . . hello, fine game you played today, aggressive yet sensible . . ." and so on.

STEALING PROPELLER HATS FROM THE DEAD

The little step-nephew cracked up and swore he'd do it, if there were any more games. And then came that glare from the head of the table, and the disapproving silence that followed. So she muttered in her best newscaster's voice, "Today in Southern Ohio, a Little League game ended over six hours ago and for some reason they're still shaking hands," and the little step-nephew, the one that was a lot like her, he lost it and sprayed sweet potatoes all over the greens, her stepdad's favorite.

Ten miles to the state line, and they crossed a bridge. Tim threw the arm into the back seat and watched a riverboat like a dog eyeballing a squirrel. Riverboats in Kentucky were the only places where gambling was legal, as they took advantage of a loophole, something about being on the water. She got Tim a book about blackjack one Christmas, but he didn't read it. He always bragged about hating books, even books on blackjack, meaning he was thousands in the red on his favorite game. Maybe he got it from his dad.

Last year, she noticed a book on her stepdad's shelf titled *Be the Alpha Dog at the Table* and mistook it for leadership tips for business meetings and board rooms, mostly due to the "terms and conditions" on the back cover.

"Handle with care. Every *bored* room battle is won before it is fought."

But today she realized it was for family dinners all along.

After the "good game" thing, she asked her mom in private why her stepdad couldn't just smile and let her joke around at the table, and she surprised Flora with a question that, at the time, seemed completely unrelated.

"Well, why can't you pretend to move your mouth when he says 'grace?'"

Flora started to explain that one thing had nothing to do with the other, but then realized, as someone who made dubious connections daily to explain her universe, she should never be allowed to use that argument.

Five miles to the state line, and tired eyelids fluttered next to her. This gave her more time than usual to think back five Christmases ago as they drove. She thought about how she was jealous of those rougher years her stepbrothers had growing up because passive aggressive glares she'd get over pork chops could have been replaced with rough but honest headlocks, upper arm grabs, maybe real anger and arguments, even voices raised to the point of cracking. That's what Tim got from his father, and that's why he'd inherited certain things. She thought about her father's hands on her shoulders, sometimes squeezing a little too hard, and how amazing that could feel, especially when she didn't know it was coming.

With no more riverboats in sight, Tim was openly snoring, so she ran through the list of things he'd inherited from his dad, things that could never be passed on to a stepdaughter. Like that long blink he'd given her at the turnpike booth when she dropped her dime. Like his tendency to be so proud when he said the word "but" right before the person did this on a television screen, as if no one else could tell by the way his voice inflection was dropping that the character was gonna say something like, "He's a nice boy and never did anything to suggest he'd attack anyone, *but* . . ." Her stepdad was big on those "buts," too, butts so big the other end of the seesaw never let you back down. One day she vowed to tell them both that only someone with English as a second language wouldn't know they were coming, but they were always so smug about anticipating them. Her favorite example:

"It's all good around our houses, but our families

simply came together too late for anything more than polite disagreements to be allowed to bubble to the surface. It seems like a mother remarrying would let you hit a reset button and bond with a new family, but . . . it's almost always too late."

One street sign said the fireworks were one exit away. Another sign said, "Soft Shoulder."

"I wish," she laughed, tensing her back muscles against her seat. Tim twitched, too, but didn't respond.

Why do I care? she asked herself. *Because you won't ever get a morning where you're late for the bus but you and your real brother are being punished and have to do the rest of the Easter dishes with islands of roast beef (never turkey) hard as rock from three days earlier and he's older than you so he gets to wash and you're supposed to dry but you can't because he keeps leaving the suds around all the edges when he moves them to your side of the sink and when you slam one back down on his side a little too hard it breaks and your dad drops his lunch box and stomps over with those heavy electrical-worker boots of his with the spikes instead of spurs to grip the telephone poles and suddenly you're flying back into the recliner to upend it with your feet high over your head and you can see that one of those spikes must have stabbed right through your laces and slipped between the piggy who had roast beef and the piggy who had none to violently punctuate a dangerous morning that you'll always remember more for your dad's stubbled cheek against your arm when you were soaring into that chair than for almost losing a toe. But, hey, at least you didn't have to go to school that day because your mom ran out when it was over and saw he knocked the wind out of you. So I guess I'm wrong, maybe you're not the one who had none. This actually makes you more like the one who stayed home.*

Just one of these moments growing up, and she might be able to have an actual conversation with her stepdad, or her stepbrother. But as it stood, all these Christmases later, she was thinking the only chance she had at replicating that dynamic was with his son.

Seeing that her stepbrother was openly snoring now, her attention turned to her own shoe hovering over the gas pedal. Inside, she pictured the ingrown nails, calluses, and scars of his father's feet adorning her paws instead of Tim's, then she stomped on her stepbrother's foot hard enough to wake him up mad.

"What the hell?!"

"Sorry, just trying to get us there faster."

She thought about her father's feet and her brother's feet, and how hands used to be feet and arms used to be legs, and it's only recently that these parts distinguished themselves by dividing up the duties.

Tim glared at her for a minute, rubbing his toes through his tennis shoe, then reached down to grab the arm from where it was working its way under their seats and attached it to her headrest.

Choking hazard, she thought. *I wish. More like a joking hazard.*

The fingertips danced around the seatbelt strap then swung on it like a cartoon monkey until they found her shoulder and dug in. She honestly couldn't help feeling something significant when it touched her, maybe not quite love, or not quite the satisfaction of her father's hand on her shoulder and the bottle rockets whistling on opening day at the ball game, but for now it was all the fireworks she needed.

***

STEALING PROPELLER HATS FROM THE DEAD

That night she tried to sleep, tried to imagine she was back in her childhood bed, indulging in the nostalgia like her stepfamily was at that moment, instead of just listening to her husband snore. She heard a noise in the closet that gave her a start, but knew it was only a disembodied arm, and her heart slowed back down.

She went to get a glass of water, feeling cold air on her legs as she descended the stairs. Shivering, she looked around the kitchen and noticed the window was open. She closed it tight, secured it, then walked to the living room. The double bay windows were also open. In fact, every window within sight was open a crack, lock spun open. Except for one near the garage.

That window had a fist-sized hole near the bottom frame.

She forgot her water and ran back upstairs to check her closet. She tried to be quiet, but was still afraid her heart would wake the house.

Her new arm was gone.

She saw a page of the instructions, torn from the book and crumpled in the corner. It read:

"May cause drowsiness. Do not use while operating heavy machinery." Then, more urgent, "Do not allow to operate heavy machinery!"

Then she saw the spray can, and she remembered she forgot something else, but there were so many rules. She started thinking about the *Gremlins* trilogy instead, the original being the scariest Christmas movie she ever saw. Still in stealth mode, she got dressed, grabbed her husband's heavy winter coat, then swapped it for her stepdad's heavier coat, and headed out the door. But first, she stopped and peeked into Tim's room to make sure it wasn't wrapped around his throat. She almost couldn't believe it wasn't. Then she started wondering if it could see over a steering wheel well enough to drive a car.

Flora walked around the house, stopping at the broken glass and saw the pattern in the snow that led away to the sidewalk, and down the street. Suddenly, the truth of the situation was obvious. She'd been wrong about these limbs the whole time. Everyone had been. She ran back to get her car keys and followed the trail for miles.

The arms made wonderful backscratchers, sure, but that was merely incidental. When they writhed around the room, they weren't searching for something to scratch.

For any arm without a body, any hand without a frame, fingers became feet. Claws became paws.

It was trying to walk. It was always trying to walk. And now she needed to know where it was walking.

***

As she drove through the quiet streets of the neighborhood, she counted dozens of broken windows, even more open windows. The snow had just fallen, and the tiny tracks were clear in the street lights. She knew these limbs were trendy, but she had no idea they were this popular. They were the hot gift the previous Christmas, and sales were clearly up again this year.

But tonight, they'd all found a way out of those homes, out of their nest of wrapping paper, under those dying, decorated trees. She followed the tracks along the roads, along highways and on ramps and off ramps, for almost three hours. Three hours by car. Four hours. Five hours. She checked the dashboard clock right before the hand prints in the snow vanished and shook her head. There was no way a hand could scurry so fast. There must be more than her own running around that night, but even so, how fast could they all move? She slowed and almost pulled over onto the shoulder when a car passed her with its neon undercarriage glowing lime green. Then another. And another. She realized she was almost to Pittsburgh, but as hideous as some of those modified vehicles could be in the Steel City, it was a bit of a stretch to imagine three drivers in a row who just needed the shadows of their mid-life crisis to emit the sickly light of an algae-filled aquarium.

But now she understood. That's how they were doing it. Maybe lingering near an intersection when the red hand lit up to say "Don't Walk," and maybe they grabbed a bumper. Maybe they hitched a ride instead. Hanging from any piece of metal down there would be easy. Cars were a veritable jungle gym for stray animals, so why not stray hands?

She took off her seatbelt as the itch became maddening, and she imagined how fast those fingers must move when no one is watching if they'd gotten such a jump on their mysterious journey before they needed to put up a thumb. She wondered if next Christmas the hot item would be leashes.

She wasn't shocked to find herself at PNC Park, home stadium of the Pittsburgh Pirates, ground zero for the original outbreak. She'd heard it all happened because of the fetid water in one of those rancid hot-dog carts, maybe the very thing veteran rockers Limp Bizkit had warned of decades ago with their cryptic album title. She thought about the long line of headlights creeping toward the baseball game cut into the cornfield at the end of *Field of Dreams* and how disembodied hands on those steering wheels would have made it a much better film.

She pushed through a twisted corner of the fence where the gate had collapsed, a new hole she'd normally assume children had worked open. She crept past the gutted press box and peered down the dark tunnel toward the field. It was dark, but she could hear the movement, hear the crunch of the snow and the unmistakable squeak of skin. She groped to find a mad-scientist lever on the wall nearby, and guessed without reading the instructions that it would light up the entire field.

She brought it slamming down, and shielded her eyes. It turned out this switch only ignited the flickering fluorescents within a row of moldy popcorn machines that lined the tunnel, but now she saw that she didn't need the lights after all.

The field was already alive, throbbing, a symphony of radiance. Not as much a pyrotechnic celebration like the Roman Candle fuses her stepfather had lit earlier, or the crescendos of sparks the stadium was built for, but more of a steady pulse. A low, green glow of hands, arms and bumping elbows, surging and twisting in the soft dirt, thumping and thrumming alone the baselines. Like a thousand Vishnus making snow angels, a fleshy pile of limbs climbed and grasped each other everywhere on the dust and dead grass of the baseball diamond, rubbing and pinching. She could have sworn she saw a group of hands engaging in sign language, and another pile making shadow animals on the pitcher's mound, some even thumb wrestled. A pair near second base were clasped in prayer, or, more than likely, saying grace. Two hands on the foul line attempted a high-five and fell back onto their elbows, duteously picking themselves up high and proud like cobras for another try. She could almost she hear the congratulatory "good game . . . good game . . . good game" as they slapped, and she smiled at the sluggish but lustrous dance that soothed her like never before, without even a touch.

She left the tunnel, and walked down the steps between the bleachers, toward the field, ashamed of the terror that had gripped her during the drive, and she took off her stepfather's coat, dropping it onto the metal seats.

She kicked off her slippers. They were gripping each other tight, but there was still room for her. Thousands of hands clenched each other close, not desperate, but like teenagers on a first date with many more to come, fingers entwined, no body needed.

DO THE MÜNSTER MASH

IT'S A HOT, hazy day. Daytona Beach, Florida, summer of '83. A young man sits on a bench facing the ocean. He's tall but skinny, shoulders hunched out of habit, not insecurity. He wears a trucker cap way too big for his head and aviator glasses that obscure most of his face. The cap, covered in candy-like splashes of paint, features a grinning pig mascot selling its soul for a barbeque smokehouse. High behind the pig is a blank, peeling billboard with the lone, scorched eyeball of a sunscreen company logo. Higher still is the dead concrete screen of an old drive-in theater, patiently waiting for the sun to go down.

Near the beach, someone is cranking "Second Home by the Sea" in their headphones so loud that everyone can hear it, one of the few Genesis songs not on the radio this year, as their self-titled album just landed the previous spring. The young man frowns trying to locate the direction of the muffled music, as well as place it in his memory. Just over his narrow shoulder is yet another advertisement, a toothy cartoon dog shilling for surfboards. Smiling cartoon animals are everywhere today, it seems. Their eyes are watching all while the young man stares straight ahead, unblinking, vacant. Everyone on this beach is leading a dog, their own personal doppelgängers, and every so often an animal shows a curiosity in this young man that is not returned.

One dog passes particularly close to him, a mutt

dressed head-to-tail in a purple pimp costume. Still the young man never blinks. He only smiles once while the sun is still up, when someone switches the Genesis song to a strange, all-German version of Peter Gabriel's "Intruder," and he realizes this person must be flying the superfan flag high to dig so deep.

"All Dogs And Their Owners Welcome!" is scrawled on the yellow boards of the young man's bench, but with his arms out, he covers three words to cancel out the owners' invite. He's done this on purpose. The boards of this bench are rotten, almost transparent. Lovers' hearts that were carved too deeply are linked by cracks, like a child's connect-the-dots ready to bring the bench down at any moment. The young man traces one heart with this thumb and wonders if it was one he scratched into a tree trunk as a boy, surviving the rebound down rivers and dissection in the mill, now hoping to finally upend the original vandal.

Everything about this young man suggests blindness. The sunglasses, indifference to a parade of half-naked rollerbladers, drooling dogs chasing balls, and girls chasing their dogs chasing those balls. In his hands, he holds a pot of dirt at an awkward angle, a tiny green seedling peeking from the center of the soil. Sometimes the young, blind man shields it from the sun.

A white American Eskimo runs by him with a dead fish in its mouth, the fish flapping faster as the dog picks up speed, dodging its master.

The young, blind man stares straight ahead.

A small, black-headed Münsterländer chases a bright red ball, and the young, blind man lazily cracks his neck toward nothing. A small, fawn-colored Pug dog trots by wearing a tiny hat with a propeller. Several people turn to laugh. Even the dog in the pimp costume turns toward the pug, seemingly ready to comment. The young, blind man yawns.

Then the Münster's bright red ball pinballs off pedestrian traffic and rolls toward the young man's shoes. The little dog slips and scratches at the sand as it frantically changes direction to lunge. For a moment, the young, blind man seems to be teasing the dog by maneuvering the ball around his feet, just out of its grasp. Then the young, blind man kicks the ball away. Hard. The dog anticipates the kick and catches it easily. With the ball finally locked in its mouth, the Münster runs back to its master, a boy with a prog-rock mix in his headphones, who misses the impressive footwork and unlikely exchange between a young, blind man and a dog he cannot see.

As the dog drops the ball, head cocked in confusion and anticipation, a tall, dark-skinned Hispanic woman walks by the young, blind man, confidence in her hips.

The young man stuffs the ball in his pocket, and the dog nuzzles this bulge, immediately forgetting all suspicion. Then, when the woman is closest, the young, blind man sits up straight and turns his head toward her, nostrils flaring as the Peter Gabriel song climaxes.

"Eindringling kommt . . . eindringling kommt und legt seine spur . . . legt seine spur."

"Can you please tell me what time it is?" the young, blind man asks.

The girl ignores him and keeps walking.

He stands to follow, and the dog runs back to his feet.

Tomorrow, he'll be back with his plaster cast, or maybe his badge. Of all his props, the badge is the only one that's real. He doesn't worry about the name on it, since most will see it for the first and last time. Staring at the animal, he thinks of his squad and their secret quota of 50 dog executions a year. Their sergeant, a Democrat, adjusted the limit to 25 if they were chained. He waits for the boy to again be buried deep enough in his music to forget about his doppelgänger, and then he kicks the dog so savagely that it folds over the toe of his work boot with one last air horn of a yelp, sailing high over the head of its master, trailing a tongue now twice its length. Because of the size of his headphones, which bob the boy's tiny ears like a Dobie, he doesn't realize what's happened until the young, blind man is long gone.

No one remembers what he looked like. The girls either.

***

Thirty years later? Another hot, hazy day in Florida near the beach. Peter Gabriel's song "Intruder" is playing deep in someone's headphones. The young man, no longer young, is sitting on a bench near the ocean, wearing a baseball cap and sunglasses. The old man turns the cap around and lifts his head. Just over his shoulder is a large sign with a grinning cartoon dog. The dog's eyes seem to be watching everyone. And everyone is leading a dog, of course. But there is something wrong with these dogs. The sign screams:

ALL DOGS AND THEIR OWNERS WELCOME!

Behind him is the dead screen of a drive-in theater, waiting for the sun to go down.

The old man cradles a small potted seedling like a baby. After a while, an attractive Chicana girl walks by.

"Can you please tell me what time it is?" he asks her.

Fast forward through several dark-skinned girls walking by the old man's bench and answering his question in Spanish. There is a dismissive, impatient tone to the parade of responses. No one notices how amazing it is that this old, blind man only interacts with pedestrians possessing a certain look. Clearly a preference, or a profiling, is going on. But no one notices there's something wrong with the dogs either, so the parade of dark skin is equally unremarkable.

No translation is necessary with a rapid-fire list of rejection:

"El tiempo para usted comprar un reloj," says the first girl.

"Joda Lejos," says the second.

"Cogida apagado," says the third.

"Vete a la mierda," says the fourth.

"Coja eso," says the fifth.

"Varfunculo," says the sixth.

The old man raises his head sharply at this last response. Certainly some kind of rebuke, but not Spanish. He's angry not understanding what the girl said, as he's clearly gotten used to a steady stream of Spanish "fuck offs" and learned to let them roll off his back.

Finally, a small Mexican girl smiles and stops to answer him. Their connection and the friendly tone of the conversation is obvious. The old man's apparent blindness also puts her at ease.

"No puede decir ested por el sol?" says the Mexican girl, number seven.

"Usted madre no lo dijo para nunca contestar una pregunta con una pregunta?" he asks.

"Eso no es lo que usted acaba de hacer?"

"Eso no es lo que usted acaba de hacer?" he smiles.

The Mexican girl moves closer. "Yo no recuerdo a mi madre."

"What's all that noise down there?" the old man whispers in English. "What are they doing by the water?"

DAVID JAMES KEATON

"I'll show you . . . " she starts, then stops, embarrassed. "I mean . . . let's see."

She steps toward him, taking his arm. He's surprised and almost drops his plant. Gently cradling it, they both walk toward the water where a pier is under construction. Suddenly, a thundering pile of tree trunks rolls out of the back of a truck and crashes onto the sand. The noise startles at least a dozen sunbathers, several of them sitting up on their towels, sliding down their sunglasses and frowning and looking around. The Peter Gabriel song climaxes:

"Intruder come . . . intruder come and leave his mark . . . leave his mark. Leave his mark."

"Feel the sun on your nose?" she asks him. "It's noon. To answer your question, that is what time it is. See how easy we did that?"

"Thank you," the old man says, in love again, trying to resist the urge to look down at her dog, for many reasons, not the least of which is the fact that she's been dragging it.

"You didn't answer me back there," someone's mother says. "I asked if your mother ever told you not to answer a question with a question."

"No, I asked that. But I guess she didn't. But one time, my father said that if I threw enough rocks off that pier . . ." He nods toward the construction. ". . . I would eventually hit a duck that deserved it!"

"What were you trying to hit?" someone's daughter asks, suspicious. "How could you even see to—"

The old man holds up a hand to stop her.

"Don't you mean to say, 'There wasn't a pier here until today?'"

His voice fades as they walk on together. Smiling wide with his nostrils flaring, the old man turns to the ocean. A dog's ragged ball rolls in front of his foot. And even though the ball doesn't bump his shoe, he quickly kicks it away as if he sees it coming. He takes a deep breath, hiding his urge to kick a dog along with it. There's no reason these days to do such a thing.

Somewhere in the dark, he carves another heart.

A small dog quickly skids to a stop as its master yanks on the leash from a hundred yards away. Another yank gives the illusion of a fully functioning animal altering its course to run down the ball, as if it wasn't digging trenches in the sand with its snout, as if the dead eyes would see the ball it was chasing. Someone's grandmother doesn't notice the quick kick the old man has given the ball, and after the dog doesn't catch it, the dead-eyed animal is dragged back towards the boy wearing headphones. Halfway there, the dog stands and snatches the ball, surprising everyone on the beach. A little girl who has never seen a dog walk on its own, gasps. The little monster turns to stare at the old man, growling, head cocked to one side, endless tongue lolling, as if to acknowledge both their games, an admission it was also playing dead this entire time.

"Was ist los?" the boy with the headphones asks in German. Then, in English, "What's wrong?"

The dead dog ignores its master, slowly opening its mouth as the sand and saliva-streaked ball drops and is stolen by the surf.

WHAT'S WORST?

"Whenever it was taken outside, some officious person was always pointing out that it was in danger of being left behind."
— Edward Gorey — *The Beastly Baby*

JASON DROVE PAST a dead baby on the side of the road.

He drove on a few more seconds, until he slowly realized what he'd seen, foot easing off the gas as he stared in his rearview mirror, engine revving down. Nothing back there except the vanishing point. He turned down the stereo as he coasted. He was driving slow enough to count ten white lines sliding under his car between heartbeats, and he felt the warmth of the crackling speaker behind his head. He'd mounted the speakers in his headrests, despite his mechanic's warnings, gutting the cushions like his old teddy bears, like a kid forced to play doctor all by himself, and he forced the speakers to fit inside, even though they really didn't, then black-taped it all shut. This gave the headrests too many sharp corners to ever rest his head on them again, but he figured it was worth all the sweat and middle-of-the-night tinkering with those hordes of mosquitoes drawn to his dome light. He never rested his head when he drove anyway.

Hell, speaker magnets shouldn't be too *close to the skull, right?*

With the balance turned all the way to the right it gave him someone to talk to, and the vibrations under his arm were comforting. And after enough miles, he even started talking for a bit. Nothing crazy. Just thinking out loud really. Until one night after a particularly good song, a speaker finally blew. Lately, the ruptured music was popping and sparking so badly he had to turn them down a bit. The right side was a little better, and he figured one would be enough though. Especially since he didn't have enough money to replace them, but mostly because he couldn't see himself ever going through the effort of cutting them open again even if he did have the cash. Although he was sure the static couldn't be that bad for his brains, he'd wrapped at least seven rolls of black tape around those headrests. That meant forever.

"Was that really a dead baby back there? No freaking way." He tilted his head, rolling it around on his shoulders until it cracked. His eyes never left the rearview mirror as he slowed down to about 10 miles an hour. Still no cars anywhere around.

"A dead baby. Not just something pink that looked like a dead baby. I know that's what I saw. Please, let that be what I saw . . . " He said that last part almost to himself, leaning over even more, the fuzz on the seat tickling his ear.

"I should go back, huh? I know it wasn't an animal. There was no blood, no fur. Nothing red, just pink. That means no one threw a baby out of a car. Now that would be worse. You'd be a little red comet, and I'd still be driving next to you, if that were the case."

A couple seconds went by, about ten white lines sliding under the car while he thought about it, then he leaned over again and explained himself to no one.

"You know, there's something to be said about someone like myself who sees something that horrible and just keeps on driving. Doesn't even phase him enough to go back. I know what you're thinking. That I'm scared. That I don't want to touch it or see it up close or something. That's ridiculous."

He turned the stereo off. It was stuck in the static between stations anyway. Second ticked by with his engine. Suddenly he had both hands on the wheel, both arms locked, both feet on the brake, subwoofer popping.

But what if someone else sees it and thinks they found it first?

Jason went back for the baby. Fast and backwards. When he got up next to it, he opened the passenger door, stretched across the seat on his stomach with his head in his palms and stared at the thing, with the car rumbling under his body. It was right there by his tire. He hands trembled a bit, and he told himself it was the low idle from the car. Not the fact that this was definitely a dead baby.

No flies, no blood, no smell, nothing, he thought. *No bugs, no red . . . just dead.*

It was on its stomach, too, and he studied the smooth, pink head and thought about rolling it over to see if it was a boy or a girl. Then he decided he liked not knowing. He considered drawing three lines on the back of its scalp so he'd never have to turn it over. Three lines, that's all you need for two eyes and a mouth. Then he could pretend he found an alien instead.

Now that was a dilemma, he thought. *What would you rather find on the side of the road? A dead baby or a dead alien? Alien. What about a live baby or a dead alien? Live baby, definitely. I'd be big hero. Dead alien and you'd end up on the slab in Area 51 right next to it.*

A strange sound came from the car, as if it was thinking hard along with him, and he grabbed it by its swollen ankle and picked it up fast before he changed his mind. It was heavier than he expected, and he thought of stuffed toys left outside to soak up the rain. He flung it into the seat beside him.

"Damn, what you been eatin'? That must be how it died," he explained to the static. "First, someone lost the thing, maybe while they were changing a tire, and when it got left behind, there was no one around to stop it from putting things in its mouth. And everyone knows a baby on the side of the road will eat rocks all night long if no one is around to stop it . . . "

He trailed off as he noticed something else in the roadside gravel as he was closing his door. He leaned out, reaching out slow so his back could crack, but also hoping someone would come along. It was a toy. Or it had been a toy at one time. It was smashed now, many times run over, and Jason couldn't decipher what it had been. He knew what it was supposed to do though, and that was rattle. Babies liked things that rattled. This was a toy that had rattled once, then burst open under a wheel, all the popcorn kernels that had made those noises now scattered in a star pattern around it. He thought maybe it was homemade, sewn together from some dying stuffed animal. He counted the extra eyes and ear on the rattle and decide it was a bunch of animals, by the look of it.

Something tightened in Jason's chest, something about the toy affecting him in a way the baby hadn't, and he shook his head hard, like a dog that got thrown in the pool or a cat reacting to a surprise gunshot, and he slammed his car door to get moving. He guessed his reaction was just from being down there at exhaust level, the fumes or something. He clicked the volume knob off, then reached over and strapped the baby in while the hiss of the stereo static faded away again. He didn't want the thing rolling over onto his side of the car when he took any hard turns. He still remembered how important it was to stay on your own side when he was on a long drive in the backseat with his brother.

When he clicked the seat belt over its distended belly, he noticed that he'd placed it onto the seat perfectly, carefully, just like any child. And right before he pulled back onto the road, his eyes took a snapshot of its face before he could stop himself. It was a boy.

"So what?" Jason said, looking straight ahead. He played with the rearview and drove on, then leaned over and whispered to it without looking.

"Hey, here's a good one. What's easier to unload? A truckload of bowling balls? Or a truckload of dead babies? Dead babies! Because you can use a pitchfork."

Jason sighed, satisfied he'd broken the tension.

"So, you from around here? No one threw you out of the car, did they? You'd have been a little red comet if that had happened! You run away? Someone give birth to you in that ditch? No, there's no cord. Can you imagine that? Some girl pulls over to have a baby and leave it behind, only she forgets the cord, right? Then, miles later, she gets pulled over 'cause the cops see the baby bouncing behind the car. Now, that's a worse ticket than not having a baby properly restrained in the car seat, ain't it?" Jason's smile dropped a little. "I should probably take you to the police now, shouldn't I?" But an hour later, Jason was still driving, telling himself that he'd done nothing wrong. He worried someone would take it to a lab, cut it in half, count the rings to solve the mystery, then wonder what the hell he was doing driving around with it for so long. He honestly just wanted someone to scratch their head and ask him why he'd hauled a dead baby around the highways, and he imagined himself on TV, symbolizing detached youth everywhere or some such nonsense. This was right up there with those headlines about teens leaving babies in the toilets then heading to prom. No, this was worse. Nobody ever did what he was doing. He'd be the boy who drove around with a dead baby, telling it dead baby jokes.

He leaned over again, still not looking.

"Okay, what's worse? Killing a baby, or driving around with it like it's nothing? Hey, you remember those 'what's worse' jokes? You know, what's worse? Fifty dead babies in a garbage can or one dead baby in fifty garbage cans? That's a tough one, ain't it? I wonder what someone would say if they heard me right now. I am a true mystery."

Jason's eyes got wide. "Holy shit! I wonder what someone would say if I took you to a movie! Do you want to go see a movie? It would have to be a drive-in though. I'd get in trouble if I carried you into a theater, especially if it was rated 'R.' They check I.D.'s these days."

He tilted the rearview to pretend someone was in the back seat listening to him.

"Hey! What's worse than finding a dead baby in the back seat of your car? Realizing you fucked it! So nasty."

He wished for a train or a red light so he'd have to slam on the brakes at least once. He leaned over and unhooked its seat belt, always without looking. He wanted to hit the brakes while he was talking to it, then act shocked when it bounced off the dashboard. He thought that would be hilarious and edgy as fuck. Especially if anyone saw it. But there were still no cars around. No one at all. He wondered if he'd missed the end of the world. This was a depressing thought, as he couldn't imagine finding a dead baby then having no one to show how unimpressed he was by such a discovery. Then he had another idea. What if he turned the baby into the authorities, but then the cops found out he went through a car wash before he surrendered it?

STEALING PROPELLER HATS FROM THE DEAD

They would be confused, suspicious as hell, but couldn't do anything about it. He'd be pretty mysterious if he did that.

Maybe they'd think I was washing blood off my car?

Jason drove faster, looking for a car wash.

He looked hard for one, needing desperately to find one, even wishing so hard that visualized blowing the candles off a birthday cake with this wish and extinguishing every candle on his first try. And what the hell, he found one.

***

It was one of those crazy car washes where you drove through the mouth of a monster clown or something equally sinister. Not that he thought clowns were sinister.

"Don't be afraid of clowns," he said. "Aren't you sick of people saying they're afraid of clowns? You will be. They're all like, 'you know what's scary? A killer clown with sharp teeth. Who kills people. Oooh, I'm so weird being afraid of clowns! You know what else is scary? Alligators with nine heads! Keep them away from me!'"

He'd seen car washes before where the garage-door entrance was painted to look like a dragon, or a dinosaur, depending on if it was a Creationist state. Whatever monster the starving-artist graffiti artists employees had come up with in-between wiping down cars, that was the theme. He was still far outside any town and surprised he found it, at least there was still no sign of highway life. This made the gyrating mechanical gorilla out front even more unnerving. The ape was painted green and clutching a bundle of deflated Valentine's Day balloons with "$5" scrawled on each one in black marker. The balloons swung around, lolling lazily in the dry wind, while the metal gears within the gorilla's shoulder creaked and strained. Wires protruded around the joints where the fur had worn away, leading to a spool of cable and a power outlet behind the human-like feet. The gorilla stood grinning through green teeth, waving Jason in. He heard hissing and clanking inside the wash, but there were no cars exiting the back. Never any cars anywhere today but his own.

Car washes were scary enough when you were little, Jason thought. *Children must shit their pants when they take a wrong turn into this freakshow.*

He looked around as he pulled closer to the entrance, and seeing no one to take his money, and an "Out of Order" sign taped to a busted change machine, he put a five-dollar bill in the mailbox by the door. The box was painted up as another smaller clown, with the inside of the flip-up painted like a tongue. Jason slammed it shut, and a loud bang made his heart jump. He looked up to see the garage door retracting and this monstrous tongue disappearing into the clown's maw. A flashing green light beckoned him inside, and Jason gave the car a little gas to accommodate.

"Now, I know babies get scared in car washes," Jason whispered soothingly to his cargo. "I used to get scared in these myself, I'm not afraid to admit. But I'm sorry, I'm not going to close your eyes."

Something thumped under his seat as the car wash took control of the vehicle.

"I heard that dogs go bonkers inside these things. Hey, that reminds me, what do you give a dead baby for its birthday? A dead puppy!"

There was another jerk as the wheels found the sweet spot in the tracks and now the machines had taken over completely. Jason took his hands off his steering wheel and the green light flashed red. Water started trickling down the windshield as the tongue rolled closed behind him and his car was drawn the rest of the way into the dark.

Jason stifled a laugh, some of it snorting from his nose to betray his nervousness.

"You ever wonder where dead baby jokes come from? Wait, no, you ever wonder where dead babies come from? Dead stork brings 'em! Just teasing. Hey, who comes up with all those jokes? Maybe you really need a dead baby around to get the best ideas going, to get the real funny stuff . . . "

Something rocked the car hard, and Jason bit his tongue.

"Ow. Hey! Why did the dead baby cross the road? Because it was nailed to the chicken!"

The car lurched like a bronco as the water pressure increased, and he sat up a bit straighter. He jumped at a wet slap on the glass and watched an octopus of purple fingers dance down to his wiper blades. That part always scared the shit out of him as a kid—the way the tentacles squirmed there for a second, then lazily dragged themselves up and over the car, leaving a steaming white trail of bubbles and slime behind them. And when the two huge, green scrubbers started slowly moving up and down his doors, his heart may have skipped and he coughed a bit in panic, bringing both feet down hard on the brake pedal. Then he sighed and scratched himself hard behind the ears in disgust. For some reason, whenever those scrubbers moved past the car, he always thought the car was moving instead of the machines. The optical illusion never failed to make him stomp the brakes like a dumb shit.

The heavy soap started spraying, and Jason looked down at his crossed arms, watching the pattern change as foam and water marbled the light across his skin. He adjusted the rearview mirror again to see how the dance of light looked on his face, then his eyes. But he saw the toy again in the back seat, and before he could hypothesize the species of stuffed animals skinned to create it, there was the blur of a tire flashing over it in his mind, and the popcorn kernels bursting, dancing, then rolling away to pop on the heat of the asphalt. Another tire rolled through his mind's eye, and the popcorn on the road popped and boiled up higher in the heat. Then another tire as the popcorn sprouted wings like blowflies as the rattling sound magnified . . .

But something didn't sound right outside the car, outside in the wash. He looked down the hood and found the problem. The rattling was the sound of the antenna on his car getting hammered by a particularly angry green scrubber. It was bouncing back and forth way too hard, bending much too far, wiggling dangerously fast. Jason sighed. He'd forgotten to unscrew it before he went in. And even though he hadn't seen the sign, he knew neither the clown nor the gorilla would be "responsible for anything lost or broken." He wondered what someone would say if he complained, "Your evil-clown car wash scared my baby to death. You owe me a new rattler. At least!"

The scrubbers were up and spinning on the side windows now, pounding away at the glass and filling the car with strobe lights and vibrations. He never saw them move like that before, never that high anyway. He could feel the tendrils almost touching each other on the roof above his head. Every sound in the wash seemed too loud, and he clicked on the radio and put his arm around the dead speaker in the passenger's side headrest, listening for his soothing lullaby of static.

"You know, I remember more jokes about killing babies, instead of jokes about babies that are already dead. Like, what's red and squirms in the corner?"

STEALING PROPELLER HATS FROM THE DEAD

A fleet of scrubbers surrounded his car. He hadn't counted them, but he was sure they were multiplying. The antenna was batted back and forth between two of them like Pong on the fastest level.

"A baby playing with a razor! Okay, what's blue and squirms in the corner?"

Now the antenna was being slapped around harder, and under the splashing and the rattling, his radio was making a noise he'd never heard before.

"A baby playing with a garbage bag! And what's green and *doesn't* squirm in the corner?"

The antenna shook and wiggled so fast that it vanished, then it snapped and was gone for good, flipping end over end into a chaotic blur of chrome, water and suds.

"Same baby! Three weeks later!"

Dead air on his radio now. Seconds passed. Then minutes. His car had stopped moving forward, though it was still being washed. It felt like he'd been in there a long time. A lot more than five bucks worth anyway.

He leaned over to talk to the speaker in the passenger-side headrest, only to jerk back his arm as if he'd been burned. He'd heard something strange, more of a feeling in his head than an actual sound. But something was very wrong. He crawled out of his driver's seat and into the back to squint through the defroster lines to see if anyone was in the wash with him. It was hard to see through the steam and foam, and his breath fogged the glass. He was sure someone had to be working on getting the tracks moving again.

Maybe they got distracted refilling the soap, blowing bubbles. Or blowing up more balloons, feeding the robot monkey.

"Nothing to worry about," he lied to the dead baby.

"This is just like when you're stuck at the top of a Ferris wheel. That never hurt nobody."

A frozen Ferris wheel, he thought. *Now* that *meant forever.*

The car started shaking violently, and he wiped the fog rolling off his skin from all the windows, checking every direction for someone inside working on repairs. He saw no one and adjusted a side mirror to watch the scrubbers down beating on his wheel wells. He wondered what they were made of, if they would puncture his tires if they cleaned the same spot of rubber long enough.

If a hundred monkeys washed a hundred tires for a hundred years, they wouldn't need to shake a spear . . .

He figured anything could cut through anything if it worked on it long enough, and he remembered a picture he'd seen depicting the aftermath of a tornado. It made no sense at the time, but the photograph revealed a sock monkey stuck half in and half out of a tree trunk, its soft head buried in the wood.

If something gets spinning fast enough, he decided. *Anything can happen. Is that what's going on in here . . .*

He climbed back into the driver's seat, then leaned over to the passenger's side, not sure whether he was talking to the static or the baby, wondering again how easy it would be to not notice the end of the world.

"What's worse than running over a baby with your car? Getting it out of your treads." He scratched his scalp hard in frustration. "Didn't like that one? Fine. Why do babies have soft spots on their heads? So you can carry them ten at a time. Like a six-pack! Hey, you know what?"

He squeezed the headrest under his arm affectionately.

"I really don't like those kinds of jokes. The 'what's worst' ones are better. Remember the little kids and their 'what's worst' jokes? Or 'what's grosser than gross'?"

STEALING PROPELLER HATS FROM THE DEAD

A strange smell rolled his eyeballs down to the passenger's seat before he could stop himself.

"Phew, someone's baby needs changin'! Changin' back to *alive,* mean."

Change machine out of order . . .

Jason tried giggling, but he'd already made the mistake of looking. And he could have sworn the baby had been staring back at him before he could pinch his own eyes shut.

And its mouth was open, too.

He shook his head to erase the image, then his back was stiff and straight in his driver's seat again, both hands on his window, pressing his nose against the glass. He wished he would have looked closer when he first found it back there on the road. Then he would have known if the eyes and mouth were already open. Then he'd know for sure if anything on the baby had changed. Or needed changing.

What's worst? he wondered. *Open eyes or open mouth?*

At first he thought maybe the eyes? But now he wasn't so sure which would be worse. But he was pretty sure the open mouth was where the smell was coming from.

But what about that sound?

He looked at the digital clock in his dashboard, trying to remember what time he'd entered the wash. Then he tried to remember the make and model of his car. Or where he had been going. Or how long he'd been inside. He had none of these answers. And the clock seemed to be displaying military time, or something equally impossible. And his odometer was creeping backwards. Something about the wash was affecting things, this he was sure of. Maybe it was as simple as the heat and moisture and pressure of a car wash's ecosystem, like a miniature storm over the Bermuda Triangle.

How long could you be stuck in a car wash without someone noticing? he thought. *Would I even want to know the record?*

He squinted out through the bubbles again and decided that the washing stage should be done by now, at the very least. He thought it should definitely be time for some different machines to come crawling over besides these scrubbers. He knew there were more machines out there. And people. He could hear them all. He crawled into the back seat again, and smeared his hand through the fog to peer out toward the mouth of the clown. A new machine lowered onto his trunk, and between the rhythm and bounce of this cylinder of shredded beach towels, Jason could see some light through the garage-door's windows, and then, past that, the shimmering dark outline of the empty road. He had to keep wiping away his breath to see, and he told himself that maybe there was a long line of cars filing past, that maybe cars were going by unseen, every time his hand cleared the steam from the glass.

He climbed into the front again and sucked in a deep breath, preparing for his space walk. Then he gently pulled up on his door handle and cracked his car open like a soda.

***

Hot needles of white water peppered his arm, and he was ready to make a run for it when one of the green scrub-wheels suddenly lurched towards him and slammed his door back shut. He forced a laugh and opened it again. But the door stopped against the scrubbing wheel and bounced violently under his hand. The noise of the wash was impossibly loud now that the seal had been broken, and his head ached with the tidal sounds of the machinery. He leaned his shoulder against the door and pushed. The door would only open a crack, vibrating so hard he bit his tongue from the force. He put all his weight against the door, gaining a few more centimeters, but not enough for even his shoe to hold it open. He pushed harder, then threw himself against it in a tantrum, worried for a moment that he might lose control of his bowels, like a baby. He thought about a video he saw once where a woman was giving birth and defecating at the same time. It had made him sick, and at the time he thought it was because it had made him realize humans were mere animals. But now he knew it was so disturbing because of the possibility of raising the wrong one as your child.

He shoved hard and a jet of hot water filled his mouth and his drowning reflex kicked in.

How do you make a dead baby float? Take your foot off its head. How else do you make a dead baby float? One can of root beer and two scoops of dead baby. How do you spoil a baby? Leave it on the side of the road . . .

The door slammed shut, and as he coughed and spit out the fluids, he was suddenly worried that fighting a door to the death might mean he'd be discovered in a car wash with shit in his pants, never mind the dead baby. So he stopped pushing and forced himself to relax. All the windows and mirrors were fogged, even the chrome on the radio knobs. He couldn't see the whirling mechanisms surrounding him at all anymore, and he started working to control his breathing, slowing his exhales so that all the glass would clear and he could see what was holding him captive, so he could work on getting out.

"You know what you never hear?" Jason practically screamed at the dead baby over the static and the bashing hurricane of the wash.

He worried the speakers were broadcasting the beat of the machines, maybe even before he got there. Maybe that's what he'd been tapping his foot to for hours.

Can you hear a car wash through your radio? If it

was loud enough. I swear I heard a hockey game once that wasn't being broadcast. No one believed me, but how did I know it went to a shoot-out and had six fights? In the parking lot.

"You never hear someone make up a joke. No one's ever around to see it happen. Just like you can smell a skunk on the road but never see it. Just like you hear the tires squeal and never hear the crash. And even though we know the dead storks bring the dead babies, don't you ever wonder where jokes come from?"

For the first time since he'd picked up his tiny hitchhiker, Jason forced himself to look directly at it. Its eyes and mouth were looking at him, just like he knew they would be. But it was much worse than he'd feared. He stared at the thing long and hard, until the baby blurred and finally faded from his vision. Jason knew that this always happened when he stared at things too long, and this was the first time it had ever happened as a defensive measure, but he told himself it was really just the impenetrable steam inside the car that had mercifully swept the baby away.

"So let's make a dead baby joke! Right here, right now. You know, just to pass the time. Now, how do jokes usually start?"

He blinked and his vision cleared, and the baby was back in his head, burrowing behind his eyelids. He waited until it faded again.

"So, a dead baby walks into a bar . . . shit! That doesn't work, does it?"

He slapped himself upside the head and vigorously scratched the back of his neck to focus.

"The best jokes always start with the words 'what's worst.' This we know. I once heard this little girl telling dead baby jokes and she kept saying the words 'what's *worst*' instead of 'what's worse,' and it's so much better that way. So what's worst? Driving over a baby on the road or . . . getting the baby out of your . . . fuck, we already did that one. Okay, what's worst? Trying to get the dead baby off the hood ornament or . . . "

Jason closed his eyes to keep it together.

"What's worst? Trying to get a dead baby out of your grill? Or trying to get it out of your head?"

Jason looked around for answers, his spit drying and foaming on the back of his tongue. He looked at the baby and saw its mouth was closed. Then it blinked.

It was time to go.

***

Jason slammed his back against his driver's seat and pulled his gear shift down hard. His foot stabbed the pedal and he straightened his arms to brace against the dash, waiting for the crashing and sparks and sunlight as he broke through the clown's mouth and splintered its metal tongue, bouncing and scraping his car out into the road in a shower of fireworks.

Nothing.

He pushed the gas down flush against the floorboards, stomping so hard he felt the pedal actually bend to the curve of his foot. He heard the engine screaming with all the power it had and he wished he could remember what kind of car he drove so he could visualize maximum performance in the commercial. He still wasn't moving.

Are my wheels off the ground? That's not how these things work. You ever notice how you never see a hockey fight during overtime? Time to focus. Let me the fuck . . . out.

He tried to remember what had happened when the red light flashed on and the car wash first pulled him in. There was no way it could be holding him up with his wheels in the air. There was something very wrong, and he was leaving. He shoved himself back in his driver's seat even farther, grunting and punching the horn with his fist, then his feet, walking his legs up and over the steering wheel onto the glass of the windscreen. Then Jason started jack-hammering the windshield with his heels. He kicked hard, then harder, then faster, almost running in midair, hearing the rubber on his shoes squeaking and watching the crazy patterns they were smearing in the vapor. He thought of a kaleidoscope, one that he'd had and loved as a boy, a toy that he just had to break open, and how two rolls of black tape couldn't fix it after he cracked it open to see what was inside. Nothing really, nothing like what he seen through the hole anyway. He tried refilling it with sand and bugs and screws and apple juice and marbles, and even after all that labor, it still never worked again. He shook the image out of his head, cracked his neck in both directions, and pushed the muscles in his legs faster and harder than he ever had before.

His sneakers kick-started a spider web of cracks between the steaming bubbles and wax splashing across the glass, and his frantic heels squeaked and spasmed. He imagined an army of spiders on the outside of the windshield, in a furious competition to finish their design first, all while he drove off down the road, RPMs redlining on the curves, trying desperately to find a straightaway long enough to gather the speed to blow the passengers off.

His ankles ached, one of his shoes slipped, and a flailing knee turned the radio back on. Static and voices fought for his attention, even without the antenna, distorted singing and crying rising up from the passenger's seat that couldn't be coming from the speakers, and Jason kicked the windshield with everything he had left. And finally, his legs locked straight behind the knees, both feet went smashing through the glass.

Coming out breach, he thought. *Got no choice, doc.*
His hands came up to protect his head.
Just don't let the cord wrap around the neck . . .
Then a snowstorm of safety glass cubes splashed his crossed arms and showered his face. The roar of the wash and the hot water riding in with it, dragging the shards across his nose and forehead. A shard stung him over the eyebrow, then another bee sting under his nostril. He fought the urge to wipe them away, knowing this would make the cuts deeper. Then he pulled his feet back inside and surged forward, trying to exit head first, eyes pinched closed, ears getting the worst of the scalding wax. His shoulders got stuck, and he sliced through his shirt working his way free, grinding the sand of the windshield into his chest and stomach as he strained and contorted his body to widen the hole. Eventually it was big enough, and he exploded out, rolling across the hood and flopped onto the ground gasping for air.

He stood up tall outside the car, watching the machines dancing and spinning around him, seemingly keeping their distance now as the pink, blood-streaked water pooled on his dashboard under the jagged hole where he'd come from, crimson and foam running down his throat, past his legs, and gathering between his toes.

He turned, and the clown's mouth started to open for him, just like the baby's had, and he finally stepped out into the sun.

***

It was only when he saw the boy lying there outside that Jason's heart started to slow to a normal speed. Gray, soggy rags wrapped around his arm, mouth frozen in a yawn, and stretched out in a grass-angel he'd worn into the ground around him. Headphones covered his ears, and the boy was slowly sitting up on his elbows and realizing that Jason was there.

The boy squinted and pulled the headphones down to his throat, absently picked dirt and stones out of the skin on his arms, then checked his watch and shrugged with a "What the fuck?"

Jason turned to watch his car exit the clown's mouth behind him, safe, wheels locked on the tracks, windshield gutted yet gleaming, and right on schedule. That's when Jason knew his car had been in neutral the whole time he was gunning it in there, that he hadn't been inside the wash any longer than normal.

So he went back for the baby. And this time, when he strode out through the scalding foam and the sting and the Turtle Wax snapping, a dead baby clenched tight against his chest, soft translucent head under Jason's chin, brittle snakeskin like an accordion around its neck. He covered the open eyes and open mouth with a loving, protective hand when the blast of the last machine came down over both of them, blowing the water out of his ears like they were candles, and he didn't hesitated to look anymore. It was his baby now.

He stopped to let the machine finish, feeling the tiny single rubber wheel on the blower rolling down the back of his neck, the hot wind filling up his eyes and roasting away any bad memories, evaporating the pools inside his ear and turning the static back to music.

What's worst? Finding a dead baby on the side of the road? Or wanting to?

He walked to the boy in the grass and yanked the headphones from his head, surprised they weren't connected. He used the rattle in his hands to lead the boy's eyes around like a drunk test, imagining how powerful he looked after his rescue. Even if he'd only gone back in to get the antenna.

ZEE BEE & BEE
(A.K.A. PROPELLER HATS FOR THE DEAD)

"Follow me, and let the dead bury their dead."
                                    —Matt 8:22-23 p.m.

YOU WANT MOANING? We aren't supposed to start moaning and pounding on the house until the sun goes down, but we're taking our jobs real serious these days. Over by the fake gas pump, I can see a shadow crouching down, and I suddenly realize it's really going to take a shit in that football helmet. All this action has the setting sun glaring behind it and turning everything black, but I can just make out the Steelers logo as the shadow's jeans roll down and fill it up like unholy ice cream all the way to the ear holes. There is no chance of the helmet being worn after this desecration, even if it's hosed out again.

Another shadow runs up and takes a swat at the one still squatting, but the first shadow just hunches down and concentrates harder, kind of like a cat still trying to get the ham off someone's sandwich after it's been busted red-handed. The "S"-shaped silhouette just gets lower and lower and lower with each blow, belt buckle jangling, making no move to pull up its pants. I hear a voice from the second shadow demanding an explanation for this insult, and I sigh. I don't have to see their faces to know who they are. We've played this game too many times already.

"It's my love letter to the city that gave birth to us," the first shadow explains, finally deciding it's a good time to run. "Love 'n' hate letter, I mean."

Our instructions were always to display precisely one character trait. This, we were told, was because it is both the most efficient way to make a memory in the allotted time, and because it was so hysterical in *Dawn of the Dead* when they wandered over the hill inexplicably wearing baseball uniforms, ballerina outfits, and Santa Claus suits. Most of the boys usually just want to wear their favorite team jersey though, and that means there's almost always too many sports fans bumping shoulders among our small band of the undead.

"I'm just saying," the first shadow laughs as it backpedals and falls down under a steady rain of backhands and elbows, "if we already have a Baseball Zombie, we probably don't need a Football Zombie. But we definitely don't need *two* Football Zombies."

"Said the Football Zombie," someone adds.

"You're not even supposed to be on a team. That's not why we got you that shirt . . ."

The fight escalates, and someone hustles them behind the shed and out of the sun-blasted blind spot behind the house. It's not even night yet, and everyone's already tired of them. But I have to admit one thing. The first shadow was right. Pittsburgh was the city that started it all, and it was the reason we were here, if you got right down to it. But I had to agree with the second shadow's violent reaction to that act of biological vandalism. It was hard to see any "love" in such a gesture, and it wasn't even my Steelers helmet that had been defiled.

And as handy as one might be during an apocalyptic onslaught, two football helmets were obviously one football helmet too many.

"Why would that fucker be wearing a catcher's mitt?"

we used to complain during our end-of-season, zombie-movie marathons, "Come on, did he get bit during a game?"

But our previous Baseball Zombie was always ready to defend those criticisms.

"It's not that complicated, man! It put the glove on later, just like me, after it died. It's just pretend."

"Then why can't I have a catcher's mitt and roller skates, too?"

Good question. Well, we were told very sternly by our employers never to mix and match. You couldn't wear a cowboy hat and carry a hockey stick, for example. You couldn't wear a Hawaiian shirt and a magician's top hat. You couldn't fumble around with a book while wearing a KKK cloak, not just because books are like Kryptonite to the Klan, but because, obviously, what would the poor Library Zombie wield if not a book? And you couldn't stand outside a window slowly and comically figuring out how to aim a gun all over again if you were, say, a Face-Painted Big Game Zombie. Yes, it would be hard to do this anyway with a giant foam finger, but that was the Cop Zombie's job. Always would be. This rule was particularly hard to follow for our latest Cop Zombie, since it was always so tempting for him to make fun of my nervous cough, something I'd been afflicted with all my life, but also a trait that made little sense to him or me. Especially me, the Truck Zombie.

"Shouldn't it be 'Hit-By-A-Truck Zombie?'" they always asked me.

At one morning meeting, I tried to explain that my name was a result of the grill impact of an imaginary 18-wheeler that crushed my chest. I even showed them the cookie-cutter impression of a Jesus on the cross that I'd pressed deep into my skin to simulate a hood ornament.

But everyone just scoffed and said cars probably didn't have Jesus on their hood ornaments, and that the coughing was for the Cigarette Zombie, not me. So maybe I should just continue to hold in my coughs? As if I could.

So I suppress my first cough of the day as my earphone informs me that the second couple is already heading for the basement. This means they will be confronting our first "plant," the hysterical yet tyrannical businessman, followed soon after by a reveal of his wife and their injured daughter. This is about an hour ahead of schedule. Remember, the sun isn't even down yet.

I pound harder, furious they've never seen *Night of the Living Dead*, or even the hundreds of imitators, like us, or they'd know that running to the basement always means doom. At the very least, they should understand that the trip to the basement should come at the end of the goddamn movie. Even *Day of the Dead*, despite that deceptive title, only displays about nine minutes and seventeen seconds of total sunlight throughout its entire running time. Practically the whole movie takes place in a basement! It's no accident that their bunker is considered the logical end and tombstone of the series.

It's also no accident that most survivors in the remakes end up on the water. Those blue-and-white waves remind people of being safe, if only for a moment, like being up in the sky.

Tonight, I let my legs give out, start crawling toward the next open window, then I snap back up. Sometimes I play it like my legs are broken. Sometimes I even put my pants and shoes on backwards to look like my body has been turned around completely below the waist due to some sort of massive impact. But tonight I decide my backwards shoes won't be enough of a hindrance, so I spin them back around when no one is looking.

Hold on, here's some trivia. I actually knew the actor who got hit by the truck in the '90s remake of *Night of the Living Dead*. Okay, he was a friend of a friend, but I heard that he was sort of a real, live mutant with no sweat glands and, legend has it, had to smear ChapStick all over his head if he was stuck out in the sun too long during filming. Often I wish he could play this game with us, because with that kind of dedication, I know he would probably take it just as seriously as I do, maybe even shame me into turning my shoes around for good.

I punch through the window, and everyone squints as glass showers their sweaty faces and forearms. Cowboy Zombie stops moaning for a second to hold the eyeball up off his cheek and glare at me. Then he flicks a glass shard from behind a sticky blue ear and starts to pound again, face slack, all business. Baseball Zombie shakes his head, brushes his jersey with his catcher's mitt, and waits patiently for me to notice him. Then he gives me a shrug under his perpetual slouch, jaw still swinging, the siege momentarily forgotten. I shrug back, then turn away to grab a pink and panicked hand before the wood covers the hole and a deafening burst of panicked hammering finally displays the proper level of respect for their situation.

Beyond the hand, I catch a glimpse of some weary eyes inside the house, and I'm glad to see they are finally realizing how long this game might last.

***

They got the idea by trying to be the last bed & breakfast in the phone book. Mags came up with the name "Z B & B" specifically to trump Youngstown's Country Inn (and a particularly idiotic driving instructor's ad with a zebra for the mascot). And it was this name, and the meaningless "Z," that started her boyfriend, now husband, Davey Jones, thinking about zombies nonstop. And soon after that, as a bit of an experiment, they were involved in an altercation at an Italian dinner theater/fake wedding combo that was touring the Midwest, "Tony Baloney's Madcap Reception." It was a gimmick that Mags called "vaguely racist bullshit," although she did eventually admit that getting shoved into a ten-tier cake while Mafioso caricatures staged a fist fight might be a good story to share at a party after enough time had passed.

"Tragedy plus time equals comedy and all that," she reminded her husband the morning after his crowd-pleasing, buttercream obliterating Pete Rose slide.

"But wait!" Davey Jones exploded over corn flakes, bloody twist of toilet paper popping from his nostril. "What if zombies were trashing the ever-loving shit out of that wedding reception? Would you pay to see that? I'd pay to see that! Hell, I'd pay to *do* that."

And *pow!* they suddenly found themselves with an untapped gold mine of couples who would rather spend the night of their honeymoon pretending to be hiding from zombies instead of tapping glasses with forks to encourage some failed actors to stage a kiss.

"Zee Bee & Bee?" Davey Jones mumbled. "Sounds German."

"Sounds more like 'Bee Bee & Bee,'" Mags laughed. "You know? Like Bed Bath & Beyond? I know that's where I'd want to be trapped when the brains hit the fan. Easy cleaning."

So, whether it was a new groom wanting to puff out his chest and protect his woman during a life-threatening emergency or the blushing bride hoping to demonstrate how she would, much to his surprise, bloom into a steely-eyed killer in an end-of-the-world crisis, business was excellent right out of the gate. A little later, when they hired me (their second cousin and tireless initiator of years of Sunday night zombie film festivals) to eagerly amp up the threat level of the scenario, word spread fast. I helped hand-pick a crew, and by the next fall, we had everything up and running.

Oddly enough, two full years after we'd started making enough money to start seriously thinking about filming our first 4:00 a.m. commercial spot, a low-budget flick popped up in the video stores called *Dead & Breakfast* that sounded a little too close to home. Everyone started muttering "lawsuit." But, luckily, it bore no resemblance to our original idea of staging an attack for fun and profit. This movie was just another attack on a house, and it took the situation more seriously than we did, even for a supposed comedy, as their storyline treated everything as if it was actually happening, something even the occasional survivalist couples that stopped by our joint rarely considered for long. Clever title though, we all had to admit.

And if that wasn't suspicious enough, a jazz/calypso fusion song about zombies partying it up at a bed and breakfast was released the same summer we flicked on our "Vacancy" sign. It was called "The Zombie and B," but, thank Christ, it had two inherent problems that quickly relegated it to our bosses' pay-no-mind list. One, it hit the radio a full 48 hours after the story of this story was first transcribed by the banker where we got our loan, (which, of course, seems like an impossible claim with the current state of the union and the fact that you're reading about all of this at exactly the same time). And two, unless you say that title out loud, stressing the second syllable of "zombie," you don't get the gag at all. You'd just think it was another love song. So the hell with them.

Anyway, this was our job. No one else's. It didn't matter how trendy this shit got or whether people were sick of zombies again this year. We were serious. And we were the last love song you'd ever need to hear.

But while we're keeping score, it was definitely *my* idea to have the evening start with Mags and Davey Jones meeting two newlywed couples at the bottom of the long driveway leading up to the house. This is where they would sign the waiver. And it was also my brainstorm ("Brainstorm! Sounds delicious!" was our crew's second-worst zombie joke) to make sure that the two couples arrived about an hour apart. This gave one couple a chance to get settled and locked in before the other couple came banging on the door. See, now this door suddenly became *their* door, just because of that extra hour. And there was always only one bed split between the two couples to encourage competition and arguments, another good reason to keep their arrivals staggered. It was amazing how much controversy could be caused by one couple getting an unfair opportunity to toss a suitcase onto a bed and claim it first.

Mags chalked this behavioral science up to the sad influence of reality television.

She eventually started profiling them very carefully to decide which couple was most likely to not want to give up that sacred mattress without a fight. We were never sure how she figured this out, and there was talk of Mags going through trash cans and peeking through windows of potential applicants, but damn if she didn't always seem to pick the right couple to step into the house first.

Sometimes, I pretend she picks me.

***

"What's going on? Where did you come from?!"

Inside the house, someone is screaming, and it's so loud I don't need my earphone to hear it. It's a Plant, not a Camel this time. That's what we called the guests,

"Camels." Cigarette Zombie sort of made up the name. Something about the title of Albert Camus's short story "The Guest" being a translation of the French word "L'Hôte," meaning both guest and host. According to her, this was "precisely" what we were asking them to be. She tried to get us to call them this nonsense for a while, but we couldn't pronounce it, and we really had no idea what the hell she was talking about. But they did become "Camus" for a time, and that made her smile (at least that's what somebody told me. I've never actually seen her smile myself). Then the term got changed to "Camels" for good, and she's scowled ever since. Even though we tried to convince her it was based on an Aesop's Fable about "familiarity breeding contempt," that one story where the Arabs first see a camel and are all terrified but by the third sighting they're putting saddles on it (because, hey, wasn't that "precisely" what we were doing?), it didn't matter. She never got on board with the new moniker.

But it isn't a Camel that's screaming. I can tell by the moderate display of acting ability. And it can't be Tom. Not yet. He should still be in his locked room, waiting to be discovered if and when they find the key in the bucket of nails under the sink. For now, he should just be happily rustling his ball of aluminum foil, maybe scratching at the door or the floor every so often, maybe making just enough noise for someone to start wondering what's in there, mouse or monster.

For a second, it's silent. Then I hear that girl, that perfect girl we all saw walking up the steps, the newlywed, making her "tisk" noise at something that disgusts her. I heard her doing it an hour earlier when I was hiding in the bushes watching her new husband sign the waiver. I remember thinking if there was some fine print in that contract she'd missed earlier and was having second thoughts about it with all those mouth noises of hers, it was too late now.

I've always hated those kinds of tongue-smacking insect noises, those impatient clicks and hisses people always make when they're annoyed. I had a girlfriend once who ruined every movie by sucking her bottom lip and making a sharp *snap! snap!*, sorta like bubble gum popping, whenever something remotely melodramatic happened on a screen. It was especially excruciating in a theater, and I found myself taking her to more comedies than I ever cared to see. And at a zombie movie? Forget about it. She would "tisk" so many times at the characters' bad decisions that one nearby theatergoer actually asked if she was shuffling a deck of cards.

I start thinking about how this blushing bride's cute little noises might screw up our game, maybe make some other zombie out here in the yard, a zombie with less patience than myself, try just a little harder to make her stop making that noise, maybe by pulling her tongue out from the root, slow and steady as a flower you don't want to break off before you get it out of the ground and give it to your girl.

In my earpiece, I can hear the honeymooners talking very seriously about a shower curtain for some reason. They're exchanging the kinds of details you would assume had already surfaced before their nuptials.

" . . . well, my dad used to flip out if we messed up the bathroom. With two boys, it got real messy real quick . . . "

"I'm telling you it isn't blood. Somebody dyed their hair in here recently, that's all."

" . . . and then when my little sister came along, she was one of those vacation babies by the way, that's why there's the age gap, well, she'd trash the place, and Dad never said peep. In one night, she changed her hair from black to red to green and splashed it all over the walls, and he just sighed . . . "

"This sure looks like blood though."

" . . . and when I tried to tell her how he used to lose his mind if we got one drop of urine behind the toilet seat, she wouldn't believe us. I mean, a little yellow on the toilet is a lot more understandable than a rainbow bathtub like a circus crime scene . . . "

"You know what? If they try too hard to scare us, I might call their bluff."

The groom has a little swagger in his voice, and that's okay. Bad things happen sometimes. Not often, but sometimes. It comes with the territory when things really start rolling and those emotions spike. Overly aggressive behavior, minor theft and vandalism, a general disrespect for the situation. But to discourage these shenanigans, we discovered early on that there were a few simple preventative measures we could take. We didn't want to hurt anyone, of course, but we did need to convince people we were really, *really* trying to get a grip on them.

So Davey Jones told us to always go for the meat.

"Meat," he said. "Not bones. Avoid the bones. If you look for spots that an actual zombie would prefer to bite into and grab that spot with your fingers, you will usually hit a part of their body less likely to inflict pain."

He was right. The skulls and elbows and knees were a lot of trouble in our hands and best avoided when possible, just as they would likely disappoint a hungry mouth, they should disappoint us, too. But nothing caused as much trouble for us as an agitated Camel. Therefore, in the wavier, it clearly states that they can be expelled from the house by any staff or Camel ("For the sake of the human race!" our Plants would declare to the rest of the survivors if necessary, if they witnessed the bounce). So the precise moment they crossed that line into purposeful injury or, like the example described more explicitly in the contract, "catching a zombie's finger under your hammer more than three times," those assholes were gone.

That part was easiest to remember. Three fingers and three strikes and they're out. And it wasn't fun to get bounced. Since they would have already turned in their car keys, they'd quickly understand this meant they could either sit in a ditch all night and watch their new husband or wife have all the fun, or they could allow themselves to be gently steered along the well-worn path of our very reasonable and ultimately satisfying storyline. However, if they were really ornery (like that little fucker last fall with the cherry bombs that we ended up ejecting headfirst through our mailbox), they would be held down and forced to take a slathering of blue paint to the face. Then, if they wanted to keep participating at all, they had to start attacking the house with the rest of our staff. We called these blue paint-brush smacks in the cheeks "getting bit," and it always surprised us how many of these clowns decided to join in with us on the pounding. I guess it was the choice between punching a door like you really meant it or . . . walking aimlessly around the woods all night. Two things a real zombie would probably be doing with his or her Saturday night anyway, but which one do you think a zombie would choose every time?

"Why the need to give everyone advice all the time?" a petulant voice sneers. "You get that from your uncle, I swear."

"Just trying to help you make the most of those nails. And why bring my uncle into . . . "

"Uh-huh. Why don't you tell us the advice he gave you the first time you got on the bus to kindergarten."

"He said, 'Be careful.'"

"Mm-hmm. Right. What else did he say? Tell them about his advice for little kids."

"Yeah, tell us," one of the Camels says.

"Okay, my uncle might have said something like, 'If you stick your hand down a girl's pants and it feels like you're feeding a horse, you're in trouble.'"

Between laughter, hammer strikes, and another "tisk," I finally recognize the voices of our Plants. It's our Irritable Couple Hiding in the Basement, Jeff and Amy. Apparently, they were forced to join the game early since the other Plants had already opened their doors. They seemed to be ad-libbing a little more than usual to fill the gaps and unexpected questions, so I cup my ear tight to listen to the banter. The rest of the zombies should be doing the same thing as me. If they're doing their job. And after another couple seconds of monitoring the progress of our script, we could safely assume the couples hadn't seen the injured daughter yet and we should stick to the plan.

Up until a couple seasons ago, this particular stage of the game would have been alerted by barking because the injured "daughter" had actually been an injured Blue Labrador (more hairless than "blue," to be honest) for a good while instead, a wonderfully irritating, half-domesticated, very snappy little monster we referred to as "shark dog." Daughter, dog, same problem. But after we lost the dog, we had to get our earphones to synchronize the plot without the barking as sign posts for the plot. It worked out okay though. Davey Jones found a whole box of them at a going-out-of-business sale, he told us. Marked way, way, way down.

But animals are sorely missed in these situations. Having one around changed the way everyone acted. Critters and all their energy, they never doubted the sincerity of our acting, not for one second. But any twist on the timeless Zombie Assault tale usually turned out to be a mistake, and with an animal in the mix, this was particularly problematic. There was a reason they kept dogs out of most of those movies. And you saw what happened in the *Dawn of the Dead* remake when they got too attached, right?

But what happened to our dog is something we blue-collar zombies rarely talk about. And, as always, we worried Amy would bring up the incident by the end of the night. She always did.

***

I'm pulling at a window frame when someone nicks some skin off the side of my thumb with the claw end of a hammer. It's the same worried pair of eyes from earlier.

I frown and count "strike two!" in my head.

At least Jeff is laughing tonight, having more fun with it. That's something. See, back in the day, Jeff used to date Amy. And Davey Jones encouraged this, thinking it would be great motivation since he'd swell up a little more around her, show a little extra plumage, and maybe that would help sell his role as troubled authority figure to the Camels. Back then, Davey even let them keep their real names to help stay in character.

It worked for a minute.

The problem was that it quickly made emotions bleed over into real life in increasingly dangerous ways. It sure didn't help that one ugly season when Amy cheated on Jeff with Jerry, a.k.a. Baseball Zombie. The infidelity made Jeff target the big number 3 on Jerry's back a bit too aggressively some nights. And during one seemingly endless barrage of moaning and pounding, Jeff broke character and mercilessly ridiculed Amy for liking "fucking athletes," even though Jerry had never thrown a pitch or hit a ball in his life, Nerf included. This, in return, caused Jerry to punch one Camel in the face last year ("barely a swat," he finally admitted after Davey Jones's terrifying two-hour interrogation), a very solid and un-undead-looking right hook that plowed through that Camel's bottom teeth like the Garden Weasel and cost the equivalent of a dozen of those tools, plus shipping and handling, to settle out of court. Don't laugh. Garden Weasels aren't cheap. We regularly use those fuckers after each weekend attack to fix our landscaping.

A lot of "dead baby mama drama," Mags called it.

These days, Tom, our military Plant, and part of our locked-room mystery during the big climax, was very quick to freestyle through the awkwardness of any embarrassing broken noses by coming up with his own stories off the cuff, usually about their lost platoon and mysterious reports of zombies imitating what they'd seen on the screen at a drive-in *Rocky* festival.

"Wait, what?" a Camel would ask.

"Could happen," he'd shrug. "Fist fights are instinctual, even when Rocky was alive."

Then he'd stand there humming nervously in a dogpile of corpses, covertly kicking at any zombie brawls to break them up and start acting like professionals, like dead men, as he held a toy phone over his head desperately searching for a signal and some misdirection.

But besides that recent love triangle, this year there was a new power struggle in our ranks. The two Bobbys, Bobby Z and Bobby B (stay tuned, lots more about those goofballs later), had both developed a strange impulse to lead us on our house assaults at all times. Each of them wanted to be the head zombie, standing on point, the first to snarl, the first to break the window, the first to use tools, sort of like the Gas character at the end of *Land of the Dead*, or at least the first to pick something up and turn it around in his hand like he was remembering something important.

But not at the end of the game, like we were supposed to. Like all the time.

You know, leading attacks, making decisions, very slowly, at least. But it all became quite a nuisance, more and more important to each of them during every Blitzkrieg. It made for low, slurring but serious arguments over cold barbecue chicken, about who broke what window first. And even though we all guessed it was mostly because they had the bad luck of both being named "Bobby," there was also some talk about one of them wanting to be the first zombie to drive a Camel's car. This was inexcusable. Not just because it wasn't in the contract, but because this would be a scene that wasn't in any of the movies, endless remakes included. Well, maybe in that *Warm Bodies* bullshit.

But tonight the Bobbys are just fighting about that football helmet nonstop. You'd think taking a dump in it would have been the last word on the subject, but it's not.

"I don't know why you even like the Steelers. It goes against our philosophy."

"The fuck you talking about?"

"That Polamalu-malu-lu or whatever his name is. His girly-ass hair would be a serious liability during a zombie uprising. I can't believe none of the announcers ever bring it up, to be honest."

"Nah, he's way too fast to get caught."

"Maybe with a ball in his hands. Without it, he's lunch. In fact, I once saw him take a hit so hard the ref yelled, 'Fatality!' instead of 'Offsides' . . . "

"Horseshit."

"I saw him get hit so hard he left his multiplication

tables on the 50-yard line, along with memories of three Christmases ago . . . "

"Never happened."

" . . . so hard his helmet rolled into the end zone and his head was still in it."

"Unlikely."

"I was there, man. And I couldn't believe they played such an inappropriate song on the speakers while they gathered up the pieces. If he ever did wake up, he'd have thought he was the lead singer of Maroon 5 . . . "

"A level of exaggeration I've sadly grown accustomed to."

"Shhh!" Another zombie tries to get them to keep it down.

"You owe me a helmet, asshole," a Bobby whispers. "A hat ain't a toilet.'

"Yes, my asshole owes you a helmet."

"You guys keep forgetting your roles," I interrupt. "Mags gave you two those shirts to represent the Army and Navy football teams for a different reason entirely, and I think . . . "

"Fuck off," they tell me in stereo. Then the weight goes out of their arms as they get into character. Just in time, too, as the second couple comes bounding up the driveway, laughing and zigzagging past the Bobbys as they make half-ass swipes at their shoulders. I'm closest to the house and the only one who sees what the Camel drops near the front door.

It's a paper towel. My heart would have jumped if it still pumped. As the brother of a child with OCD, I suddenly suspect this might change some things, perhaps everything.

A guest with such an affliction might not be ready for prime time, might not be ready for the trials and tribulations of our particular game, certainly not ready to fiddle while Rome burns. I start to think this might be one of those guys who doesn't want to get dirty enough to convince himself it's really happening. Well, then he shouldn't have signed up, should he? This should make me angry, even angrier than the Bobbys' constant nonsense, but for the first time since I started shuffling up the driveway tonight, this Truck Zombie is scared.

"'I Bite,'" someone says.

"Nice work. Hold on. What?" someone asks.

"Bite who?" someone else wants to know.

"No, I'm just saying that would be the perfect name for a zombie movie. Or the shortest zombie story ever. It's even better than *I, Zombie* because it's like the shortest sentence in the goddamn history of the English language."

"I thought that was 'Fleas: Adam Had 'Em.'"

"No, that's the shortest poem in the goddamn history of the English language."

"You bite, eh? Hmm, I like it."

"Yeah, 'I admire its purity,' as the man once said."

"'As the robot once said,' you mean. You got that from *Alien*."

"Actually, 'I bite' is not the shortest possible sentence. 'I am' will always hold that distinction."

"'I Bite Therefore I Am!'"

"You sound like Dr. Seuss."

"Not a real physician, by the way, but the world can use all the doctors they can get."

I stop shambling and stare up at the house, thinking about the Camels discussing that blood in the tub. How something like that should scare us more than it would scare them. Then turning back to our mob, I see her.

She's keeping to the rear, head down farther than anyone else's. At some point tonight, I will have to tell her how I feel. It is expected, of course. In the movies, end-of-the-world confessions are almost required. But this isn't why. I was inspired earlier today during our smoke break by the perfect advice I'd heard her giving a co-worker about something entirely inconsequential. Whether to eat or hurl some expired eggs was the original subject of their conversation. I'm not sure which side she came down on, but her answer was universal.

"Do it," she said. "If not now, when?"

***

The smoke breaks were probably her idea; our precious Cigarette Zombie (a.k.a Coffee And Cigarettes Zombie, a.k.a. Term-Paper-Grading Zombie). She was a creature whose assigned character trait was, once she broke into the house, to try and desperately smoke every butt and chug as much coffee as she could. But also to do this really, really slow. This was all a result of trying to relive her previous existence as a grad student, according to Mags anyway. I never thought it was fair that she was the only one claiming to be a "Grad Student Zombie," as we were all, without exception, University of Pittsburgh drop-outs, kicked-outs, and failed-outs, every cursed one of us.

We usually took the smoke break behind "The Joshua Bush," the squat, lonely shrub in the middle of the field near the fake gas pump. This was where most of our debates occurred. It was not named after the U2 album like you might think. You'll figure it out later.

One of the smoke breaks was usually scheduled right after the reveal of the Plants in the basement, since that surprise should occupy the Camels for a good half hour. But the timing was off tonight, and the second couple had just arrived, so we decided to hurry up and eat lunch as fast as we could.

We were always tired of barbecue chicken and sheep

entrails by the end of the evening (Romero was right that these were always the best meats to simulate cannibalistic feasts), so most of us usually stuck to fruit or vegetables at lunch to balance our diets. Ever see a zombie with rickets? It's not pretty. Looks just like me actually.

Since we are out of earshot, we don't have to whisper or moan anymore. And after passing around the box of fig bars, our discussion turns to the word "zombie" again, and how hard it is to not acknowledge exactly what we are every time we play the game. It seems impossible, but the existence of zombies should be a new discovery every single time, especially in the movies, just like my peanut-brained feline when he used to think every waking moment was his first day on Earth.

I might agree, but I don't say so. The topic makes me uncomfortable. It's usually taboo to say the word "zombie" out loud, a strict rule that British romp *Shaun of the Dead* mocked quite effectively. But contrary to popular belief, the much revered 1978 *Dawn of the Dead* was actually the first movie to break this law. But the worst infraction was, of course, in the later installment, *Land of the Dead*, where a visibly bored Dennis Hopper seemed to be speaking not just directly to the audience, but directly to the movie's fucking trailer, "Zombies, man, they creep me out," he shuddered. Everyone else did, too. Shit, I still cringe when I think about it. You'd assume he would have been thankful to have a script written for his complete comfort and indifference and try a little harder. Hopper had it so easy on that shoot. He had to be the only villain, zombie movie or otherwise, to ever spend 90% of his screen time in a luxury hotel sipping whiskey. He probably thought he was doing a buddy-cop flick the whole time.

While I'm waiting for the fig bars to come back around,

it's just a matter of time before someone is dwelling on labels again and stirring that familiar pot of discord.

"Then why are you, say, 'Lumberjack Zombie?'" Baseball Zombie asks with his mouth disgustingly full, pointing through then over the Joshua Bush and sputtering around a mumblecore of masticated mush. "We're encouraging that word every day, you know? Why resist it?"

"We don't count, asshole," Lumberjack Zombie scoffs. "And I'm Seattle Zombie now. Don't forget it."

"Don't let them see you guys kissing this time, Jack. Talk about breaking character."

"I ain't Jack. 'Seattle Zombie,' damn it! Recognize!"

"Who was kissing?" I ask, heart wanting to pound, eyebrows way too interested in the answer.

"Cigarette Zombie and one of the Bobbys," someone mutters.

"What's wrong with that?" Cigarette Zombie laughs. "Zombies should want to smooch just as much as they'd want to find a catcher's mitt. It's former-human nature. Come on, they're actually fucking in *Dead Alive*."

"You mean *Braindead*?" someone corrects her.

"Whatever."

"Hey, anybody been in the shed lately?" one of the Bobbys asks. "I think we got a Meth Zombie cooking back there. That's all we need. We've been moving way too fast as it is."

"No. Not whatever. *Braindead* is the original title."

"Whatever."

"I schooled your ass. Admit it."

"Yes," admits Cigarette Zombie. "You have indeed taken me to Ass School."

Cigarette Zombie turns away, but Josh, the instigator, a kid who was, technically, supposed to be our Sushi Chef

Zombie, until we started calling him the "Sour Towel Zombie" instead (because he smelled like a ripe bath towel at all times, as if he never heard of a dryer, even before the Apocalypse hit), he plops down next to me and keeps inching closer and closer to my shoulders, which are up high around my neck and defensive as always. He was always way too into these debates, and surprisingly unfunny for a kid named "Josh."

"That's right, baby," he laughs. "You have definitely been taken where asses are regularly schooled."

"Dude, take a step back, please," I hiss. "You're stepping on the punchline. And for the record, they don't make toothpaste strong enough for the undead."

I elbow him toward Cigarette Zombie, and she elbows him right back.

"You know what Sour Towel Zombie reminds me of?" asks Cigarette Zombie, looking up from the brown parts of the apple she was eating around, "He's like *Night of the Living Bread.*"

"How's that?" Sour Towel Zombie, a.k.a. Josh to his friends, a.k.a. Nobody to everyone else, sneers, ready to jump on any inaccuracies of the obscure parody of the film that started it all, Romero's straight-up Zombie D.N.A.

"Like the bread on the lawn, man! Every time we look away then look back, he gets a little closer."

"Yeah, seriously," I agree, then cough. "Back up, sucker. You're in my bubble."

"You know what I never understood before?" Bobby still wants to talk about the suspicious equipment he saw in the shed. "Crystal Method. That band's name? Crystal *Meth*od. Get it? I just got it."

Then somewhere around the bush, the conversation takes a dark turn.

"Okay, sure, they may hope it'll be like trying to deep

throat an old, splintered baseball bat. But that's just wishful thinking. It's more like trying to inflate a decade-old New Year's noisemaker. But sucking instead of blowing."

"Is this Corpse Blowing 101 again? Jesus Christ. When does the semester end?"

"Wait a minute. Does it even count as a 'deep throat' if there's a convenient exit wound?"

"Those days are over. As we've been drying up, don't tell me I'm the only one who noticed his balls are on the wrong side of the tracks lately."

Laughter.

"Whoa, what do you mean?"

"Okay, you ever smack one of your Hot Wheels too hard and the wheels ended up near the windows?"

"Que?"

"That ain't right."

"The wheels on the cock go 'round and 'round . . . " someone sings.

"Quiet!" snaps the other Bobby, and we hunch lower around the bush instinctively as Cigarette Zombie lights up for her few puffs, signaling the break is almost over. She's smoking less and less as the world runs out of her beloved Camel Blues (what else would she smoke?).

"Why don't you just quit?" someone asks.

"Because around you idiots all day, I need a smoke so badly."

"Smoking 'badly' would be, like, sticking a cigarette in your butt," I say before I can stop myself. She gives me a withering stare.

"Who are you? Grammar Nazi Zombie?" she asks. "Fine, I want so badly to smoke."

Embarrassed, I look around our circle. Besides the Plants, Jeff, Amy, and their daughter, or dog (and, of course, Mags and Davey Jones, who are supposed to burst into the house later tonight), there are about, what, a dozen of us these days? Yeah, that's got to be right. I remember the number because of that carton of rotten eggs in the house where Mags drew every one of our faces onto the yellow shells to remind us not to eat them. They're a great consistency if you wake to fake some brains, but only when they're ripe enough, and only if they're free-range.

The rest of the crew, well, first there's Jerry, a.k.a. Baseball Zombie, a.k.a. Somebody's Little Brother, I think. That's gotta be the only reason he got the job. Then there's the kid with the unlikely name of We Ma, a.k.a. Cowboy Zombie, a.k.a. Wii "None" Ma, the result of filling out a driver's license application and putting "none" in the space for a middle name, which the clerk mistook for just another crazy Asian appellation. To show her own cultural sensitivity, Mags vetoed Davey Jones's attempt to make our one Asian kid the cleaver-wielding Sushi Chef Zombie. Then there's Lumberjack Zombie, a.k.a. Seattle Zombie, a.k.a. Zombie Two-Shirts, a.k.a. Steve? I don't think I ever met that guy, actually, and probably couldn't "recognize!" no matter how many times he said it, which was a lot. He's been known to wear two shirts to try to look bigger, or so I heard. At least that's the only possible explanation for a nickname like "Zombie Two-Shirts." He was also called Sensible Shoes Zombie for a while, when he found the perfect trainers and told us how he was shuffling "ever so comfortably!" Then there's Matt, a.k.a. Security Guard Zombie, a.k.a. Rent-A-Cop Zombie. His title doesn't really fit though, since he sports a huge beard like a gnarly surfboard hanging off his face that he could probably hide half a chicken inside. We were still petitioning to make him Shoplifter Zombie instead (which would have probably been called "Sticky Fingers Zombie" instead, if we didn't all have sticky fingers) just so we could fire Glen, a.k.a. Midlife Crisis Zombie, who was currently balls-deep in exactly that sorry situation. Then there are Michael and Rachel, a.k.a. Indian Zombie and Indian Zombie, respectively, one Native American with a feather behind his ear, one European with a dot on her forehead, a target that sometimes doubles as a bullet hole. Michael loves his one characteristic—never showing emotion—claiming it suits him perfect as, supposedly, he has never shed a tear in his entire life. "And now, if you think about it," he loves to tell us, "it's way too late." And Rachel, well, she doesn't just stick to citing various Eastern religions. She's also been known to ironically quote the Bible to us when the Camels aren't in earshot. Matt, too, of course, in honor of his namesake, and they both always do it in a deep, movie narrator voice (but for some reason, he always bursts into scripture at precisely 8:22 Eastern Standard Time). And there's Mark, a.k.a. Fast-Talking '50s Newspaper Man Zombie, who never really fit in with us at all, and who walked off the set one day and never came back. He said our plots were predictable, our jokes stale, our lifestyles as unhealthy as our metaphors, and he just didn't have the stomach for it anymore.

Then there's Nate, a.k.a. Third Stage Zombie, a.k.a. Inevitable Head Torch Zombie. He's the slippery, oily, decaying ghoul you'd always see towards the end of the film, the zombie that's having a tough time putting one foot in front of the other. He's one of those zombies who's swimming in that limbo right before his muscles stop working entirely. Funny thing is, Nate used to walk awkwardly on the tips of his toes back when he was alive, back when we used to call him Obsessive Compulsive Zombie, a.k.a. The O.C.Z., back when this game was all just speculation.

Sucker came up with a killer drinking game though.

But, yeah, his adopted role here is a no-brainer. And no brains means he's starving. We try not to look at him. He reminds us the game can end.

And then there are the wild cards, sitting directly across from each other, as always, our two Bobbys, Bobby Zelienople and Bobby Balldinger, a.k.a. Bobby Z and Bobby B. They aren't playing zombies, not yet. At this point during the game, we aren't even supposed to see them. They're supposed to represent the military show of force that always appears in the third act to screw everything up and dash any hopes of rescue.

But they can never get this right.

They like to pretend they get bit by a zombie right from the get-go, already turned, always way too early. They want to be both, and neither, apparently. A proud tradition in most zombie films is that the military is never to be trusted under any circumstances, and they do relish that role. Too bad they can never wait for their cue. Sometimes they play Army, sometimes Navy, sometimes Air Force. But their rivalry probably started when, right after we started making the big bucks, Mags bought them both Armed Forces football jerseys instead of just Army and Navy T-shirts so they'd be more visible at night. Then someone brought the Steelers helmet. Big mistake. Now their competition regularly comes to blows. Thank God no one brought a football.

Tonight, however, neither Bobby wears a jersey. Just some gray Ts. They claim they're playing the roles of National Guard volunteers who are sick of their uniforms. Nobody bothers to argue. Rumor has it among the two higher-ups this is gonna be their last season if there are any more problems. Well, defecating in a football helmet probably sealed the deal, even though they tried to pin their recent behavior on some shocking news from the real world; the untimely motorcycle, train, Segway, and hot-air-balloon collision (and subsequent third decapitation) of their favorite Fantasy Football father figure, beloved number 7 (but number 1 in their hearts), cereal endorser and serial rapist, Big Ben "Has Been" Roethlisberger, a.k.a. Hand-off Burger, a.k.a. Rapist Burger, a.k.a. Roethlisraper. But now and forever Headless Road Burger Zombie.

Some say you can still see the motherfucker lurking around bathrooms.

The Bobbys glare at each other, arms crossed, pinched mouths and smirks crawling like caterpillars around their faces. We all know it will be a long night for us, but they won't disappoint anybody just tuning in. More about them later, I swear. Lots more.

And Cigarette Zombie? I never got her name. And I can't really remember when I first noticed she was stumbling alongside me as I sighed and kicked cans and probably pounded the house embarrassingly limp-wristed. I wish I would have been paying more attention.

Finally, there is the "live" staff inside the house, the big finale. Mags and Davey Jones, the long-suffering proprietors and our secret bosses, both buried so deep in the plot that they rarely come up at all, even for air. But we all know who's in charge. Ever hear the song "Maggie's Farm"?

Yep, she's the brains behind Pa.

But weren't we talking about poor Jeff and Amy, our Plants in the basement? I don't know who is playing Jeff and Amy's daughter this time, whether it's a scarecrow, a tackling dummy we borrowed from the 6th graders' practice field, or a splintered cowboy silhouette we took off the neighbor's barn and shaved down to toddler size.

But I'm hoping Amy doesn't bring another dog. This is always a concern. Her and that damn dog.

One of the Bobbys starts mocking me by clearing his throat when it's obvious he doesn't need to, so I try to distract him with a question that's been on my mind lately.

"Did either of you notice anything weird about that guy?"

"Which guy?" asks Bobby B, never looking up from Bobby Z. We used to call Bobby B "Cloverfield" because of his freakish height and tendency to destroy any beer can or small village he was squeezing. But he was less effective attacking a house that you might guess, so the "Cloverfield" thing was dropped. No one could have anticipated this monster's rivalry with Bobby Z, who carried at least a foot and 50 pounds less than him.

"The Camel," I whisper. "He was moving a little shaky, looking around too much. I don't know."

"Well, maybe they're getting more cynical, harder to snow," Sour Towel Zombie offers. "We've got to be famous by now."

"Yeah, but . . . "

"The Camels shouldn't know too much if they want to play the game right," Sour Towel Zombie interrupts. "But they shouldn't know too little, either."

"They need to be the porridge that's just right, is what you're saying," Bobby B scoffs with the perfect level of disgust. He's Rembrandt in the art of the scoff. Maestro of the mock.

"Exactly!" Sour Towel Zombie shouts, holding up one finger to punctuate this. "With so many movies showing the usual pattern of behavior in a house under siege . . . "

"I know, I know," I say impatiently. "And this is why the puzzle pieces have to be juggled sometimes. I get it. I understand all this. But there was something about that guy that just . . . "

"See," Sour Towel Zombie goes on, finger still up, "these movies are basically just home invasion stories. It is the house that is most important. Not them. Not us. The Camels could just run away, and it would all be over, the movie, the game, everything. But by protecting the house, any house, things escalate nicely. It's the most natural thing in the world to protect a house. And that's what we're doing every day, all day, even by tearing it down . . ."

"So, technically," Cigarette Zombie jumps in. "The first zombie movie was that book about the two guys who kill a family for a silver dollar. If a book was a movie, of course."

"What?" asks Rachel, a.k.a. European Indian Zombie. "No, no, no. That was Capote, technically the first true-crime novel you're thinking of."

"Bed and Breakfast at Tiffany's"? Cigarette Zombie laughs. Clearly Rachel was in her house now, her wheelhouse at least, by daring anyone to challenge her book knowledge.

"No, I meant his other book."

"In Cold Blood, right?" Sour Towel Zombie laughs. "No, that was technically the first pop-up book. Worst pop-up book ever! You open it up . . . *Foomp!* There's the house. Turn the page . . . *Foomp!* There's the basement where they killed the dad. Turn the page . . . *Foomp!* There's the crime scene upstairs where they raped the daughter. Open up the little flap and . . . whoops, you tore the page. Good job, kid, you fucked up your book already. Children will love the book you got them, when they're not crying."

"The girl wasn't raped," Cigarette Zombie corrects. "That's why she was shot."

"Lucky her," European Indian Zombie mutters sarcastically.

"Never mind," I sigh.

"Wait, if you think this Camel might potentially take things too far," Bobby B says as he stands up, "maybe we should introduce the military presence a little early."

"Here we go . . . "

"Yeah," Bobby Z agrees. "Maybe you can shit in his lunchbox and give him a heart attack!"

"Wait," Bobby B laughs. "Did you just say 'hard' attack?"

"No," says Bobby Z, standing up, too, trying to be the one to signal our break is over. "You fuckin' heard me."

"Sorry. I'm just trying to figure out what a 'hard attack' is and how I can make sure you don't ever give me one. Faggot," Bobby B says, smile slipping as Sour Towel Zombie steps between them.

I don't even know whose turn it is to shove our poor Sour Towel into the bush when he gets close enough to pick on, but, for some reason, I jump on the opportunity. I push him so hard, he almost flips over twice. I don't even wait for a Bobby to get on all fours behind him, the usual drill, and I can tell both of them are a little disappointed.

This shove is very uncharacteristic of me, and I cough nervously to let everyone know it. No one says anything, even though they've done their share of flipping that kid turtle-like into the bush at least three times apiece, then subsequently failing the Voight-Kampff Empathy Test by leaving him there to struggle.

But then things are suddenly even worse when a disappointed Cigarette Zombie quietly helps a dour Sour Towel Zombie out of the broken branches and back to his feet.

Things are awkward until we all crack some knuckles and put on our game faces and hunch over and start lumbering back toward the house. I'm the last one standing up straight as I think about what I did and who I did it for.

STEALING PROPELLER HATS FROM THE DEAD

***

Someone is sick, coughing instead of moaning. Coughing for real though. And Soul Towel Zombie is telling anyone who will listen about the movie *Gates of Hell* and how that poor actress had to swallow still-warm sheep entrails for the effect of vomiting up her entire intestinal tract on film. Cigarette Zombie stops coughing, then lights another cigarette off the orange nub of her last one before she drops it.

"Now that's a chain smoker," Sour Towel Zombie laughs. "When you light one off one and they're both yours? Time to quit! And why don't you ever flick 'em for dramatic effect?"

She blinks long but doesn't answer, and I leave them crouched down next to the porch as I navigate the gas meters and gutters. It's my turn on scout duty, recon, psychological warfare. I scratch around the aluminum siding until I find a good window to peek inside. I can see the beautiful bed, the carefully made bed, the bed with the big, pink, fluffy comforter and someone's shiny, new suitcase dead center in the middle of it.

Then two Camels appear, the women, all arms flailing away and gesturing to the bed, both apparently explaining why it should be hers. I snicker. They must have already located the other bed, the damp mattress in the corner of the unfinished family room (or "Tetanusville," as Mags calls it, "Spiderville to the locals."). One of the Camels eventually leaves, defeated, and the other walks to the bathroom and clicks on the light over the mirror. She checks the lines of her face, then places a sickly green Tupperware bowl of a squirming something or other on the edge of the tub to soak. I blink a few extra times as I realize what it is. Then the other Camel storms back in, still yelling, and I take off.

When I come back down the Joshua Bush, everyone is shuffling in a circle, killing time between attacks, but Cigarette and Sour Towel Zombie are arguing.

"I've seen that movie!" Cigarette Zombie almost yells. "There's way worse than that."

"Like what?"

"Like *Beyond Re-Animator*, zombie schlong vs. rat during the end credits. Or even your precious *Braindead*, uh, I mean, *Dead Alive*, where the dude's rectum flops out and then runs amok around the house? Hell, it even tries to groom itself in a mirror at one point, like comb its gnarly little head with tiny bladders or whatever."

"Yeah, that scene's okay," Sour Towel Zombie has to admit. "But everything in that movie is overshadowed by the Greatest Moment of All Time."

"Which is?"

"Sigh. I shouldn't even have to say it. Do I have to say it? I won't. Okay, I will. The lawnmower scene, fuckers. If my own death came at that moment, in that film, I would be okay with it."

"Next time, just sigh instead of saying the word 'sigh,' douchebag."

"Sorry, it's hard to resist when you're breaking the Fourth Wall with your face every weekend. And the fifth . . . and the sixth . . . "

I try to get their attention by shuffling the wrong way in our circle, against the natural flow of traffic and migration of the mob. They dodge me easily, glaring but mostly keeping their yawns glued open. Nothing like that summer when there was a hornet's nest under the porch, angrily activated every time more than two weak-ankled feet bumped the steps, an extra obstacle that made us dance around in a seriously comic, quite un-undead-like fashion. We almost changed our name to the Zee Bee &

Bee & Bee & Bee & Bee as a tribute. And it took at least three smoke bombs to get rid of the nest for good. But every so often, a sting will still surprise a thin-skinned ghoul into breaking character with a high-stepping wince at the most serious of times.

"Hey, guys?" I whisper. "There's a suitcase on a bed."

"Good," says Bobby B. "Are they fighting over it in a beautiful passive-aggressive way?"

"No, more like actually fighting."

"Sweet. What are the men up to? Did they trash the place already?"

"I can't tell. We really gotta fix it up better next time, make this place look less scary out of the gate, not so . . . foreboding."

"Speaking of foreboding," Sour Towel Zombie cuts in, "I love how the people on *The Walking Dead* couldn't wait to get to a place called 'Terminus.' The only thing more suspicious-sounding might be Youfuckedville, right outside of Necropolis, North Screamtown!"

"I like how the Daryl Dixon Is Dreamy fan club ensured we had to watch him rescue and or cradle babies on every episode," Cigarette Zombie snickers. "And people were still surprised when the finale had him breastfeeding a newborn."

"Whatever," someone squeaks from the back. "Everybody loved Daryl on that show, but to me he'll always be the punk who betrayed Blade."

"Get what's left of your minds back in the game!" Bobby Z snaps. "Have the men found the key to the closet yet? That's all we need to know." Bobby Z hates it when we talk about Daryl because we're pretty sure he wishes he was the guy, and no one wants him to keep working on that homemade crossbow. He'd kill us all. All over again.

"No, just the nails, near as I can hear," I say. "But they

may have run out already. There hasn't been any hammering for a while."

"Great. Good job," Bobby Z says sarcastically as he grabs my shoulders. "Now turn around. You're going the wrong way, fucknuts."

"But, uh, I did notice a couple things that were kind of weird . . ."

"Yeah, you already said that. Something about a paper towel. Good detective work. So the Camel washes his hands too much. It's just habit."

"No, it's the female. One of them has a pair of bloody underwear soaking in the tub."

Everyone stops shuffling.

"And?" Bobby Z asks, mouth working.

"What do you mean 'and'?!" at least three zombies chime in simultaneously.

"So, what? You think she'll be more on edge? More likely to defend her personal space?" Bobby B wonders. "Who cares."

"No." I speak slow, like a child, seeing that some of them might not know what I'm getting at, or are just pretending not to. "What I'm saying is that she must still be . . ."

Bobby Z shoves me over before I can finish.

"Dude, don't fuck this up. It's the only job I've ever liked. I can't go back to the unemployment line like this."

My shoes pop off, and this lightens the mood.

"Hey, that reminds me!" Bobby B laughs. "What do you call a zombie melting in your bathtub?"

"What?"

"Duane! Get it?"

Bobby Z smiles a big, blue smile and starts to stumble around next to Cigarette Zombie so he can put his arm around her. I start grinding the last of my teeth. I've never seen a season with so many love triangles, dead, undead, or otherwise.

Wisely, Bobby B keeps telling jokes, trying to break the tension with oldies but goodies. Sometimes he cheats and modifies old "dead baby jokes," but the world was ripe for recycling these days.

"What do you call a zombie with no arms and no legs?"

"Matt."

"What do you call that same zombie in the pool?"

"Bob."

"What do you call that same zombie hanging on a meat hook?"

"Chuck!" Bobby Z is trying hard to answer them before Bobby B finishes the set-up.

"Or it could be 'Art!'" Baseball Zombie interrupts it. "That works, too."

"Shut the fuck up and watch the house." Bobby Z now has his arm around Baseball Zombie's shoulders instead. "Go on," he says, sweetly.

"What do you call a zombie stuck under your car?"

"Jack. Go faster."

"What do you call a zombie head stuck in your mailbox?"

"Bill. Hurry up."

"What do you call a zombie with one leg?"

"Eileen. Come on, don't you have any new ones?"

"What do you call a zombie with no arms or legs in a pile of leaves?"

"Russell."

"What do you call a zombie with no feet?"

"Neil."

"What do you call a zombie in the middle of a baseball field?"

We know them all backwards and forward, but even Baseball Zombie isn't fast enough for that one.

"Second base!"

"I like it better when Davey Jones does them," says Cigarette Zombie. "He's always so serious about it."

She's right. He used to fire them off as a sort of calisthenics before the game, something to get our minds right, get us down to that "just . . . one . . . thing" he was always babbling about, like De Niro in *The Deer Hunter*. I actually overheard him tell Mags once in a weird, gravelly voice that this place would be his legacy, and "no less than my *Lord of the Flies*."

Yikes. Rumor had it that Davey once tried to be one of us, way back when, back when the shit hit the fans. And like most hardcore fans, he took it the hardest. Supposedly he would attack the house all by himself. And he was a miserable failure. Refunds were demanded. But that didn't stop us from calling him "The O.G.Z." sometimes, just to fuck with him a little bit.

It's quiet for a while, until Bobby B starts cracking knuckles for another troop surge. I point to the Camels' car at the bottom of the hill, still trying to rekindle the discussion.

"Look at that. What kind of vanity plate says MARCH-7?"

"Is that today's date? How tempting would it be to fuck with that car if that was today?"

"Did anything important happen on that day? I mean, besides . . . "

"We all know what happened on that day."

"It's a secret message!" Bobby Z yells. "And it's telling you what to do!" He shoves me again, and now we're all running toward the house. "It says 'get moving!' That's a fucking order, soldier!"

Ironically, "original birthplace of the genre" be damned, it's really hard to be a good zombie in Pittsburgh with all the hills. But tonight in Toledo, Ohio, even though the landscape is much flatter, it is still much too tempting to run. We relocated to T-Town a while ago. No shame in it. It's cheaper, and those lazy bastards film all the new movies in Canada for tax purposes anyway.

Cigarette Zombie is originally from Pittsburgh, and she once said the only reason she smoked was because the coughing reminded her of home, all the brick buildings still stained black from the dying factories and people blowing their noses to seal up potholes. One afternoon, when we were the first two to get to work, she sneezed black and swore to me that there was a "little bit of Steeltown in all of us now."

"Just a little bit of blood left in all of us . . . "

Then she turned and spit a little splash of tar onto a nearby butterfly.

It was beautiful.

"And one more thing!" Bobby Z trumpets, running harder to get in front of Bobby B. "No one says the word again for the rest of the night! We're over the limit! Now march!"

What word? "March"? I snicker to myself. *March 7th was our D-Day, meaning Z-Day, not the Fourth of July like they'd predicted.*

Sour Towel Zombie pushes himself and his gangly legs, and he catches up with Bobby Z an unlucky thirteen steps before the porch.

"You know," he snorts. "I thought I was watching a zombie movie the other night, but it just turned out to be a documentary about some lame-ass rapper getting shot nine times. But he's got to be one of us, right? Ain't everybody a zombie at this point?"

"Fuck him," Bobby B answers him before Bobby Z can get mad about such egregious use of the holy word. "That guy's a pussy. All rappers get shot. Doesn't mean shit. Bullet holes? Please. It takes more than that to prove you're a tough guy. You can't even see a bullet hole, on anybody. You usually just have to take their word for it, especially when they tattoo over them. Now, if he'd been shot with nine *arrows*, that would be a different story. That would be impressive. Can you imagine it? Him stumbling past the DJ, crashing through the turntables at the party, nine arrows sticking out of his body like a porcupine? Maybe one in his face? Now that's tough."

The house is about five feet away, and we can hear the hammers again. They can probably hear us, too, and we still aren't in character yet. Davey Jones would flip out, but we can't help it. Our music, book, or movie conversations usually keep going until someone is definitely proven wrong about something. With as much ridicule as possible.

"Less like a rapper," I offer. "And more like the cowboy in the western who stumbles into the campfire after an ambush with an arrow in his . . ."

That's when Bobby Z punches me in the mouth, and I feel my two bottom teeth tip a little toward my tongue. Amazingly, I jab him in the throat before I can talk myself out of it, and we both tumble onto the porch. The other zombies dogpile ontop to pull us apart just as Davey Jones's furious mug appears from behind a cracked flap of wood in the doorway.

"What the hell?" he barks. "Knock that shit off! And why the fuck were you guys running? Real zombies don't run! Wrong movie, assholes!"

"And then I saw his face . . ." Bobby Z sings. ". . . now I'm a believer."

"Wrong Davey Jones, asshole!" someone giggles. Our boss hates that band, of course.

Sour Towel steps up behind me and sarcastically flexes where his bicep would have been, an ironic tattoo of the character Tattoo from *Fantasy Island* renting the space instead.

"The Original Gangsta Zombie has spoken," he whispers.

But Davey Jones is right. We've always chosen to emulate the shambling, drunken interpretations of the walking dead and never subscribed to the latest, more popular, run-amok versions in, for example, *28 Days, Weeks*, and *Months Later* or the last five *Dawn of the Dead* remakes. And we usually followed this code religiously. But sometimes we had to remind a few extra-excitable staff (like our very first, now-deceased-for-real Cowboy Zombie) not to howl "Brains!", the war cry first heard in *Return of the Living Dead*. It was almost irresistible sometimes, but mostly we could successfully fight this urge.

Mostly.

The angry face of our boss is gone before we can respond, and I stand up without any help, wiggle a tooth, wipe a nose, then turn to find a Bobby scratching at the door, already forgetting what he did to me. I join him reluctantly.

Yes, "no running" was an old rule, but a necessary one. First, there's the indisputable fact that when it's dark, trees are a real danger. Like Sour Towel Zombie always says, "Run too fast through the trees and you can lose your virginity!" Like that poor girl who was spread-eagled and penetrated by a stop-motion spruce in *Evil Dead*. But the biggest problem was it also got dead people too excited about crashing into the house by the time they got to it. Tempers were always too short when people moved too fast. That's why the "walking" dead could always count on such a huge snowball of new memberships every weekend the world ended.

I scratch harder even though it's all wood instead of windows now, and at least three splinters slip under my fingernails.

I count each one as it goes in and feel nothing.

***

Most of the game never changes.

The hammer is under the sink. They usually don't find it right away. And when the windows run out of glass from our fists, there's a stack of replacement plywood and wooden doors for them to find upstairs, to give the impression of an interrupted renovation before the Apocalypse. And under the other sink, of course, the bucket of nails. But to get the power going, they have to use the car battery in the cupboard.

And like scientists in the movies will tell you, things change quickly when any creature starts using tools.

So, when the television is up and running, they'll see our eight-hour videotape of fake news broadcasts (a VCR hides in the wall looking like a fuse box, its cable looking like cable since nobody notices those tangled octopi anymore). And first on the screen is The Newscaster In Denial, expertly played by my father. Then comes the interview with the Frustrated Scientist, Mags's uncle Mark actually. Finally, my sister interrupts the broadcast with her creepy Casio keyboard rendition of an Emergency Broadcast Signal. It was spot-on, but she cried when I said she couldn't do the theme for the news, too. "Sometimes too much music ruins a movie," I had to tell her. To plead her case, she cited *Shaun of the Dead* as a film that showed the necessary reverence for any random collection of old vinyl LPs. She insisted that it didn't matter what songs were referenced, just as long as there were plenty of pop-culture references. Kids loved that shit! But I explained to her, if she thought hard enough, she'd remember Shaun's record collection wasn't that random at all, that there was a lot of Prince in that collection. I said to her, "And, sure, maybe the *Batman* Soundtrack ended up splintered in someone's eye, but that movie was a parody and doesn't count anyway, especially with all the blunt objects as weapons. There's been few things less satisfying in a zombie situation than a cricket bat substituted for an ax."

"How about I sit on the roof and do, like, a soundtrack?" she peeped, all excited.

"Too much music," I had to repeat.

"How about too many movies?" she said through her teeth and stomped off.

***

Once the real arguing starts inside the house, there are two choices.

Basement or roof.

Okay, three, actually. There's always that mysterious locked door and whatever's scratching and rustling inside it. But one of our Plants, usually Mags, will argue hard for the basement. 'Cause the basement is doom. The basement has always meant doom, and not just when we were scared of the dark as kids. And if the couple chooses the basement, come morning, everyone in the house will greet them at the basement door all zombied up with a resounding, "You lose!" Translation, "Time to eat your fucking faces." Kidding.

But they should know these things if they've seen any movies. Remember, *Day of the Dead* was just one big basement, and that movie should have taught them all they needed to know. Wait, maybe that was *Alien 3*. Which movie was it where someone said, "This whole place is a basement" and the hero smirks in response, "It's a metaphor," right as the writer rears his ugly head in the middle of a perfectly good script? Sour Towel Zombie tried to argue this line was from the movie *Dog Soldiers,* and *that* was the film that said it best when the token last final end girl reveals to the platoon stranded in the deserted farmhouse that the monsters were never in the barn as we assumed they were, but simply hiding in the basement the whole time.

"They were always here," the girl explains as her foster family of werewolves slowly rises up behind her. "I just unlocked the door . . . and it's that time of the month."

That time of the month? The point is that shit is always dangerous. Period.

Back when he first overheard this theory, Davey Jones grabbed Sour Towel Zombie by his damp, wrinkled collar, the maddest we'd seen him up till then, which was no joke. Must have had something to do with that dog. Always the dog.

"You're not werewolves, you fools!" he spat. "You can never change back."

But before those all-encompassing basement debates begin, the Camels will find the TV. One time, I saw a scowling newlywed click past our fake news and click on the real news instead. It was just for a second, right before a Plant slapped his hand away, but long enough to catch the real news anchor sniffling:

"They're calling it the end of . . ."

You could see the question in his eyes. The end of what? The end of something, anything. That's all anyone in the audience needs to know. You only need to watch any news broadcast for three to seven seconds tops.

Then the show was back on with my dad in the anchor seat, reading his script in his best solemn smirk, but still accidentally correcting the real news that he couldn't help but sneak glances at off-camera.

"They're calling it Judgment Day," my dad said. "Not to be confused with *Judgment Night*, a fine film and cautionary tale about bad traffic and a siege on a *mobile home . . .*"

The evening of that big scare, I slumped down by the gas meter to ponder through our break, and one of the dead, likely a new hire (I thought it was Cowboy Zombie at the time, although later he denied the whole conversation), plopped down wearily next to me. He was wearing the Pittsburgh Steelers helmet, which was crushing his ten-gallon hat, a direct violation of the "one characteristic" rule, and it shadowed his face more than usual. I noticed he had one of his shoes off and a bloody fish hook stuck in the ball of his foot.

He wiggled it free and held it up in the moonlight.

"Can you imagine what this must look like to one of them?" he asked me in a voice unfamiliar. "That wiggling bait with the line stretching up to infinity, catching the sun every so often like a lightning bolt? If you were swimming by, you would know something was wrong, but there is just no way you could resist taking a bite."

***

The puzzle is called "The Executioner and the Four Hats," and it's new this year.

Apparently, Mags got the idea from a kids' book, a bush-league knockoff of Sobol's *Encyclopedia Brown's Mysteries* series called *Dictionary Blue's Bafflers*. A day earlier, Mags and Davey Jones had us all get together for a brainstorming session on how to apply this puzzle to our job in an interesting way. We started the meeting in the house on our loosely-screwed-together, easy-breakaway dining-room table, but we all felt so creatively stagnant in there that we had to move the meeting to our home away from home, away from home, the Joshua Bush.

Our bosses told us they wanted to "kick things up a notch" because the state of the economy and the housing bubble and global warming and all that had them worried this might be our last season. At the table, Mags had ineffectually tried to explain this complicated puzzle with a pen, a Wheaties box sporting the new Bruce Jenner, and a lonely saltshaker, but we'd just stared at Mags, mouths agape, of course, but more agape than usual. So outside huddled around the Bush, when Davey Jones tried acting everything out with some Halfway Homeys (imitations of the popular but racially-insensitive Hispanic bubble-gum machine toys that cost half as much as the actual Homies and came with feeding-and-caring instructions for when the child took one into their home, a.k.a. their Halfway House, a.k.a. their "Halfway Homey Home"), that was when the puzzle finally made sense and the ideas started flying much easier. At least we closed our mouths a little more.

"See, we got three little dudes in a line and a fourth one behind a wall no one can see," he said. Luckily, he used the Beefier Halfway Homeys (the ones from the 75-cent machines, which almost made a Whole Homey) for his demonstration or class would have been ridiculous. Not as ridiculous as a demo with the Homeys that cost a dime though, as they would have been *way* too small to see, just torsos really, literally Half of a Halfway Homey! Anyhow, according to the boss, Halfway Homeys represented the infiltration of the fake Hispanic gang members into the gigantic, beautiful mall of *Dawn of the Dead*, the pivotal '78 film, since those actors' faces were spray-painted brown instead of blue, making them "a much more serious threat to the heroes." Or something.

"Now, look close," he went on. "They're all wearing a hat . . ."

"Uh, no they're not," someone laughed.

"Well, the salt shaker is. Sort of," someone admitted.

"Just bear with me," Davey Jones grinned as he patted a dusty shoulder. "In the puzzle, the 'prisoners,' they're all wearing a hat. Here, if you look real close, you'll notice I've grass-stained two of the Halfway Homeys green, but left the other two brown. The green prisoners represent zombies, or 'red hats.' The brown prisoners? Just pretend they have blue hats on for now. On the other side of this wall, or 'pine cone,' is the salt shaker, which is actually another prisoner wearing a blue hat. Even though it's silver."

"What the fuck are you talking about?"

"Yeah, when did they become prisoners?"

"He means us, I think."

"No shit! Let me out!"

"It's the salt shaker that's fucking me up. I've never gotten past it."

"Now, if it was the original puzzle," explained Davey Jones, ignoring the grumblings, "then you'd say, 'An executioner is gonna shoot all four of them unless a prisoner can declare with certainty what color hat he's wearing.'"

"What hat? There are no hats!"

"Bobby, please, get your head out of your ass," Mags sneered. "He just told you that the green ones represent red hats, and the brown and silver hats are actually blue. So, one more time, how do they know what color hat they're wearing?"

"You mean the hat on their own head?"

"Yes. Sort of. All the hats, really."

"You could just take off your hat and look."

"No. They're tied up."

"I'd just shout out 'blue' or 'red.' You got a 50/50 chance."

"That's not an option."

"I'm confused."

"That salt shaker mocks me."

"Medic!"

"Can they talk to each other?"

"No."

"Why can't they look around?"

"They're tied up."

"That one isn't tied up." A finger flicked over a Halfway Homey holding a bundle of tiny oranges. "It's selling itty-bitty fruit at itty-bitty intersections to support its itty-bitty crack habit. Look."

"Tiny crack ain't no joke."

"Fuck this."

"Please don't screw the lid on the shaker any tighter. The grinding of salt in metal is making me crazy."

"We give up."

"Okay!" Davey Jones shouted. "The answer is the guy second from the end because he knows if the guy behind him doesn't say anything, then that means he sees one of each color hat on the guys in front of him and therefore knows by the process of elimination that his own hat is the opposite of the one he can see."

"Uh . . . pbbbht . . . okay?" someone said through a lip-flapping sigh, speaking for us all.

"So, here's the million-dollar question," Davey Jones said. "How can we play this same game with zombies instead of all this bullshit?"

"We can't," Cigarette Zombie said through her teeth, standing up tall and underlit by her glowing matchbook. "You'd still need something like a hat. That's the only reason the puzzle works. A hat or, at the very least, something that you can see on the others but they can't see on themselves. Like that poker game where you stick one card to your forehead."

"Maybe if everyone had been bitten?" Sour Towel Zombie offered, standing up, too. "Like they're zombies but don't know it? But, like, the others know?"

Pause.

"Never mind. This shit makes no sense."

"What if one of the guys in the line was blind?" asked . . . was it the Baseball Zombie?

"Yeah! Wait, no. That doesn't work either," Davey Jones said, clicking his teeth impatiently.

"You only need one prisoner or zombie or whatever tied up, right?" Cowboy Zombie asked as he tipped over the first Halfway Homey, the one with the tiny spray can and skateboard, so its tiny face was in the dirt. "The first one can be a corpse or a zombie. Only the one with the answer, the Camel, or the prisoner, would need to be immobilized."

"I got it!" shouted Bobby B. "Bury them up to their necks!"

"In the house?" asked Mags, eyebrow up.

"Maybe," Bobby Z went on for him, snickering now, too. "What if we rig the floor so that they fall in up to their chests and can't turn around."

"Like *The Money Pit!*"

"What if one of them was mute instead?" European Indian Zombie asked, quite sincerely. "You know, so they could see who's a zombie but can't say anything?" She reached down to make a Halfway Homey jump up and down like it had something urgent to say. It was palming a tiny basketball.

"No, no, no, then there's no puzzle." Davey Jones clicked his teeth even harder. "The last Camel in the game has to be unable to answer the question because he or she sees one of each, zombie and human."

"Maybe we should just stick with hats," Bobby Z laughed. "Have beanies that say 'zombie' on them or some shit."

"That's a horrible idea," Cigarette Zombie scoffed. More like coughed. "Why not just give everyone propellers instead?"

"Yeah," I agreed, scoffing nervously with her, but more like coughing.

"Maybe it's no use. It's just not gonna . . ." Mags started to say.

"Fuckin' forget it!" Davey Jones gathered up his toys, stood up over everyone a long second, then stampeded away, knocking over lamps.

"Whoa, O.G.Z.," someone snickered. "Chill."

"He should understand that if there's a chance of something happening, no matter how remote, then it has already happened to someone else," European Indian Zombie said to us all, palms out and all wise. "And if you think you have a great idea, someone is already doing it somewhere."

"Did Zombie Rama tell you that?" asked Bobby B, kicking dirt in her direction.

"Zombie-O-Rama. Get it straight."

We all got up and followed Davey Jones up to the house. Inside, he was pouting cross-legged in front of the TV, staring at the Emergency Broadcast graphic. Seeing us, he turned off the television in disgust and stomped to the refrigerator. *Thud, thud, thud, rattle . . .*

"You guys don't get it!" he practically shouted. "Any of you ever see the movie *Things Change*? Well, things change."

"Uh, isn't that a movie about a shoe shiner for the mob?" asked Sour Towel Zombie.

"What's your point?" Davey said, cracking open a quart of orange juice.

"I don't see how that applies to us. I mean, the title is cool and all, and I get what you're trying to say, but . . . "

The refrigerator door slammed, and that shut him up. Our boss said this "Things Change" line a lot. In fact, he said it so much we expected to see it on a T-shirt someday soon, instead of "Army" and "Navy." Davey Jones tipped his juice towards all of us like a disappointed dad.

"Pulpier, people, that's the key. Like this," he said, holding up his O.J. and slipping into De Niro-mode again. "This? See this? This is us. If there's gonna be copycat zombies everywhere playing our game, we're gonna have to step it up. We're gonna have to do it with more pulp, yeah, pulp. Surprise them with something to chew on when they only thought they were drinking."

"Wait, what's us?" Bobby Z laughed. "That? That missing kid on the side of the carton?"

"Exactly!" Bobby B agreed. It was the happiest we'd ever seen them, both smiling at the same time, but we still had no idea what anyone was talking about.

"But orange juice is hell on us zombies to drink," one of them went on. It may have been me. "Maybe it's a zombie's diet of cold barbecue to stain our lips for the cameras, but the heartburn is ridiculous."

"Totally!" Laughter.

"That missing kid on the carton is ugly as fuck. I think it's a set-up."

"You know what? Maybe we just need weapons again," Davey Jones said ominously. "Like the old days."

The room got quiet. We used to have Laser Tag gear on our chests, then some more electronic targets on our heads. Then we moved to paintball for a while. Then, after the incident forever referred to as The Blinding of Zombie

Seventeen, a.k.a. Gamblers Anonymous Zombie, we got everybody goggles. We looked just like the Underwater Nazi Corps in *Shockwave*, according to Sour Towel Zombie.

"Wasn't that originally called *Deadcorps*?" someone corrected him.

"What? Like a 'Dead Corpse'?" he said. "Kinda redundant, homey!"

"No, 'corps,' like the military."

"Never heard of it. There's lots of movies where zombies come up slow-mo out of some kinda water though."

"You mean like the movie *Zombie*," someone made the mistake of suggesting.

"What do you mean?" Sour Towel pounced.

"You know, the movie with the zombie fighting the shark underwater." Silence. "You know, that famous scene where the splinter goes through that chick's eyeball?"

"It's *Zombi* with an 'I,' not *Zombie* with an 'I-E!'" Sour Towel shouted.

"How do you know I wasn't saying it with an 'I'?" whoever it was asked him.

"And it's *Zombi 2*, not *Zombie*."

"With an 'I,' right?" Bobby Z taunted him. "I mean, I hate to bring it up, but you forgot to say it with the 'I' just now."

"I was saying it with an 'eye.' And a splinter. Get it?"

"I can't wait to kill you."

"Again?"

"Hey, remember that cute finger-footed eyeball monster the mad scientists made in *Bride of Re-Animator*?" I offered, playing peacemaker. "Did you guys see that movie?"

"Don't remember."

A punch caught me in the chest.

Peacemaker, my ass, I thought, holding in the cough. *More like a pacemaker.*

"Didn't your dad take us both to see that in Junior High?"

"I don't know," Bobby Z snapped. "I'm not my dad's mom."

And with a statement as confusing as that, the subject of eye injuries and bush-league Italian George Romero imitators was finally forgotten, at least for a day.

But there were more problems than that with our scandalous Laser Tag legacy. For example, in the fog, lasers took away all the suspense of aiming at anything. You'd just gently line up the glowing red stripe until it was touching their face, kind of like you were slowly stretching out a tape measure to see how long you could lead it before it finally collapsed (the record will always remain 23 feet, by the way, tape measure, not laser), so we abandoned the whole "shooting zombies in the head" thing forever. Plus, it made us seem more like zombies from the *Return of the Living Dead* movies instead of the original Holy Trinity. As you probably figured out, this wasn't a new dilemma.

"However, at least one of the writers of *that* classic parody slash reimaging was involved in the making of the original classic," Sour Towel Zombie reminded us like an insufferable schoolmaster. "So maybe a shot to the brain not being enough to stop them was always part of the plan."

Right then, Davey Jones kicked open the door and stepped outside onto the porch. He had the orange juice in one hand and a very real Spencer repeating rifle in the other. Later we would mistakenly remember this weapon as an "AKA-47," confusing the huge laser site on top of it for the distinct gas mechanism of the Russian weapon.

"Whoa, boss," Bobby B said. "You ever see *Do the Right Thing*?"

"You guys better start taking this a little more seriously," the man with the gun said.

He let this sink in.

"Because I'm gonna hide this weapon in the house. And tomorrow, if someone can find it, it'll be fair game."

"Uh, that is not a fair game," Bobby B said.

But Davey Jones was done talking. He loomed like doom in the background, sulking and sipping his orange juice, glaring at us occasionally, while Mags pursed her lips and handed out paychecks and W-2s and told us not to be late tomorrow.

Which is today.

But before that meeting officially adjourned, I decided to climb the antenna and check the roof for loose tiles, figuring it was safer up there anyway. The object of the game was, will be, and always has been to be on the roof come sunrise. Just like *Dawn of the Dead*, the roof was hope. The roof was life. Never shopping malls, like Roger Ebert, lesser reviewers, film students, or historians keep insisting.

They have always made the mistake of thinking more about those movies than the zombies in them.

***

There are always some Easter eggs sprinkled throughout the game. We changed them around sometimes, but one staple is the footlocker stenciled "U.S. Army" (my sister did the decoupage), a big ol' metal box that rattles nice and provocative, as if it contains some answers. It turns out to be hiding a broken television remote rather than a solution, however, if they ever do manage to wrestle it open.

"What's in the box?!"

In my right ear, I hear one smart-ass Camel imitating

the seventh sequel of *Se7en*, a.k.a. *Se7en and 7*, for the benefit of his new bride as he shakes the footlocker like a bartender making a highball.

"I never understood that first movie," his wife is saying. "After the initial murder, I thought we were gonna find out an actual sloth was doing the killing, and doing it real slow. What a disappointment."

"Never underestimate the insatiable appetite for an unnecessary sequel though, especially in the zombie universe. *World War Y* and *World War X* should be clear evidence of that. You'd think those were prequels, right? Nope."

"He was better in those movies, though. 'What's in the socks?!'" she squawks.

The wife's nasally Brad Pitt impression causes at least three of us (Cowboy and Cigarette Zombie, too, I think) to stop scratching the window sills and stifle our laughter. I'm a bit wary of any zombie discussion or self-awareness from the Camels so early on, but then we hear Amy, our Plant, back in our ears, steering them back to the subject at hand: looking for the key. The Camels aren't wired for sound, but the Plants are. Us, too, although no one remembers which holes they used for the microphones.

"Remember that embarrassing night when some Camel's kid found that old porn stash hidden behind the mirror?" Cowboy Zombie whispers in my left ear.

"Found what?"

"There was a hidden recess behind an old mirror that had a ratty pile of old Super-8 John Holmes videos and *Oui* magazines."

"Treasure!"

"Don't you mean 'booty'?"

"Oh, I thought you meant a porn 'stache in the mirror," Cigarette Zombie snickers. "Like a giant mustache in the kid's reflection? That would have scared the shit out of anybody."

"I found my dad's snuff porn and rape movies once," I offer. "Mom flipped out on him."

"What did he say?" Cowboy Zombie asks, taking the bait.

"He said, 'Don't worry, I hide the rough stuff much better than those, baby.'"

"Nasty."

"Hold up, you said it wasn't porn, remember? I thought your dad was just embarrassed about his zombie movie collection!"

"Zing!"

"Fuck that. Zombies got so unfashionable they're fashionable all over again!"

"Which makes us the backlash to the backlash to the backsplash."

"Shhh . . . "

We're suddenly distracted by another scuffle behind us. It's the Bobbys, of course. One of them is yelling something about a discrepancy in the paychecks we'd received the night before. Cowboy Zombie doesn't even bother to break them up anymore, but Cigarette Zombie always, *always* tries real hard to make the peace, especially when a certain Swaggering Cowboy Zombie is watching her, or sometimes a Baseball Zombie, both, however, indistinguishable from the Forearm Flexing Zombie.

She never does this for a Nervous Cough Zombie like myself.

Sounds like a lot of zombies, doesn't it? It isn't.

"See, you Bobbys are frustrated because, back home somewhere, you each have a brother. And this brother acts just like the other Bobby," she explains, eyes uncharacteristically wide. Her arms, too.

"So why can't we just *switch* brothers, so there's no arguments? Huh, Psychoanalysis Zombie?" Bobby B mutters, back-peddling from Bobby Z.

"Hey, one semester of psychology is no joke," Cigarette Zombie goes on. "It's just like my own stepbrother situation. I'm the same age as the one who acts like my older brother, my blood brother, and he's the same age as a stepbrother who acts just like me. But we were forced to pair off because of our age, and we always wished we could switch until we realized, guess what? It makes perfect sense."

"What's your point?" Bobby Z asks, five fingers now around Bobby B's throat, the other five fluttering near his mouth, still adding up the extra taxes deducted from his check.

"It's because you're brothers!" Cigarette Zombie huffs. "You were meant to argue like this. Think about it, stupid."

"It's like that movie . . . " a new voice offers.

With his other hand, Bobby Z quickly closes another throat before Sour Towel Zombie can finish.

"Enough with the *Dead of the Dead of the Dead* movies, motherfucker."

"Wow. That's the original title for *Diary of the Dead*, actually! Well done!" Sour Towel Zombie squawks. Then, "Sorry."

"You're not allowed to talk the rest of the day, S.F.B."

Sour Towel Zombie's fingers drum the handle of the cleaver in his holster, then they relax. He'd long since grown used to Bobby Z laying hands on him on a daily basis. Most of us had. And the nickname doesn't make him flinch at all anymore either. That's what we used to call him, the "S.F.B.(T.)," as in "Sour Fucking Bath (Towel)," previously "Serial Finger Banger," in order to mock the limits of his sexual experience.

"You know how most people comb their hair before a

date?" Bobby Z would ask everyone real loud. "Well, he clips his fingernails."

But this never fazed him. He owned his endless tales of finger blasting and wore them like a badge of honor, so we just went back to talking about his towels. I'd like to say he deserved the endless abuse, but Bobby had attacked all of us at least once by the time we were picking out nicknames, so most of us just laid low, lower than usual anyway. And whenever Mags would tell Sour Towel Zombie that he was "this close" (fingers about an inch apart) to being fired because of his mouth, I thought about my first lunch with Sour Towel (a.k.a. S.F.B., a.k.a. S.T.Z., formally Sushi Chef Zombie, officially, according to his birth and death certificate, "Josh Something Something") and what was perhaps his finest moment.

It was when we were both working at that video store, back before the Netflix and the Red Boxes and the movies playing on your wristwatches and milk cartons, and he went back to Burger King to complain about there being no crust on his Hershey's pie. So they gave him a whole one in return, a whole goddamn Hershey's pie, not just another one of those chocolate slivers in the triangle box that they usually threw at you. And he happily shared that whole pie with me at work, both of us sneaking bites under the counter all night. When I asked him why he did this, he said, simply, "The crust is the best part." He was right, and he felt like a friend of mine that day.

But just like the topographic challenges of Pittsburgh I was talking about earlier, and how it started fucking up our commitment to stagger correctly infecting us with the urge to bolt . . .

It's been downhill with him ever since.

***

The thing people forget about taking off your jacket before

a fight is that you're not doing it because it's a throwback to an 18th Century duel or something. You're doing it because it makes it a lot easier to punch someone in the face.

At the end of the night, with all the zombies winding down behind the barn, things always seem so calm and content. No one ever anticipates that bloody jackets are going to be dramatically removed before our shift is over. And yet it happens every goddamn time.

Even Sour Towel Zombie's endless movie trivia exchanges seem oddly soothing at these moments, the almost quiet before the Idiot Storm, full of sound and "funny," signifying nothing.

"So, I finally watched *Day of the Dead*. Way better than *Land of the Dead*, which is ironic since rumor has it that *Day's* script resembled *Land* before funding was pulled."

"Yeah, what's up with all the mental cases? That's a director who needs his vision limited or else he would eagerly populate any post-apocalyptic arena with noble retards."

"You've seen his glasses . . . "

"Speaking of glasses!"

"You're funny."

"Or he'd eagerly populate his world with Middle Easterners being called 'spics' for some reason, like in *Day of the Dead*."

"Yeah, that poor Arab in the opening scene was, apparently, doing an alligator call by mistake, judging by what came running. 'Helloooooooooo . . .'"

"You know the band Gorillaz sampled that on their debut."

"'Is anybody there? Helloooooooooo . . .'"

"Florida's got plenty of gators, dude, so it wasn't that strange to see one."

"I think you're getting your racial slurs confused."

"'Hellooooooooo . . .'"

"No, I think the director was confused, since I distinctly remember a Mexican Army sergeant calling a Middle Eastern dude a 'spic.'"

"And a 'jungle bunny' at one point."

"Clearly Romero was in such a hurry to load that merry band of survivors with every race, creed, and crayon in the box that he got a wee bit confused."

"No shit, I think the mad scientist was an Inuit."

"And that evil 'Sarge' was screaming more than *Braveheart*, 'Fuck youse, Frankenstein!' Jump cut to drunken Irish helicopter pilot singing theme song from the Lucky Charms commercial."

"Wait, are you trying to say that writers used such broad strokes as a short cut to characterization?"

Silence.

"Moving on . . . "

That's when Bobby Z takes a swing at Sour Towel Zombie and loses his watch in the process. At least we think it's his watch. Then someone materializes between them wearing the stinky football helmet (Baseball Zombie maybe, which would make even less sense), and Bobby Z wrinkles his nose and takes a swing at that stupid Steelers logo instead. The helmet absorbs the blow easily, but the zombie wearing it spits out a mouthpiece to let it dangle over the guard.

"Who the fuck is in there?" Bobby Z asks, making a grab for the chinstrap. Then the helmet headbutts Bobby Z back onto his ass and into a blinking, momentary daze and blessed silence.

Up at the house, but deep in our earbuds, Amy is talking about the dog again, and everyone is moaning and groaning. Moaning and groaning more than usual, of course. But worst of all, not getting paid for it.

The dog again. Always the dog with her.

Once, Cigarette Zombie called the dog our "Sword of Damocles." And she's called it our "Gun Over Chekov's Fireplace" at least twice, and we all preferred that analogy instead. All except Sour Towel Zombie, who settled on "Dog Over the Fireplace," arguing that if you ever saw a fucking dog over a fireplace in a movie, it better go off.

Back in the day, Amy used to play the game outside. But she couldn't narrow down her personality to just one character trait, so Davey Jones moved her to the basement and the second act. Originally, he wanted to call her Invisible Shower Zombie because of her tendency to tip her head back and run her fingers through her hair, eyes half closed, at the most inappropriate of times, but that name didn't translate well to a horror movie, at least not the ones we preferred to pattern our lives after. It would be right at home in a De Palma credit crawl though, we agreed.

When Amy first brought the dog into the game, it seemed like a great idea, a good one for her to focus on anyway ("Dog Whisperer Zombie!"). But after a couple of weekends, everyone agreed that having an animal around a situation like this was just too soothing of a presence and negated the mood we were after. That's why they bring in puppies at old folks' homes, to sooth the dead, as well as the dying. And while it *did* help to cause a little of the anxiety we worked for, rather than alleviate it, it was still the wrong kind of anxiety. Much like the doomed canine in the novel *I Am Legend* (which contained vampires that acted like zombies, something they did even worse in the movie), it took our precious Camels right out of the story.

They just worried about the dog too much.

It was like they didn't want the dog to think anything bad was really happening and tried to protect the animal from the threat of the thumping outside. Petting and petting and trying to distract it from the monsters that were making it shiver and pin its ears back, not unlike what the guy did for his son in *Life Is Beautiful*, the most adorable little Holocaust ever, but easily twice as corrupt.

It comes down to this. It's too emotional for a dog. A dog has no reasonable place in any self-respecting horror movie. Or our game. Not unless they're gonna play.

But even worse than all this is the fact that a dog puts everyone in a perpetually good mood. It just never seems like the end of the world around one, especially when it keeps wanting you to play fetch with its favorite squeak toy. Ours was a rubber mailman that it had long since chewed the legs off that Mags dubbed "Lieutenant Dan." They still keep the toy in the house, even though Shark Dog is long gone, because it fits in good with our crippled crew. And because the memory of a dog long gone can be more effective than the real thing. In fact, just in case a Camel, say, rips my pants off during the game, I keep a picture of the chew toy in my wallet. A spooky caption, supposed to bring back memories of the Y2K scare (the second-to-last worldwide crisis, but ridiculous to adapt into a role-playing game) reads:

"Here lies our dearly departed Lieutenant Dan, scoffing at strange 'New Year' celebrations of another successful orbit of the sun. This soldier considers the Earth flat, so he has two reasons not to chase it."

I can hear Amy barking in my ear again. Mags is real close to her, so we can all clearly hear what's happening through her microphone, too. Amy is acting out a somber tale of how the dog was cruelly trained to fight other dogs, as well as zombies, by locking battleship chains onto its collar, how this made its head and neck so strong that it could even walk through walls without flinching. Then, between sobs, she's suddenly comparing the dog to

Vonnegut's short story "Harrison Bergeron," a story that's not about zombies at all, making it a completely unacceptable tangent for anyone but us. Amy's weeping sounds more authentic than usual tonight, and the Bobbys stop pulling their shredded leather jackets back over their shredded arms so they can listen, too.

". . . then it ate one of the nails, and Matt tried to coax the nail through its body out the hind end with a powerful magnet, which caused . . . " Sniffle. " . . . a tragic perforation of the groin. Then the bucket of tools upended, and nails peppered the makeshift operating table between its legs, narrowly missing everything but the testicles, and . . . "

Mags must have started glaring at her, because she trails off, then adds cheerfully:

"But that's a whole 'nother movie!"

"Whole 'another'?" Mags mocks.

"Don't worry though," Amy goes on. "The dog's fine and much happier living with my uncle. He's got a farm where he can run and dig. But remember when it ate that spider?" Sniffle. "Then it ate all those ants. Everyone joked that the dog just loved to stop hearts. And I'm sure it's still stopping hearts somewhere, but in a different way, you know? With love." Sniffle. "Some people say a dog still roams these woods . . . "

"That is the worst ghost story I have ever heard in my life."

It'll be the last time we'll hear Amy's voice, a ridiculously romantic but fitting eulogy.

But Mags will sneak in one more line tonight before our game is over.

"I've got it!" Sour Towel Zombie bleats from behind me. "The only name for a zombie movie that hasn't been used yet!"

"What's that?"

"*The Dog of the Dead.*"

"Already been done. *Pet Semetary*. I'm saying that with an 'S,' by the way."

"Hey, is *Weekend at Bernie's* technically a zombie movie?"

"Nope!" Sour Towel Zombie is an inch away from Cowboy Zombie's nose, mouth wide and working around his answer like a jawbreaker. "Well, to be technical, he really was a zombie in the *second one*. Remember? The sequel with the voodoo music?"

I'm pulling back a strip of wood to peek inside the house when I smell a sour towel breathing down my neck instead.

"You got your earphone in?" the Towel asks. "Come on, what's going on in there?"

"I don't know," I whisper. "But they're clearly having way too much fun. Look at that! Are they playing Twister or what?"

"Shut up. Dude, zombies would dominate at Twister."

"Listen, what is that they're singing?"

"Huh?"

"They're singing along with a videotape. One of the Camels must have brought it. Shit, they found the VCR. Hmm, looks like porn."

"I've seen this one! It's called the *Wild Naked Latina Sing-Along Wrestling Fun Party*." Awkward silence. "Uh, that's what I heard anyway."

"And what the hell is that goulash of a title supposed to mean?"

"It's a bad translation. In Portuguese, the title actually reads much more accurately as *The Fifth Horseman of the Apocalypse*."

"Now that's a movie."

"So, what are they singing now? Translator!"

"'In the widening gyration, the falcon cannot hear the karaoke . . .'"

Sour Towel Zombie stops breathing down necks and suddenly stands up straight.

"Perry, I've been keeping track of the lights," S.T.Z. tells us, voice cracking a bit as he attempts to be creepy. "'And the way I calculate it, when you turned off the upstairs light, that left the house completely dark.'"

No one looks at him. He's done this before.

"Come on! Nobody? No one recognizes that?! It's from the original home invasion story. No, no, not *Night of the Living Dead*. We're talkin' *In Cold Blood*, haters! That's really where it all began. And our blood is cold as fuck."

"I'm sure there were plenty of home invasions before that one."

"Yeah, wasn't that James Caan movie *Thief* based on a book called *The Home Invaders*? Hmm, I wonder what that was about," ponders Cowboy Zombie, hat brim tipped sarcastically, if that's possible.

"You're all wrong. William Seabrook's 1926 classic about Haiti? *The Magic Island?* It had a chapter entitled, 'Dead Men Working in the Cane Fields.' They dug up some poor suckers and resurrected their sorry asses for cheap labor."

"Just like us!"

"Voodoo zombies shouldn't count, fuckface."

"Come on, no one can deny our proud heritage began on a summer day in 1932 with *White Zombie*."

"Whoa, 'white zombies?' Fuckin' racist . . ."

"Nope, sorry. Lovecraft's 'Herbert West: Reanimator' serial was written way earlier than Seabrook's union-busting manifesto. It was completed at 5:37 a.m., six days before Christmas during the strangely warm winter of 1921. Approximately."

"Speaking of racists, you ever read that thing? Holy balls . . . "

"Enough already, I have the answer!" Cigarette Zombie bellows triumphantly. "The first zombie was most certainly Mary Shelley's *Frankenstein*. Mary Shelley's Frankenstein's monster, I mean, not the doctor. 1818, bitches."

"Don't you mean, *Frankenstein (a.k.a. The Modern Polyphemus)*?"

Someone snorts.

"She's right. Truly our Patient Zero," someone else says, serious as a "hard" attack, and there's a quiet moment of respect. Someone in the distance tips a beer to splash their drink on the ground.

"Fine. If it wasn't the first, it was sure the worst."

I look around, suddenly worried. Whoever was wearing the football helmet has vanished into the dark, and the Bobbys suddenly remember they need to be fighting at this point in the story, so they go back to dramatically taking off their jackets again.

This time, the snakeskin of their forearms sloughs off completely within the sleeves, so, sheepish, they put their jackets right back on. Their skin, too.

***

If and when they open the door to the upstairs closet, if they've done things in a certain order, there will be a man hiding in the dark who is afraid to come out.

He might have a stash of whiskey and some delicious, honeymoon-type foods, or maybe some wine, cheese, and fruit, or, hell, there may even be a vending machine bag of pork rinds and Sterno. It all depends on Mags's profiling earlier in the week. But once they let him out, he'll happily lead everyone up through a hole in the attic, up onto the roof, up to the beautiful blue sky, and anyone left will watch the sunrise while bouncing apple cores and soda cans off our shrunken heads below.

So when we stand back and look up to the top of our

Bed & Breakfast and see nothing but crows, we know the Camels are still doing it wrong.

"You know what I wish?" Sour Towel Zombie asks us. "I wish this house would take off into the sky at the end of our game. Like it did in *Bad Taste*. Remember that? When P.J. was one of us?"

He won't stop talking, and Bobby Z gives him a grunt and a Hurts Doughnut to get him back into character. Those doughnuts usually break a bone or two, but this time, S.T.Z. resists a little harder than usual. It's that kind of night.

"In fact," he goes on, defiant, "I wish we could have a guy stuffing shit back into his skull after his brains fall out. That was the best part of the movie. The zombies themselves were kind of lame, but the guy literally with shit for brains? He sort of reminded me of someone. Who am I thinking of . . ."

Bobby Z holds up a finger to stop his mouth, then starts taking off his jacket again, as sloppy and *Weekend at Bernie's*-like as he can in case a Camel is watching. I look for signs of life between the boarded-up windows, listening for any fake screams or hammer cracks.

Now, if they've done things in the wrong order, as we hope, hope, hope they have tonight, the Big Plant inside that closet will have stuck the Hillbilly Heaven-brand bubble-gum machine "rotten teeth" gag into his mouth, and the milky contact lenses into his already-milky eyes, and he will proceed to scare the living shit out of them when they open the door.

Well, sorta the "living shit."

However, if the Camels have done things really wrong, as we suspect they have tonight, or if Mags or Davey Jones are just feeling spiteful, the Big Plant in that closet (or the biggest guy we got left) will be wearing a police uniform.

This is because everyone, everyone, even those with just a passing knowledge of the films, everyone knows you never trust police, fireman, security guards, military (especially the military), or any authority figure for that matter, during your garden-variety siege of the undead.

But some people don't know the movies at all, and most people don't know them as well as they think they do. Just like that guy we hired who played one of our very first Plants. He insisted on yelling, "It's the end of the world!" with an exaggerated Irish accent, quoting the drunk in the diner from Hitchcock's classic *The Birds* by mistake. Mags was like, "Dude, birds aren't zombies. Even *those* birds."

Okay, it was an end of the world movie, sure, and maybe Tippi Hedren had a look in her eyes by the end that most of our corpse family would find familiar and comforting, but the soothing Technicolor of those scenes just never projected the correct level of dread. So, yeah, they had to start jamming fake rubber teeth in the Biggest Plant's mouth to discourage any more creativity.

All of a sudden, Sour Towel Zombie is grumbling and sputtering like he's never done before, showing a level of commitment to his role that we've never known, and some of us are getting nervous. Bobby Z starts putting his jacket on again, even thicker skin crumbling from his arms and leaving a nasty pink-and-gray halo around his shoes.

If he does that one more time, I think. *That dummy's arms will stay in those sleeves forever.*

"What's up, Halfway Homey?" Bobby Z belches at S.T.Z. "You trying for an Oscar or what?"

Bobby B lurches closer to get a better look, too, and his eyes widen.

"Hey, I think he's really hurt."

We all stumble over and suddenly notice a glowing red dot over his fluttering left eye.

"Uh, I think he's been shot."

"What?"

"Are you serious?"

"I didn't hear nothin'. What the fuck . . . "

"What the hell is this?" Baseball Zombie shouts. "There ain't no zombies in *Deliverance*!"

As we watch, Sour Towel Zombie begins to wind down, creaky foot over foot over foot, like a weary robot desk toy. Then one knee is on the ground. Then the other. Then he's clutching a handful of grass like it's the answer.

I remember something Cigarette Zombie once said when she was sticking up for him, something about his endless movie references just being his way of hanging on by his fingernails to a world long gone. Maybe she was right, and maybe we all did that, too. But no one ever seemed to need a savage headlock as often as that kid.

He looks up to us all one last time, his left eye now closed completely, the other one dilated 8-ball black, as red fingers of brain and burger roll down the side of his neck inside a spider web of blood. He points up to his beloved European Indian Zombie, the only one in our crew he ever dated more than once, to quote a final beloved movie before his arms hang limp as balloon strings a week after a birthday.

"It should have been you, Gordie," he croaks.

His face hits the ground so hard it disappears up to the ears.

***

"Our hearts have stopped," the news anchor sighs. "But our brains just keep going."

Right before we break through all their half-ass defenses and into the house for good, I hear a strange voice on the television. Not my dad or my sister's, certainly someone I'm not related to in any way. A Camel must have found the real news broadcast and left it on, I realize. If they found the real news, they would have already known that hearts were stopping everywhere, of course, and theirs should have, too. But seeing a real, live broadcast, and hearing it out loud, as well as hearing all of us pounding on each other instead of the walls, this may have empowered them to accept everything as authentic enough to finally fight for the house.

Which is what they should have been doing all along.

As I resist running, I'm still convinced that one of the Camels has a pulse, even though no one wants to hear about it. But I know at least one of them came into our game alive as hell. I'm not running, but now I'm certain.

The paper towel the Camel dropped when he compulsively avoided the door handle was my first clue. I tried to tell the staff, but denial has always run rampant in our workplace. And now, judging by the gasping and bubbling in my ears, that same Camel is probably upstairs with Underwater Zombie's head in the toilet, trying in vain to drown him. I already miss Sour Towel Zombie. At a moment like this, he would probably name-drop the Nazi Zombie movie *Shock Waves*, the one movie we'd ever seen with an aquatic undead army. He'd name-drop that shit, like I did just now. We both loved that flick to death, huge fans of the tasteless ending where hapless victims are forced to hide in ovens (ovens, can you believe it!) to escape the undead S.S.

To my right, Bobby Z has broken into the living room, and now he's choking out one of the other Camels, a guy who's trying desperately to warn his new bride of real danger through all his coughs and sputters. When his eyes roll back forever, Bobby Z helpfully moves the Camel's mouth to plays ventriloquist as the bride gets low and tries to hide.

"'Hey, baby!'" Bobby Z shouts, still talking for her lifeless consort. "'We ain't got no heart, but I love you! You remember our song at the reception? Our first dance? "Stars are dying in my chest until I see you again?" Hum it! That's everyone's song now, baby!' Wait, where are you going?"

Bobby Z gets the Camel down and out for good with a definitive knee that flattens his windpipe, cartilage crackling like bubble wrap. Maybe a little more satisfying than bubble wrap, judging by Bobby's smile, but it should be noted that popping bubble wrap was pretty goddamn satisfying for our crew, especially when we got big orders of novelty teeth and barbecue sauce. Then Bobby starts turning over furniture to find the bride. When he gives the Camel a heel to the temple on the way by as an afterthought, I hear a "Tisk!" from the corner and suddenly remember a certain newlywed's familiar but annoying habit. If this was poker, it would be her "tell." Or the card stuck to her forehead. Bobby Z seems on the verge of finding her with the next chair he'll flip, but he's having a lot of trouble with one of his hands, which is now flapping alarmingly at the wrist. If Sour Towel Zombie was here, he of all people would understand that it's just like Frankenstein said in *Day of the Dead*, the doctor not the monster, I mean:

"We are them, just functioning less perfectly."

With some extra effort, he upends the couch, and there she is tucked behind it, squirreled under some red cushions, burrowing deep like a tick. Okay, more like a "tisk."

I watch her reach out to her poor husband, lying broken on the floor, her fingers tickling the collapsed crater in his throat, as if trying to coax it to inflate. Some air does hiss from him as if her fingernail finds a tire valve, and over a gurgle, he struggles to point a quivering wedding ring toward her face.

STEALING PROPELLER HATS FROM THE DEAD

I suddenly remember that familiar, sinking feeling you always get when you find out the girl you love has a boyfriend, that feeling when you can tell something has changed her mind about saving the best conversations for you, and she decides to bring up their relationship out of the blue with a sneaky, off-hand comment like, "Yeah, my boyfriend likes cold chicken and barbecue sauce, too." It's the feeling that spent most of your adolescence hiding in your stomach, curled up under your shirt like a dead animal you were trying to sneak into the house. And when I say I "remember" this feeling rather than feeling it, that's not a mistake. It's because, without a pulse, I'm long past actually feeling anything.

Then a dripping Camel starts stomping down the stairs, rifle slung over his shoulder, dragging the other dead bride behind him, her head tracing her path like the train on her wedding dress may have done the night before. I'm not sure what he did to Underwater Zombie, but it's clear we're losing staff pretty fast.

Right as I begin to suspect I'm being watched, I notice Davey Jones sitting in the one upright and intact chair in the room, watching us all in amusement. He's clapping his hands slow and sarcastic like I'm told Orson Wells did in that movie I never saw without the zombies.

"You guys did awesome," he laughs. "By that, I mean you *died* awesome."

Fuck him, I think. *Always playing disappointed dad.*

How many times can you disappoint someone before you begin to look forward to doing it? About nine actually.

For no good reason, I think back to when I was looking forward to seeing the movie *Species* (not a zombie movie at all, despite the teaser and the green oversaturation) and how me and Sour Towel Zombie got there early in the morning on opening night. And how the movie turned out to be terrible. That was disappointing enough, but the real problem was that I already had plans to see it with a new girl later on. So I kept it to myself that we'd gone already since I didn't want to admit to a new girl that, much like a toddler, I couldn't wait five fucking hours to see a movie. So I suffered though it twice. But then she liked it so much she wanted to see it again the next night. Me, her, and, hey, here comes the boyfriend I never knew she had! And sitting there through *Species* for a third time, dead animal in my stomach building its nest. But I never stopped smiling, thinking this was the only time my punishment fit the crime.

Davey Jones hands me an orange juice to snap me out of it. Always an orange juice with this guy, but mercifully no De Niro shit right now. We always figured the O.J. cartons were because of the alcohol shortage and all the bottles wasted on Molotov Cocktails. For a while, we had even tried one of those popular Zombie Cliché Drinking Games. I think it was really Third Stage Zombie's idea, but we won't be playing that game again anytime soon. The endless complications of such a thing when applied to our production included . . .

First off, "Do a Shot When Arm Reaches through Window" was problematic because it made lightweights hesitate to push through the glass when they needed to. Next, "Knock Drink Out of Nearest Knobby Hand if Martyrdom Slows Down Movie" caused too many instances of fights, brooding, then more fights, not to mention wasted booze. Oh, yeah, and "Shotgun Beer if/when Motherfucker in Uniform Pulls Double-Cross, Shotgun Two if Motherfucker Carries Shotgun"? Yeesh. That rule included Army and Navy T-shirts, so with those drinking flying, were pretty much 'faced as soon as the Bobbys punched the time clock.

And by "punched," I mean punched. Mags was on her third time clock.

And, of course, "Claim Beer of Closest Corpse if Character Shows Confusion about Living or Dead Status of Approaching Loved One" just caused severe depression as we pondered our own sad situation. Oh, yeah, there was "Drink Ninety Beers if Hero Displays Cowardice, or if Some Pussy or Sucker MC Saves the Day," too, but no one ever did that in a real movie, so don't worry. Crazy shit like that only happened on the page. Before the red pens.

And who could have possibly known we were asking for trouble with the tried-and-true staple "Drink Nonstop for Duration of Tom Savini Cameos"? Well, you should try it when the man himself visits one weekend with a cease-and-desist order about copyright infringement.   That was the last night we played it, and we were so hammered after chug, chug, chugging until he finally stumbled off our property with his jet-black goatee twitching that we almost had to change everyone's name to Fetal Alcohol Syndrome Zombie in the morning.

***

"It's a tangled web you weave," someone in a book or a movie or a song once sang.

Or maybe it was "wove." Still weaving? Whatever. Either way, that was the night I learned never to stray far from the zombie genre again. Not to overthink what we were doing. In fact, to keep things simple, me and Cigarette Zombie still watch at least one zombie movie together every night. In front of our own TVs though, miles apart. Synchronized start times are exactly 9:00.

Even though, as of today, it was likely we had finally seen them all, I was hoping we could just start over at the beginning of the stack.

It was the perfect way to watch them, hundreds of

videotapes we'd stockpiled from every dusty, out-of-business video store in the state, VHS cover art bleached white by decades of sunlight cooking them through the windows, not a single title left legible. We avoided the DVDs. Something called "digital rot" had made them a real crapshoot. It turned out nothing lasted as long as anyone predicted.

We didn't have to talk about the movies though, before, during, or after. That was just fiction. It was enough just to know that she was watching a movie at the same time I was, so I could imagine what parts would make her laugh or make her sigh. I didn't need to hear her do it.

I was sure she laughed when there was no one there to verify it.

Still weaving my way through corpses, I see a shadow wearing the nasty, brown-rimmed football helmet again, crusty mouthpiece flapping like a tongue, stiff-arming everyone in its path. Picking up speed, it lowers a shoulder and puts Mike, a.k.a. American Indian Zombie, backwards through a boarded-up window before he can react. Then it dips its head, crashes headfirst through a door, and is gone, leaving behind a piece of shredded tube sock and skin in the teeth of the wooden frame like a ring around the worst dreamcatcher ever.

Suddenly surrounded by unfamiliar faces, pink and blue alike, I recklessly reach to grab someone somewhere on their body where I shouldn't, even though I know this would break the rules and normally end my game right there. Mags is sitting next to Davey Jones, balanced on his armrest, and I notice both her feet are facing the wrong way while I want to shout, "Hey, that's *my* job!" She's singing the Rolling Stones and giggling.

"You make a dead man come . . . "

American Indian Zombie, a.k.a. Mike, is sobbing and climbing inside the house, then back outside. I turn to offer a sympathetic hand, and he shoves me away. He points to the clutter of the trashed room as if to explain that's why he's crying. "The legacy of the White Zombie," he mutters like that goofy, old commercial right before the Camel's next gunshot brings him down, ragged jawbone and pinwheeling ear flap riding the bullet and half his turquoise necklace out the hole in the wall and into the night.

"Control 'Z' and 'Z'," someone screams behind me, and I understand the desperation. Those are the buttons on the keyboard to click "undo."

Then the Camel squeezes one eye to take aim at me, and I hold up my hands in surrender.

"Whoa, hey, wait a second," I say as he peeks through his squint. "Uh, so, did you know there are zombies in the Bible?"

He cocks the rifle, ejecting a shell. I keep trying to distract him as I back up.

"I mean, besides Jesus? I see you're skeptical, but listen, I'm telling you, it's true. Hey, where's Matt? Oh, he's the dead asshole with the flashlight. He'll tell ya. Okay, I can't remember the exact passage. Let me go find a bible. Should be easy to locate. This is a hotel, right?"

The Camel lowers the rifle, eager to debate.

"Did you know that the reliability of the Bible rests on 5,300 manuscripts, source material, and eye-witness accounts?" he asks me. "Therefore, if discrediting the Good Book is your goal, there are more facts behind it than any other classic historical document or source of literature, including Homer and Aristotle."

"Dude," I blink, then shrug. "Zombies in the Bible, though. That's all I'm sayin'."

The barrel of the rifle taps the floor as he considers this, and it gives me enough time to dash out of the room best I can. I start thinking about the movie *Stab 3*, of all things, and the unforced error that girl made when she ran down instead of up. Behind me, I hear the shot, and I know without looking back that European Indian Zombie, a.k.a. Second-Year Cultural Studies Drop-Out Zombie, a.k.a. Rachel, has just taken a bullet through the red dot on her forehead. Right where it belongs.

And at this time, I make the mistake of running for the basement door.

***

The basement stairs turn left at the bottom. In theory, you could stand on the top step and not be seen by anyone hiding down there in the dark. So that's where I wait, counting to a hundred. I think back to the one time in my life when I shared an apartment with a girl and how I used to come home late from work and stand outside my own door, key in my hand, waiting forever to go in. I had no logical reason for my actions, at least none that I could reasonably explain to anyone if they were to walk up and see me frozen there. I would have been busted if she were to open the door before I did. I don't know why I did it. I just couldn't face her sometimes. I think that must be it. I think I just needed to be alone on the steps for as long as I could because I knew things were ending.

There was plenty of time for that now, too.

Five hours on the steps of that apartment was the record, but I don't break it tonight. I only count to one hundred and one, one hundred and two tops.

Cigarette Zombie is sprawled out on the basement floor, her eyeglasses two jagged hoops of blood and shards. Seeing this is worse than seeing her shattered skull because I'm reminded of a story she once told me about her father first realizing that she couldn't see clearly. She had been skiing with her dad, and they were standing at the snack counter between slopes. He asked her what she wanted, and she couldn't see any of the choices on the giant cartoon menu behind the clerk's head. Cigarette Zombie confessed to me that she had tried to be sly and get her dad to read the menu for her, trying to make a joke out of it. But he saw right through the ruse and took her to the eye doctor soon after. She said she was ashamed of her lie until she wore the Coke bottles to school and the kids started picking on her, just like she knew they would. She said she'd rather lie, or stumble around blind and bumping into things any day of the week, instead of reliving that first day of 3rd grade. And when she saw Davey Jones's call for "playing zombie" in the Help Wanted pages decades later . . . well, maybe that had nothing to do with anything. Except maybe the getting-paid-to-stumble part.

"The job just sounded hilarious," she swore, and I wished I was hilarious.

Reaching for her broken glasses, I see another Camel curled up against the far basement wall, another one of the brides, her black, doll's eyes watching me close.

How many fucking brides are there around here anyway? I wondered. *The house is infested. Mags should hang some Bride Strips.*

I must have looked past her when I first came down, possibly mistaking her for part of the structure, the same thing that used to happen to Cigarette Zombie all the time back in school. She told me she couldn't see anybody at all until the second or third day of class, even after she got her glasses.

The Camel in the corner must have found the car battery at some point, but I can see she didn't use it to power the portable radio like she was supposed to. From the looks of things, she seems to have been trying to cook the chicken we stored down there, the meat we kept to fake human entrails. Either that or she was trying to bring a chicken back to life. I've seen that on a farm actually, a dead, frozen chick discarded under a heat lamp, then running amok an hour later. I imagine the Camel down here in the dark before she died, sparking the jumper cables over a pile of barbecued fowl. Sour Towel Zombie would have loved that shit. But he definitely would have warned her of the dangers of zombie poultry, as detailed in the buddy-cop zombie film *Dead Heat*. Then he would have warned her to watch where she was standing because of the horrific consequences of reanimating anything more than once, as demonstrated in the same terrible film he'd only seen nine times.

And arguably reenacted here every weekend for about 300 bucks a head.

I creep closer and raise her chin out of the shadows. She allows me to do this, and I see that she is striking. I knew a girl once who defined love at first sight as, simply, "The Whoosh," something about the rush of blood from the brain to the places on your body where you need it the worst. She had to admit this sound in her head didn't translate as well out loud.

I remember Sour Towel Zombie scoping out this girl in the driveway, months ago when she was signing the waiver, but I guess I forgot to really look at her until now. The End of Days will do that to you every time. Fuck up your priorities.

"Check her out," he whispered, elbowing me too hard. "A sable hat? What, is she Russian or something? 'Cause if she is, I'd fuck her all the way to *Gorky Park*."

"You do that," I said.

"We could watch *Red Dawn* while holding hands."

"That doesn't even make sense."

"I'd leave a stain on her head like Gorbachev."

"Sounds more threatening than romantic."

"She'd call my cock 'Glasnost' . . ." and on and on and on until someone finally told him that "Glasnost" wasn't the name of the movie he was thinking of.

"You need more salt," the Camel bride whispers to me and I almost fall. Her dead eyes are bloody milk and stare right through me where there are no holes.

"The chicken needs more salt?" I ask her, confused.

"No, the driveway," she answers softly. "We almost slipped when we ran up to the house. There was nothing about that in the contract. We could sue you, you know."

"You know what you can use instead of salt?" I offer. "Kitty litter."

"Does that mean instead of kitty litter you can use salt?" She smiles, maybe seeing me now, maybe not.

"Yeah, you could try it. If you want your cat to poof out like a pine cone and run around with a red ass." I smile back. I feel like we're connected.

"More salt . . . " she says again, looking past me now. " . . . just tell someone you need more salt . . . someone could slip." She punctuates this with one dreamy "tisk," then slumps. I put my head to her chest. No heartbeat. Nothing. Doesn't mean a thing though. You have to check when they're talking. As I pull her arm up to my mouth, I fight the urge to tell her that she already slipped, and that we don't need any more salt. Or pepper. We don't need anything.

She'll taste perfectly salty just the way she is. And blood on your wedding night is expected.

I grab both her feet in one hand and raise them high, crossing her legs at the ankles and holding them above my head. With my other hand, I pull off her jeans. I imagine her lifting up to make it easier. I look around the basement nervously, knowing that, particularly these days, being surrounded by an audience of the dead doesn't necessarily mean you're alone. Greedily burying my nose like a puppy in its first bowl of kibble, I root around for any other sign of life. It's all very scientific. And I find it, the evidence, something I noticed earlier when I tried desperately to convince everyone there was somebody alive playing our game tonight instead of just the same corpses pretending they were married.

It's a white string trailing from between her legs, and I think of the tiny strip that pops the batteries out of a remote control. This makes me worry. I sure as hell don't want four double-As flying out of her crotch and bouncing off my nose. But without batteries, there was no chance that she would move for me again.

But I pull the string out with my teeth anyway, searching with my tongue for a ring on the end, hoping it's a pull-cord that activates her like a doll. But all I hear is a hiss, and I don't know which end it's coming from. The tip of the string is stained red, bright red, the kind of red they warn you about in First Aid class, the kind of red that's full of oxygen, close to the heart, in need of immediate attention. That's what I'll give it.

Coming right up . . .

I bury my nose deeper, work the last of my teeth, and I drink her deep. The blood is delicious, but we knew that already. But it's also alive, that sharp copper and electric charge like you're tonguing a 9-volt, like sucking a handful of pennies when you're a child, almost crying because you can't bite down. Except these pennies let you chew them, these batteries let you split them red and wide open like hard candy.

An urge to cough and ruin everything builds in my chest, and I swallow her some more to keep it down, her thick and soothing nectar rolling down my throat, convincing me that I've finally suppressed my nervous hack forever, this barking reflex that once killed the mood when I last tried something like this in high school, a sneeze even thrown with the coughing that night, to guarantee disgrace. The cough was not really a "reflex," but once diagnosed as a "reflux," which is an even worse Duran Duran song, an affliction now, of course, worsened by our diet of too much orange juice and barbecue chicken. Yes, always chicken and O.J. around here. And, yes, chicken looks a lot like our skin, and barbecue looks a lot like blood, and we gobble that shit for the sake of the game. But don't believe what they always say. Only chicken tastes like chicken. This does not.

I drink deeper.

This blood is the goddamn cure for everything, and I know I will never cough again.

Confidence building, reflexes suppressed, I move deeper into her body to solve a mystery. I don't even glance around this time, as I know this bride is utterly mine. I've earned her. Hell, in most countries, technically we'd be married at this point. Blood this bright is legally binding. That's what the Book of Leviticus tells us anyway, right?

I push some skin back with my cleanest fingernail and watch it pulse out of her and into the sliver of light. Not a bean or a grain of rice or a tiny gold BB like the kids at school always claimed. No, it's a claw. A cat's claw has been hiding under that hood all along. Who knew?

"Get under the hood!" A girl said that to me once, that night I tried this in high school. And I made the mistake of saying, "Well, then it needs driven!" and she laughed at me for forgetting the "to be" in that sentence, a common grammatical mistake in and around the Pittsburgh area she would forever christen the "Hamlet," just one of many crippling conditions afflicting a typical conversation-addled Yinzer Zombie. After that, I could do nothing right, even before the sneeze.

My bride slides away from my mouth, and I take this as more evidence of life, and, for a crazy second, I consider putting some salt under her ass for traction, or maybe for flavor. Of course, cat litter works just as well.

It's quiet down here, and I'm glad we have a second, because tonight reminds me of a lot of things. Like my former-best friend's most misguided attempt ever to prove I shouldn't be worried about my girlfriend losing control if she got too drunk at a party. When she passed out on my 21st birthday, he methodically, robotically fucked her while unconscious, wearing a football helmet in case she woke up. The fact that he photographed himself holding a clipboard somehow didn't make it okay, even if he was sure I would excuse it all in the name of science, and maybe she's be more responsible about things. Nope. She was gone after that. Him, too, whoever he was.

I'm telling you though, it's a claw I'm chasing right now! It doesn't just *look* like a claw, pop out, then retract like a claw. It *is* a claw. I know shit is weird out there in the world lately, but right now I'm sure it has always been a claw under there. Push hard enough on any part of a human female and a claw might just come out and greet you.

My sandpaper tongue starts working this shard of rock-hard flint. If I do this long enough, I'm convinced it will have to ignite. No need to blow the gas pump for a climax of our movie.

STEALING PROPELLER HATS FROM THE DEAD

I knew someone once who had a cat with thumbs, which "wasn't *that* strange," she told me. The cat, I mean. Just kidding. But when she took a paw in her hand and pushed in all the secret spots, nine more claws curled out into her palm, making, what, about ninety claws total? I actually screamed. So did the cat. Then we both ran. She only went after the cat though.

Inspired by these memories, but maybe more out of instinct, I chase this claw around in a tiny circle for a while. It does laps with my tongue, proving to me that even if she isn't alive, this part of her has to be. I chase her claw around, feel the point sharpened to infinity, stabbing hard into my sense of taste, mapping out those scientifically disproven sectors of sweet, sour, salty, and bitter, feeling my own blood mixing with hers, and I gasp as I swallow to keep up with the surge. The claw grows longer, and I flick and grind harder, racing the only exposed and glistening muscle found on us human beings, ripping long lines like a gardener through any tastebuds that may remain, maybe buried between sweet and sour after all, gouging out the last one that sensed bitterness for good.

Cunnilingus on a corpse? Sure, that sounds nasty out loud. But only if you don't understand what a goddamn romantic coming-of-age moment this is.

I want to bite. How can anyone not want to bite when they do this? Something this small, the way it slips behind your teeth? It fucking *tries* to get bit. Wanna bite. Can't bite. Gotta bite. Don't bite! Impossible. It's like the oldest story in the world, "Boy Eats Girl."

No, it's like the commercial for that cherry lollipop where the owl with the glasses works it down to a tiny nub on the end of the stick. "One . . . two . . . three . . . crunch!" You're way, way, way past licking almost immediately. It is simply begging to detonate between your teeth.

Cunniliguscorpus? Is that a thing? Ever been there? Fifty miles just outside of Corpus Christi . . .

My tongue licks and leaps like fire. Yes, this is how they invented fire. I'm sure of it.

Whoosh.

But you know how I know she's alive? Because just like the other girl I tried this on back in high school, I know I will never get her off, and the fire will never come. Which is fine with me because it means I will never have to stop. Maybe we were always supposed to bite.

Someone should have told me.

***

My tongue is tracing a line of sweat and salt down her wrist, and I'm chasing and licking and flicking her up, up, up and inside out, when three muffled gunshots upstairs stop me cold.

There aren't enough of us left, I realize. *Or enough time to finish the game.*

Then the Camel bursts in with the rifle and bounds down the stairs, taking them two at a time. When I see the helmet he's wearing, I suddenly understand he's been creeping around outside the whole time, even stumbling along in our circles without us ever noticing. Once maybe sitting next to me and pulling a symbolic fishhook from his lip and acting all wise. It was him. And he's been coming and going at will, not following the rules, which is the most disrespect for our kind of movie that I've ever seen. But it's okay. I'm still smiling because the shit-covered Pittsburgh Steelers football helmet finally found a home.

When he reaches the bottom, the Undercover Camel targets me again. The firing pin clicks . . . and clicks. Empty. It clicks again. Still empty. He drops the rifle and scrubs his palms against his pants.

I drop the bride's ankles and stand up tall, smile all red. At first, I'm embarrassed my face is such a mess, then I imagine I was eating cereal instead. Human beings who have otherwise mastered the art of consuming food are always surprisingly tolerant of having milk and corn flakes running down their faces.

I walk towards him and gently put my hand on his back. He's cold, colder than us. And not because he's dead. He's cold because he's been sneaking around the woods all night, listening to our conversations, discovering our weaknesses, or, at least, our shitty taste in movies. He's been cheating, is my point. Just like Cigarette Zombie at that dance after the 8th grade football game where she pulled aside some girl and tried to get the girl to confide to her about her ex-boyfriend, a kid she wanted to steal, after he'd gone outside to sneak a smoke in his car. Yeah, just like that. She tells me stuff. And this is something he has been doing all night. And I'm telling the Undercover Camel all about her 8th grade dance, too, right as I'm telling you.

"She told me that she was planning on snaking him away from her, and Cigarette Zombie denied everything until the girl put her hand on Cigarette Zombie's back and felt the cold still floating over her skin. Right then, she knew that Cigarette Zombie had been following him to his car for some smooching, and then tip-toeing back in through the darker door at the far end of the gymnasium . . . "

"Huh?"

"'Huh,' what? She tells me stuff."

And I'm still telling him stuff when he stops listening and reaches out to turn my arm around at least three times before he starts working to tear it free from my shoulder.

But Bobby B is crashing down the stairs now, too, with

Bobby Z clomping close behind. The Undercover Camel quickly and correctly recognizes the combined unarmed forces of two assholes united as a more significant threat than me, and he releases my twisted arm. Bobby B starts to leap very unzombie-like toward the Camel, but he catches him in pre-flight, just off his second-to-last step, and takes him down hard to the concrete floor, ribs popping inside both their bodies like knuckles under a desk. The Camel punches Bobby B like a jackhammer, just like Dirty Harry did to that motorcycle cop in *Magnum Force*, something that usually happens to Cop Zombie at least once a season.

"It's the only way to punch someone," according to Davey Jones's dad, Barney, a.k.a. "Barnaby Jones," a.k.a. "Basketball" Jones, like the Cheech & Chong song, or so he claimed.

So it's looking bad for Bobby B, at least until Bobby Z catches the Camel's fist between punches in a very cinematic pose, and then wrestles him onto his back. I step closer to the dogpile, (we're in more dogpiles of bodies than "dog's breakfasts" these days, look it up), and I don't know how I ever thought the Undercover Camel's hump was cold to the touch. I can now feel the heat coming off him in waves as he struggles for his life. I decide Bobby B must feel the life in him, too, as I watch him crawl towards the tornado of flailing fists, elbows, and "motherfuckers!" as if it's a bonfire, his palms out to soak up all the warmth.

Bobby B actually looks up at Bobby Z in brotherly love, and I'm glad I'm there to see it. But glancing from one filthy mug to the other, I can no longer tell them apart. And it's not just the decay or the old purple paint still smeared on their faces. There are other colors now, too.

For a couple tense seasons, before Davey Jones

outlawed it, the Bobbys used to alternate painting their faces black as a shout-out to the civil-rights-era racial commentary of the original trilogy, though more likely a misguided gamble for their own survival because of the previous political climate. Tonight, I hate to think about the possibility, but there's a very good chance one of the Bobbys shit in our community football helmet as a way of painting a face brown and trying to claim one of the leadership roles the minorities usually dominated in zombie films. I sure hope not.

Clearly, they didn't remember the end of the first movie very well.

But a lot like the black cat I used to own, every day was a Bobby's first day on Earth.

"Bobby . . . Bobby," I say, and I have the attention of both of them for the first time in our short lives. I try not to waste it. "Like she said outside, you two are kinda brothers, you know?"

Everyone stops the killing for now, so I keep trying to make this count.

"Okay, you know how doctors ask everyone first thing when you get to your appointment if there's a history of cancer in the family? There's a good reason for that. It's not just because bad genes and diseases are more likely for you if your uncle had them. It's because you are actually the *same* creature. Your mother? Your father? Everything you are came from them. You are not just a relative. You are another. This is what you are. Everyone knows this but you, and you. And you."

They both look at each other, then down to where the Undercover Camel's shirt has been yanked up to expose his furry belly.

Sometimes during our film festivals, there will be a few grumblings about zombie movies and how easily they always seem to tear apart a human body, how hard that would really be in real life, and how zombies should never have some kind of super strength—and not just because they're dead, either. Now, I would agree with this. Up to a point. Because what zombie scholars have never understood until recently, until they began to reclassify Brian Yuzna's film *Society* and give it a decent release, is that it is relatively easy to reach into a man's stomach and turn him inside out. In that movie, the young hero (Billy Warlock from short-lived *Baywatch* fame) squares off against the toughest ass-grabbing alien in the neighborhood, and right before the bad guy is going to jam his fist up the hero's ass . . . he turns the tables by jamming his fist up the alien's ass instead. Oh, snap! Then Billy works his hand up through the alien's body to grab the inside of his face through his eye-sockets with sort of this reverse bowling-ball-grip maneuver. Then he pulls the whole nasty mess out the other guy's rectum. "Rectum? Damn near killed him!" No one says that in the movie, but, seriously, the dude's dead. The entire cast is shocked into silence, and the movie can do nothing but roll the credits. This impossible climax is closer to the truth than people think because it's even easier to do these things when a group of us are pulling in all directions, and easiest of all when there's simply one more pair of hands to help push in the same place you are pulling.

This is why, when Bobby B punches deep into the Camel's gut, Bobby Z's fist follows right behind. They both open their hands to fan their fingers at the same time, and of course the skin splits and stretches like taffy just like we always knew it would and they tumble forward, and they're suddenly swimming in that shit and blowing bubbles and heads darting under like ducks in a pond. No. More like brothers in a tub.

I rub my eyes, watching them splash around, looking eagerly for the red that never comes. Turns out our name for them was perfect. Everyone knows camels are full of water.

"No, I believe it. They could really be camels we're dealing with here," a dripping, sputtering Bobby says from the soup of the torso. "Even crime scene investigators are confused between a dead man's and a dead monkey's blood. At least for a day. You ever watch them scratch their heads bald when there's a murder at a zoo?"

"We're all brothers," the other Bobby says, affectionately rubbing spaghetti in my hair. "You, too, kid . . . "

"So, please, don't let us dine in vain!" my other brother laughs.

***

The three of us are back outside and rounding the shed when a Bobby's head opens up like a Thanksgiving turkey and a gunshot echo swirls around our ears. I fall backwards, then look over to see, amazingly, Cigarette Zombie stumbling with the rifle balanced on her small shoulder, broken glasses back but askew on a broken princess nose. She's talking to herself and seems to be finishing a debate with someone from earlier in the night, probably one of those Super Bowl fans that sometimes would wander over from a neighboring motel, The Whole Year Inn, a.k.a. The Hole You're In (third to last in the phone book), a joint that was under attack daily instead of just on weekends but never thought of it as a game.

" . . . something about girls in football jerseys disgusts me," she says, "I mean, I'm all for subverting gender norms but . . . I just don't buy that she actually likes football . . . maybe should have called them 'The Stealers' instead of . . . huh?"

She looks over her glasses at us, then under her glasses.

"No, really," she insists. "That's what spell checker wants to do with the name Pittsburg Steelers every time you type it."

Then she flicks the cigarette to ignite the fake cardboard gas pump, sorta the climax to our show when everything goes right. Our zombies might not be afraid of imaginary fire where fire is supposed to be if it wasn't for budgetary constraints, but they're certainly afraid of not being afraid of shit they're supposed to be afraid of.

"What?"

Imagination be damned, Third Stage Zombie steps up ready to burn. He sighs, and accepts his role as Inevitable Head Torch Zombie. The Last Bobby Remaining can't help but smile, and I wonder if he started that jersey argument when he was wearing the helmet, or if that was someone else. No one is sure which Bobby it is that's left standing or where their Army or Navy T-shirts have gone. But these things don't matter anymore. Never did.

However, I am pretty sure that shit-eating grin belongs to Cloverfield, a.k.a. Bobby B, since this zombie apparently has the balls to bust out the forbidden Steelers number 22 tonight, the black home jersey of cornerback William Gay and the only official NFL gear left in the Midwest without holes in it. I couldn't tell if he was wearing it down in the basement earlier, as he's lost a good foot of his freakish height on some busted shins. For the record, this jersey was a very passive-aggressive engagement present from his best friend years ago, back when they were still best friends, Bobby Z, who brought with it the unspoken dare that even the most rabid football fan might not have the guts to wear a "Gay" jersey in public. But whichever Bobby this is that's smiling at me now, I think it's telling that he probably waited until the end of the world to finally put on the uniform. The big pussy.

I reach out with my good hand to see if Cigarette Zombie will accept it. One time, when she was telling me stuff, she showed me her chapped, flaking fingers and told me about a problem that followed her all her life, not just since she'd been dead. She said that her knuckles started to crack and bleed in kindergarten, and that her mom made her wear oven mitts filled with Vaseline to school sometimes. Before the glasses, I shuddered. "It's a good thing kids aren't cruel or anything," she'd scoffed.

I try to move towards her slowly, but I'm sure that to the untrained eye, it must seem like the desperate lurch of some monstrosity, arms out, fingers flexing as it growls.

"Remember the mittens?" I ask her as she prepares to run and break the rules, something terrible leaking and bubbling around her midsection. "Where are you going? I know how you feel! Trying to build a house of cards, you would crush everything you loved!"

"I wish," she laughs, finally recognizing me after all, legs trembling. The she falls. It's the first time she's ever laughed, I swear. If I told you she laughed before this moment, I was lying.

The Last Bobby carries the radio. It still holds a charge. There's nothing but static popping from the speakers, and I think of Sour Towel Zombie overanalyzing his thirteenth favorite zombie movie, *The Beyond*. In that film, it was a static from some giant red boombox that caused all the trouble. That cinematic siren call was likely mesmerizing, and if it was only half as seductive as the silken, irresistible voice of Poor-Man's Lance Henriksen, a.k.a. Stephen McHattie, as the DJ in the film adaptation of *Pontypool Changes Everything*, we would all be at its mercy.

So the static first called the ants. Then it called the monsters. Then us.

"Brains!" someone screams in the distance.

"Wrong movie, cocksucker!" The Last Bobby screams back.

There's no denying that we all miss the bastard. We're sounding just like him. Yeah, we'll miss him right up until he stands back up.

One time when I was a boy, I brought a record to Show and Tell, an authentic vinyl 45 I'd borrowed from my aunt, and I played Sweet's song "Fox on the Run" in its entirety for a roomful of 3rd graders. Watching their eyes when the guitars kicked in made this the single most triumphant moment of my life. Then the next kid unveiled a toy shark based on the movie *Jaws*, where you stacked body parts in its rubber-band-hinged lower jaw and gently tried to pull them out until it snapped up and bit your hand. As we gathered around to play with the shark, they'd already forgotten about my song. And so did I. Later, I understood exactly why they'd ignored me that day.

It was because they wanted to be scared, not sing. That's why we always keep our radio between stations.

I turn up the static as loud as it goes, our dog whistle to call everyone together for the last scene.

***

The sun is coming up, and The Executioner and the Four Hats is being acted out by whoever's left. We are seven zombies now, unrecognizable from each other in voice and appearance, with no discerning characteristics, which makes for terrible storytelling, except maybe for the cowboy hat that's still being passed around when someone falls and it rolls off their head, sometimes with their head still in it.

We used to slather on a bit of latex paint, mostly greens and blues, finally settled on purple. But at some point, we switched over to more dangerous oil-based paints, then to spray paint, which, in the home-improvement world, is very painful and pretty much means "forever." But why not?

Forever just got a lot fucking shorter, and spray paint smells delicious. That's one part of our brain we never lost, our noses. Part of our noses, I mean. Who cares?

And now there's five of us. Nope, back to six. Whoops, back to five. Nope, back to six. She loves me. . . she loves me not . . .

I think it's Cop Zombie who is now getting his dome unceremoniously bashed into Brunswick stew when he turns his back on us one too many times and we all run him over. "Friendly fire," they call this on the front lines. We're gonna have to change his name to Fratricide Zombie next time, if and when he reassembles the purple puzzle that is his skull. Cop Zombies get it worst, for good reason.

Speaking of puzzles, we got the perfect number now, so I set it up as accurately as I can remember from Davey Jones's baffling demo. I drag a corpse into a closet, another corpse onto the floor in front of the closet door, and two more corpses into kitchen chairs to be securely strapped, hair tenderly tousled if they got any left. I'm a quick learner.

I hold the rifle to the first corpse's stone-cold forehead and whisper that it has ten seconds to live unless it can tell me whether it's alive or not. Someone behind me protests that we never found a way to make this stupid game-within-the-game actually work. So I explain, mostly to myself, that the solution is written on our faces. I tap the words I've scrawled in blood, soot, and magic marker above the eyes of the three nearby bodies to illustrate my point:

"Zombie," "Not Zombie," and "Propeller."

But with everyone dead, there's no answer to my

question, of course. This has happened before, and we've always played through it. The dead can talk about movies, sign waivers, do their taxes, take too many smoke breaks, even need glasses to glare over and under. But sometimes you might have to move their hands for them, you know?

See that? Watch me do it right now. Oh, yeah, remember before how I said we were all unrecognizable? That's mostly true. Except for the smell.

I make Sour Towel Zombie wave goodbye to the body hogtied in front of him, then I click the gun against his ear. He doesn't blink. I study his fingers. Dry as bone. That's because they are bone. I remember how excited he was when this all started happening. He said that being dead was a blessing because it meant no more oil on his fingers, which, in turn meant fewer fingerprints on his precious DVD collection. He was also excited that this calamity occurred before Blu-Rays really took off, or the Red-Rays, and that nasty recall because of the digital rot, of course, all of this negating the need to replace his movies for a sixth time. But he still had plenty of videotapes waiting to be upgraded when his heart first stopped, and he let me and Cigarette Zombie add them to our stacks when he saw how much this meant to me.

I put the gun to another skull and ask it the million-dollar question.

"Are you alive or dead?"

But I know I won't get an answer. Remember in art class when they taught you that a person's eyes are exactly halfway up the head, right down the equator of the face? Not high on the forehead like you'd expect? This helps us understand exactly how much of the cranium can be missing on a zombie before it can't play games anymore. If you see that half's gone, so is the part of the brain behind the eyes that keeps important plot points moving.

So I can tell already, even from behind, that I'm not getting an answer. Half is bad. Half is over. Half is halfway home. And when it comes to the brain, or even shit for brains, if you lose that much, your cup will always be half empty.

We'll need to put the "Zombie Help Wanted!" sign back in the window.

I eat some cold barbecue chicken, a.k.a. "hand in a baseball glove," but I don't know where the hand starts and the glove ends. This is a detail that was never accurate in the movies either. We don't eat brains. We don't eat meat. We eat anything we can, but mostly each other.

I look around for her.

I'm thinking a little bit of swagger with my stumble might help me make my move this time. Okay, so down in the basement, maybe I didn't "make a dead girl come" or whatever, as our wedding song should go, but that's setting the bar unreasonably high. I remember the claw, wondering where it came from again. Maybe like the crisp husk a dead ant leaves behind, hardening into a claw is just the next stage in its evolution.

If evolution means dead.

But that transformation couldn't have happened to the newlywed so quickly. Cigarette Zombie though? She died the same day we all did.

But none of this matters because a little experience, especially with a married woman, will do wonders for your confidence when you need to grow some guts and take a chance! Even more so when, instead of those guts, there's a hole in your stomach that whistles in the fucking wind.

I won't care what I find inside her.

Turning Sour Towel Zombie's head toward me, I

explain that the only time I agreed with him without question is when he declared the best zombie movie ending of all time as the finale of *Dellamorte Dellamore*. At the end of that film, the camera pulls back, and it turns out that the hero and his idiot manservant were just tiny sculptures in a snow globe all along. It wasn't the image of the heroes as toys and the giant plastic snowflakes coating their heads that haunted me so much as the tiny piece of broken highway crumbling at their feet and the edge of the cliff that dropped off into the dark. This ending always made perfect sense to me, and I never considered it a cheat, like the bullshit equivalent of it all being a dream or whatever.

My dad disagreed though, before he died for the last time, ejecting the movie immediately after that coda and breaking the videotape across his knee . . . and his knee off with it.

"How long would you last in the Zombie Apocalypse?" I once asked him.

"Eh, about the same as I lasted before the Zombie Apocalypse," he joked. For the record, this was the second-worst joke ever if you're keeping track. The worst joke came next.

"But I'd last fifteen minutes if I thought about baseball."

***

We climb onto the roof. Tonight, there are two of us still able to walk. Because if one is left, two are left, and you can make anyone walk that you want.

In the distance, the fields are full of stick figures marching across the pumpkin orange horizon. They're a couple miles away yet, but they're moving so slow, just like they're supposed to. It'll take them the rest of the day to get here.

But these zombies aren't playing the game. They don't seem to have any respect, or love, for their predicament. I can tell by their casual gait. It's too slow, even slower than us. I can tell by those heads that hang lower than mine ever has. They want to pretend they're us, playing the game, which isn't the same thing at all, I swear.

I just don't understand them. This lack of love for the genre. It's like Romero's last zombie pumping invisible gas for invisible cars. Why did it even bother going to work? What do you mean, "Why?" Okay, I'll tell you why.

It's because this place really was a good idea, even before shit went down, when we were still just pretending. Ask anybody. Then move their mouth to answer you.

I hear wood crack and pop. Splinters. A zombie's worst enemy. Looking over the edge, I watch a dog walk through our house, straight through the wall under me as if it's made of smoke and bad breath. A dog. Not a zombie's worst enemy, but certainly not our best friend.

It exits the other side, crashing through another wall weakened by a decade of pounding, moaning, and the weight of slumped, tired shoulders. The entire west side of the house explodes all around the dead animal's path, filling the sunshine with dust and pulp and drywall snow.

We can't rebuild that.

You ever leave a snow globe in the sun by accident? The water turns yellow, a beautiful color really, especially when the sky overflows with it, as ours does now.

But the dog could give a shit about these things. It just shakes the shards and nails out of its fur without missing a step or slowing down. Then it turns to run through the walls again, momentarily trapped in some wires and chains.

I have no doubt it will break free and drag our world behind it like a dog house.

***

A shadow will be moving closer without me having to tug on it, and I will block the sunrise with my good hand to see. At such a bad angle when the sun comes up or the sun goes down, I won't know who anyone is, as usual, but this time I will decide it's her.

Even at the end of everything again, both of us together on the roof like we're supposed to be, I will clear my throat to ask her a question.

"Let's just wait and see what happens," she will answer me.

I will sigh and take this to mean that, apparently, another dead man with a better single character trait than my nervous cough could be shuffling down the hill at any moment.

"Let's take things slow," she'll say.

"Any slower and we'll stop," I'll laugh, helping her move her jaw on a tough word like "slow," so I know she means it. I'll move in close to her lips and resist the urge to ask her where she stole the hat because they're all our hats now. I'll watch her lips work to stay unstuck, and I'll remember when she reminisced about a game called Zombie Kisses she played back in junior high. It was a bit like Spin the Bottle, except when she was slouching in their circle instead of ours she was hiding an ice cube under her tongue.

Scattered across a piss-yellow ocean of dead grass, I won't be able to tell if they're walking anymore. Even the sun moves faster than us these days, so they may never arrive. Plenty of time to clean up, maybe play another game before the world ends again.

Then everyone will be coming out of the house, cheers and applause if they're able, squinting up high at our life raft to see who won, not even bothering to gather up any parts of themselves that they will lose again and again.

Then they will start to walk in that tired orbit if they can, following each other forever, talking about movies, hands and heads be damned.

I'll spin the propeller on her hat instead of spinning a bottle, but I won't wait to see if it stops. I'll turn to her.

I bite.

"And when he was entered into a boat,
his disciples followed him."
>—Nervous Cough Zombie 6:06-6:09 a.m.

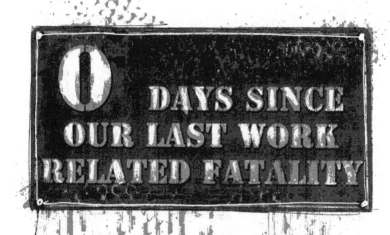

THE WORLD'S SECOND SHORTEST ZOMBIE STORY

THE FOREMAN DRAGGED his ladder over to the sign, unhooking the "7" and dropping it to the factory floor. He left a zero swinging above " . . . Days Since Our Last Work-Related Fatality." The next morning, the foreman dragged out the ladder again, hands shaking as he hung the "7" back up.

THE BALL PIT
(OR CHILDREN UNDER 5 EAT FREE!)

"Build a wall with the bodies of the dead and you're saved."
—Accept, "Balls to the Wall"

11:11 a.m., November 11ᵗʰ, 2011

HIS WATCH STOPPED again, but that was okay since the calendars had stopped, too. He spun the smaller hand on the watch face until it rested on a good time, then the smallest hand until it rested on a good day, one of those easy-to-remember junctures where he used to make a wish when he was a kid, so it would always be like a birthday whenever he looked down and he could imagine the planets lining up right along numbers. Then he wound the watch back up tight and kept on winding.

His name was Ralph, pronounced "Rafe," so he'd always gone by "Raff" instead. And today, Raff was working his way through a toy store because most reasonable people refused to set foot in one, even now that things had died down a bit. He crept along, kicking empty boxes and discarded assembly instructions out of his way. From outside the building, there'd been some signs that this Toys "Я" Us had been a shelter for some time, some of the signs more subtle than others. First off, someone had gone to a great deal of trouble to climb up on the roof and turn both backwards "Rs" around to form their own distress call. But what they chose to spell with the remaining letters wasn't a typical cry for help.

"Yours Rots," the message read, a huge, multi-colored ransom note looming over his head. Raff tried not to look at it too long.

The remaining clues were a bit more optimistic. Blacked-out, taped-up windows, rows of empty bottles and rain buckets peeking out along the edge of the roof, crude peepholes drilled into the steel freight doors. And surrounding the building, trucks parked at all sorts of strategic, glass-obscuring angles.

Except for the one door that was wide open.

He hesitated, looking up at the store's wide-eyed mascot for help, but he could only picture his grandfather's trophy-hunter magazines, particularly the page where a man had wrapped a limp giraffe's neck over his shoulders like a python, tongue lolling. In high school, the kids had called Raff "G. Raff" to harass him, of course, instead of the much cooler "Riffraff" nickname he'd always hoped for. He actually missed the giraffe taunts and infantile locker graffiti sometimes, but not today.

Raff shouldered the metal door aside, heart hammering at the crinkling rainbow of candy wrappers and crêpe paper that billowed over his shoes and out of his way like a snow drift. A lone maple seed helicoptered down onto his shoulder, and his brain said "spider" even as his eyes proved it wrong. A spider was the second-worst thing Raff worried about these days. He remembered an old saying, "If you want to live and thrive, let a spider run alive." For most of the world's populations, it turned out the opposite was actually true. He flicked the seed away, then glanced around but saw no evidence of trees encroaching on the abandoned structure. But his brain had no room to ponder the trees.

Candy.

All the color washing over his shoes was another sign, another siren blaring in his head, but one that signaled "good" and "bad" equally.

Probably more like bad, he thought.

A rainbow of wrappers like the ones covering the floor was a semiotic situation as ominous as any crime scene ribbon these days. It was a literal red flag, and Raff scratched the sweat running down the back of his neck as he considered his next move, exhale trapped in his chest, foot frozen mid-step. But he still had hope. Mostly because of the Fun Dips. He could see a pile of their wrappers recently gutted to get at the delicious vanilla Lik-A-Stix, but every cell of the fruit-flavored powder packets were still intact. This suggested intelligence to Raff, a preference for a certain taste, not the gluttonous hive mind that had become so common with every remaining . . .

A shadow turned the corner, dragging a smaller shadow behind it, which, in turn, clutched a mangy, stuffed gator to its swollen belly. Raff started breathing again. He finally had his answer.

Leading the parade was a naked child, 8 or 9 years old, sex impossible to determine. It was pulling a forever newborn baby whose mouth worked silently in protest, a car seat strap buried halfway into what had once been a pink, chubby thigh. Sometimes the baby gummed the stuffed gator between struggles, and when it did, Raff felt his brain slip just a bit, like a hiccup, before sanity mercifully resumed. He slapped himself to remain there.

Then Raff leveled his gun.

But he couldn't do it. As it shuffled closer, he took turns aiming at the toddler, then the newborn horror it was dragging. He rubbed some more sweat from his face into the heel of his hands and settled on the gator.

He fired, blowing off its tail in a spray of green and white fuzz, and the tiny, lumbering train of infected pulled each other closer. Then one began to cry. He didn't know which one was wailing, and he prayed a pull-string on the gator was responsible. He didn't know they could cry, but he suspected that's why they were such an issue. But that was probably half the problem.

The one in the lead stumbled, then slowly climbed a nearby sale bin to stand back up, bare feet slapping the floor as it worked to steady itself.

Toddler indeed, Raff tried to laugh. *How perfect is that word now?*

He pushed his gun back behind his belt. No way he could do what had to be done. He'd convinced others that he could, even laughed at their impotence when it came to stepping up to this worldwide dilemma. But now he knew no one could.

He looked at his watch. It had stopped a couple years ago, but he needed it to keep making wishes. Raff tried one final wish, mouthing it silently so it counted, then ran back outside, turned a corner too fast, and fell face-first over the rim of an inflatable pink-and-purple castle and vanished into the giant gumball kaleidoscope of rubber that overflowed its moat.

He sank slower than he would have thought possible. He saw the skeletal hands of webbing stretched between the balls as the light faded, strings snapping free from his flailing limbs, flinging tickling insect shells all over his face and arms. He rode this sticky rain of husks down to the bottom.

8:35 p.m., July 4th, 2019

It was a spider that ended the world, of course, a fact that forever justified humanity's inherent fear of arachnids.

STEALING PROPELLER HATS FROM THE DEAD

The Brazilian Wandering Spider to be exact, a fairly innocuous perpetrator loaded with fat, labia-like fangs and a ridiculously potent venom. The bite of this spider was known to cause priapism, in the genitals first, a zombiefication of the penis and clitoris that offered no pleasure, no relief, and often resulted in impotence.

So it was ironic that scientists first began experimenting with this venom to cure this embarrassing condition. The resulting tiny, red pill that promised relief from performance anxiety or endless pillow-talk rationalizations turned out to be a rather anticlimactic end to the human race, beginning at the groin with a stiffness that quickly spread through the muscles until any and every act above and below the waist became painful, then finally maddening. The victims resembled the "zombies" from film and television more than anything, but this was only a superficial similarity. Tucked away inside their bodies was a Herculean struggle to walk, speak, or communicate in any way. And this is what caused the other, more alarming symptom; a murderous rage that channeled itself into a morbid hunger for everyone, anyone moving faster and more smoother than they could.

And just like the spider, it was a bite that carried the disease.

Because of the flashpoint of the affliction in the genitalia, these semi-paralyzed ghouls initially stumbled around with awkward erections. However, this terrifying sight wasn't nearly as common as people expected, as the muscle damage was so severe that a penis was the first thing to break off on a traffic jam in a revolving door.

Raff remembered a news report from the first week of the infection, before the tiny, red pills were recalled, the story of a conspicuously aroused male playing aggressively with his children in a local Chuck E. Cheese ball pit. This man was severely beaten by onlookers, even reportedly bitten by some kids who had joined in the melee, as the crowd suspected him a pedophile or some other breed of incestuous monster. And because the staff was already indifferent about the endless glut of bodily fluids that marbled the colorful rubber and slippery walls, this man's blood covered enough of those balls to infect at least three birthday parties in the following weeks.

Raff couldn't remember his name, except that he was later referred to as Patient Zero, although some of the less responsible newspapers called him "Patient *Nero*" in their headlines, the gag being that he "diddled while Rome burned." Raff wondered if he missed his nickname, too.

It really wasn't his fault, Raff always thought. *They bit first.*

But the world saw things differently. And they were all his children now.

11:11 a.m., November 11th, 2011

When he came to his senses, he realized his stopped watch was gone. Leather strap worn through by sweat and wear, it had sank somewhere into the dark corner of the ball pit. But Raff didn't swim around after it. In a way, he was relieved of the self-imposed burden of estimating the time, and the pressure of all those wishes, and he was content where the numbers would be forever frozen.

Wishes for everybody now.

Raff had been bitten in a place like this once, long before the infection. Not by a spider, but by another child. It was when he was young enough to still think you could drown in a ball pit. Children were like sharks in a ball pit.

They owned these ponds, he thought. *Lord of the*

Fucking Flies below the surface where their parents couldn't see or hear.

Kids got to do whatever they wanted under the rainbow cover of squeaking rubber.

So Raff panicked at first, grabbed the sagging walls of the castle to pull himself out, fingernails drawing lines through the magic marker of a makeshift sign that hung next to the price tags on the trampolines. It read, "10 years and Under Only!"

The Terrible Tens.

That's what they called it. Ten years was that magic number. Right around ten and a child was suddenly impossible to deal with. Older than that, and disciplinarians began treating a problem child as a teen. Any younger than that, and you couldn't raise a hand to them in public. Let alone a gun.

This is why, even though the silently raging, murderous adults had been dealt with quickly and efficiently throughout the world, all of the afflicted children still roamed free. There was an infected child in every garbage can some mornings, and there was very little people could do about it, or *would* do about it, for one simple reason.

Nobody wanted to shoot a child in the head.

But as he breaststroked and frog-kicked through the balls and spider webs, desperate to keep his head above rubber, Raff suddenly had an idea. It was an idea that might change everything. It was the kind of idea that could maybe let everyone live with the problem. His idea was sort of like a moat, but better than a moat. You'd need a castle for that, inflatable or otherwise. And even though Toys "Я" Us apparently sold them, for Raff's idea, all you had to do was own your own swimming pool.

He imagined every empty, below-ground pool filled

with hundreds of colorful balls. He knew exactly what infected children would do when they saw something that enticing. The same thing normal children would do. The same thing he did. They would walk on in, tumble over the edge, and then they'd never come out. Hell, no one was using their pools anymore anyway. Raff's own pool had about a bathtub's worth of green water and larvae. Pools had always been for the kids.

And once everyone followed his lead, they could take back the rest of their world again, the playgrounds, then the schools, then the toy stores, the places where the children still gathered, where they still had a stranglehold on our emotions. It was true. Any house that made the mistake of leaving a swing set up in their yard would have the little monsters slow-motion fighting and falling down the slide by morning, then fighting over your neck soon after that. And once that happened, the casualties were severe. Because the same man who would shoot a raccoon off their roof, even shoot a man when it became necessary, he would just watch from his window, helpless, impotent, as a child sank its teeth into the fish-belly skin of his wife.

Raff straightened his legs to let himself sink deeper into the balls. And once he was finally standing on the bottom, his nose filled with the sharp smell of rubber, then he smelled something else. He pushed up and floated silent a moment, satisfied he was alone, then sniffed the tread of his shoe in a sliver of sunlight. It wasn't his shoe he was smelling.

The bottom of the ball pit was littered with bugs, webs, and feces. Amazingly, this didn't disgust him. He was surprised children still defecated, and the heavy scent reminded him of family, of responsibility. But more than anything, it reminded him of a feud his mother had once with their neighbor, Buzz, and his Rottweiler, Buzz Junior.

Back then, while he and his brothers sat wide-eyed on their trampoline, smacking the surface to send the dogshit higher and higher, their mother would call up the neighbor and yell into the phone, sometimes over the fence, "Hey, Buzz, who are you kidding with your ruse? Your whole 'Go potty, B.J., go on and go potty!' every time you send that garbage dog loose into our yard? These logs it leaves behind ain't no 'potty,' Buzz . . ."

As he bounced on the bottom of the pit, breathing it all in deep, he thought about how the world could use ice cream trucks or bundles of birthday balloons for his master plan, his final solution, cruising the streets at a steady three miles an hour, to Pied Piper them all over the side of every swimming pool and head-first into the promise of the squeak and color of a concrete-rimmed time capsule. Any ball would do, too. They could fill them with basketballs, beach balls, soccer balls, Nerf everything and anything, footballs, kick balls, even those Easter-egg-colored, thin-skinned balls that never seemed to serve any purpose except to either fill a giant mesh silo in the middle of the toy store and imply some sort of party that never came, only to one day ride the boiling oil in your moat.

Raff kicked hard up off the bottom, swimming strong for the light and thinking about the movie *Gone with the Wind* of all things, how everybody in that huge house was crying when Rhett held vigil over the corpse of his daughter, Blue. When his wife left the room, Raff told his daughter that Rhett had been trying to raise her from the dead, and that if he'd had just one more day, he would have succeeded.

One more day.

That's when he heard the squeak of tiny shoes kicking in the ball pit with him. Then more squeaks of fingers scratching rubber. Then he saw the red hands clawing their way through the sunlight toward him, and he realized that his plan was gold. Of course it would have worked. This pit was proof. It was loaded with them right now and always had been.

Something wrapped around his thumb, and again his brain screamed "spider." But he came back up with his previous watch instead. It was still stopped cold, of course, but that was okay since the calendars had stopped, too. He spun the smaller hand on the watch face until it rested on a good time, then the smallest hand until it rested on a good day, the last day, where he would never make a wish again, making it as disappointing as every birthday cake he ever extinguished. He didn't wind it this time.

Then he stretched his arms and let them flood over him, the babies riding the sticky balls on their navels like their first day at the beach. He remembered a comic strip from his childhood called *Mark Trail* that depicted a dozen types of spiders on one panel, all hopping from trees to rocks to webs, both spindly and hairy, living in harmony. He laughed at the time, but the epidemic had made that illustration a reality.

All the spiders were sharing their webs now. And this pit likely had as many eggs as balls.

The smallest ones got to him first, and his last thoughts were something like guilt. As they swarmed him and gummed his hands and shoulders harmlessly, he realized this was worse than the deep bites that would follow. Only children under five could gum you like that. Under five years old, and the baby teeth fell out fast.

That's why you never reach for your gun, he thought. *When a mouth is teething your shoulder, you're suddenly a father all over again. You feel guilty you can't feed them. It's the one thing left in the world that wants to hurt you but can't, and this is the part that's infectious.*

Its mouth worked and worked, desperate but unable

to break his skin, a gum line that would never sprout a smile. But, impossibly, in that moment, he wished it would

DOPPELGÄNGER
RADAR

DID YOU SEE the weather channel on the TV back there?"

"Back where?"

"At the gas station. There was this big-ass red spot coming right at us, but the TV feed froze."

"Not a cloud in the sky."

"How do you know it was the Doppler radar or the weather or whatever? Maybe that red spot was something else. Have you seen these new, high-tech Fish Finders? They find more than fish. Crabs, pirate ships, the endless parade of Marching Chinese . . . "

"What the hell is that? Marching who what?"

"It's a propaganda thought experiment they came up with during World War II to scare Americans. Uncle Sam swore that if the Chinese people lined up five abreast and marched into the ocean, this platoon would never, ever stop. Because by the time it got to the end, they'd have had babies big enough to keep on marching."

"Anyway. Just take it easy on the corners when the storm hits. We're still missing some tread on these tires."

"We're fine."

"Fifty bucks says you roll this thing."

"How are you doing back there?" the driver yells to the old man on the gurney.

"I'm fine," the old man says, annoyed.

"I know you're fine," the other paramedic says. "That

gurney is for people who *aren't* fine, not a free taxi service so you can go to the gas station and get cigarettes."

"Come on, Jack . . . " the driver says.

"Come on nothing, Rick. We know this guy," Jack snaps. "Just like his wrinkled ass knows our routes, knows the insurance, knows which crew has seen too much of him this week."

Jack reaches to turn off the siren, but Rick stops him.

"You know when it's time for a paramedic to quit?"

"When?"

"When they start losing . . . *patients.*"

"Zing!"

"Get it?"

"Oh, I get it. I don't need to see the word spelled different to get it."

"Good."

The old man clears his throat with some effort.

"Just because you drive this meat wagon around in circles all night don't give you the right," he says. "You shouldn't talk to us like that."

"Like what?" Jack asks.

"Like you're not down here with the rest of us."

"And what's that supposed to mean, you miserable old fuck?"

"That's enough," Rick sighs.

"Bullshit," Jack says. "Ten dog attacks today alone, and we're carting around this fool."

"Don't worry," the old man says. "I'm sure you'll get plenty more."

***

"So, what's up with all these dogs anyway?" Rick asks, watching the old man walk in, then turn around and walk out of the emergency room, lighting up a smoke, not even trying to fool them.

"Let's find out," Jack says, putting the CB back in its holster.

"Don't you want to go in and get your hand checked?" Rick asks.

"Barely scratched me. That old bastard wasted his last tooth on me. An old man's fingernails are a lot more dangerous than his rotten teeth."

"Well, you shouldn't have shoved him," Rick mutters, turning on their siren and stabbing the gas.

They park just past the comet trails of blood on the pavement, then rush toward the girl unconscious in the grass. Jack has the trauma dressings and tape. But after one look at the bites, he runs back to get the intubation kit, too, along with his bag of shots, or the "Halloween bag of suckers" as Jack calls it; Fentanyl, Versed and morphine. He's relieved to see her chest moving.

"Did you see a dog?" Jack asks a kid on the scene stuffing an ice cream bar in his face.

"Huh?"

He checks her injuries. Deep, ragged bites on her forearms, massive tissue loss on both legs. He checks her eyes for a response, then her blood pressure. Rick gets the gurney off the back and compacts the legs and wheels to prepare to load her up.

"I don't like her eyes," Rick tells Jack. "Shock. Or worse. Be ready when we move."

"Where are we on the map?" Jack asks. Rick seems confused by the question, then understanding washes over his face.

"Yeah, let's get her out of here before they crash the party."

Too late. Another ambulance comes flying in hot. There's no siren on this one, as this truck's been converted into something a little different. The side of the box reads:

"Highway Wildlife Services."

Under that, a smaller, handwritten sign:

"Nuisance Wildlife Control Operator. Skunk Specialists!"

"There's no dogs, sorry," Jack tells the guys that hop out as he rolls the girl back to the double doors. He leans down to her ear. "Ma'am, did you see the animal that bit you?"

"Jack, what the hell?"

"Sorry, it's just . . . I just think something strange is going on here. I mean, does that look like a dog bite on her calf? Or does it look like someone wanted it to look like a dog bite?

"Just clear her leg so we can close it up. You're driving."

"That ain't no dog bite," one of the Animal Control guys offers. Former paramedics themselves, they're always in the way, but today Jack surprises them by wanting to chat.

"That's what I've been saying, man!" Jack agrees. Then to Rick, "Let me stay in the back. I could ask her some questions like—"

"Dude, you're scaring me. Get up front."

"But was she really attacked by a dog?" Jack asks, blocking Rick from climbing in the back. "I mean, who saw a dog?"

"That kid saw a dog."

"No dog," another voice says.

"What the fuck are you . . . " Ricks starts, exasperated. "Okay, tell me this. How do you fake a dog attack?"

"Well, first you'd still need a dog."

"I thought you said there was no dog."

"That kid saw a dog."

Rick slams the doors and throws stones out of there. He checks the sky for rain and still sees nothing, so he takes the corners hard.

"Jack, obviously you think you have some idea of what's going on here. Why don't you share this theory."

"I don't. But we've got what? Twenty bites in as many hours? I think people are confusing dogs with something else."

"Like what?"

Jack doesn't answer. He's blowing on a stethoscope and checking his own chest. Rick starts laughing.

"Hey, you know how they say dogs start to resemble their owners, or people start to resemble their dogs?" Rick asks. "You know, they always say pets are like doppelgängers, right? Maybe that's what's happening."

"That makes no sense."

The girl on the gurney starts convulsing, but Jack does nothing to help her. The driver turns around in a panic.

"What the fuck are you doing?! Check her pulse."

"Doesn't matter."

"Do your job!"

"No pulse."

"How do you know?"

"Because I don't have one either."

After a moment, the girl stops moving, and Jack crouches down next to her. He pulls a sheet over her face so there's something to fall to the floor when she sits back up. He hopes this will finally scare his partner enough to roll the ambulance on the next turn.

THREE WAYS
WITHOUT WATER
(OR THE DAY ROADKILL, DRUNK DRIVING,
AND THE ELECTRIC CHAIR WERE INVENTED)

"For a full twenty minutes by the clock, the Premier might be said to have rehearsed that lively operation known as flogging a dead horse."
—John Bright, 1872, speaking in Parliament

TYING HIS HORSE to the fence, Tom clapped its neck goodbye and turned to the smoldering farmhouse, hand over his gun. He frowned at muffled laughter and shattering glass as a dust-covered man, skin split and gnarled as jerky, bumbled from around back.

The man stopped and shook his head to sober up. Tom's gun was out, slowly tracing his outline. Hands high, no attempt to clear leather, the man moved backwards, stopping with his tailbone against a sagging stone well. Eyes still locked on the gun, the man tried spitting, but nothing came out except a sputtering rant Tom had heard too many times.

"You better watch your back, boy. Sleep with both eyes open 'cause one day when you least expect it, I'm gonna be right behind you, and on that day . . . "

Tom fired, his nostrils eagerly sucking gunpowder as a Catherine wheel of blood and dust exploded from every worn seam and crack in the man's hat.

"No, you're not."

The nearly headless corpse collapsed backwards into the well, its last sliver of throat lolling with the reckless weight of a newborn's skull, just as another man, all smiling eyes, teeth and orange hair, crashed out the front door.

"Hello, Red," Tom said. "You finally thirsty enough to leave?"

Red glanced toward the well.

"Where's Joe?" he asked.

There was a splash as the body finally hit bottom. At the unexpected sound of water, Tom's eyes went wide and Red's smile slipped, his right hand flexing over his holster, cracking the knuckles of his trigger finger with his thumb, click, click, waiting, waiting.

But Tom couldn't help turning toward the first sign of water in days, and Red pulled, burying a bullet deep in his chest.

Tom backed up to sit on the edge of the well, curling like a bug. Red walked over, then stopped to notice his shooting hand was bleeding.

"The hell?" he muttered, fingers wiggling. "How'd you do that?"

Red blinked in shock at the bloody thorns riddling his skin, then upended Tom to join the man he killed.

Suddenly, a skeletal, emaciated boy was standing there. When the second splash came, the boy's eyes bulged at the sound, and he reached for the bucket. Red couldn't believe a child had survived. He fired again so things started making sense again.

The boy slumped and Red caught him with a forearm, dumping him down the well next. Another splash.

"Ain't you supposed to be in school?" he yelled after the boy, followed by, "Tom, do you see him, too?!"

Then he whistled over bloody fingers, and Tom's horse turned the corner, ears cocked, dragging a dead limb. Without hesitation, Red walked up, put his gun behind the horse's eye.

Boom.

The horse thumped forward on its knees, then collapsed into a thick mushroom of dust.

Another man walked out of the house. His mouth cracked and pulsing like a fish on the floor.

"Why'd you shoot that horse?" Eggsucker asked, heading for the well. "Where's Joe? Hey . . . did I hear water?"

Red smiled and stepped in front of Egg, grabbed the bucket off the crank, and dropped it into the dark. The handle spun as the rope unrolled, and Egg licked his split lips in anticipation.

The bucket hit the bodies at the bottom with a distant thud.

"Nope."

Crushed, Egg sat down hard, kicking dirt like a kid.

"Sorry, son," Red said. "You heard it. Dry as bone, just like the rest. Now go get Mud."

"You can't have mud without water," Egg sneered. Then, "You know, usually when you hear that thud at the bottom of a well, it's because you're dropping honey buckets by mistake."

"Dropping what?" Red asked without interest.

"Honey buckets. It's what they call a bucket that moves shit in the wrong direction. Sorta' like an outhouse. 'Cept you dump in the bucket and drop it down. And when the well fills up and there's no more splash, you're done."

"Then that's exactly what this is," Red laughed.

***

Bobby Wendler walked through dead, cracked corn, holding the long sleeves of his dad's shirt up to his nose to stop the bleeding. Two shadows cleared the hill to block the sunset.

It was the Ranger and his mother running towards him.

"Where were you?!" shouted McKenna. "I thought you were gonna' check that last well for water!"

"I'm okay," huffed Bobby as the Ranger grabbed his shoulders.

"Look at me," the Ranger told him. "Now, where's my deputy?"

"He said to tell you he found Red. Told me to tell you we'd all meet up after and skip town."

"Red?" The Ranger's head dropped at the name. "Where?"

"At our house. Him and his gang."

"We're leaving," the Ranger said, releasing Bobby. Bobby tugged on the Ranger's hand to show him a thorn he'd pulled from his pocket.

"No, look. Tom can beat him now. I fixed him. They sleep *a lot,* and last time they slept, I filled up his holster with thorns to slow him down."

The Ranger shook his head and turned to McKenna.

"We're leaving Agua Fría. Right now. As soon as we get your horses."

"But if they already . . . "

"Listen, I swore I'd get you, and that's what I'm gonna' do. Three days without water is the limit."

"What about Tom?"

"If he found Red, he'll be staying."

***

Red and his gang walked through the woods, Mud rubbing the scabs on his knuckles as Egg shuffled with his eyes closed, hands out, fingers brushing hollow trunks. Egg started pounding on the bark, and the gang looked to see the letters of Egg's name carved deep into every tree, in some spots covering every inch, up to six-feet high. Egg ran ahead, then stopped at the base of a gigantic dead tree.

To their amazement, he shoved it down easy.

Red frowned, looking Egg over with something resembling respect.

"Wanna' see it again?" Egg asked them. Then he stepped up to another tree and shouldered it over with a splintering crash.

"Holy shit buckets," Mud said.

Red marched forward to push down his own tree. It didn't budge.

"No," Egg said. "Try this one."

Egg clapped a white trunk as Red strode over, still squinting. Wrapped around the tree was Egg's name again, cut a fingernail deep into the bark. Red leaned into it with his shoulder, and it creaked, wood shards popping like fireworks.

"How long you been putting your name on these, Egg?" asked Jackass.

"Uh, about six . . . six . . . " he stuttered. "Sixteen . . . years."

"Why?"

"Dunno'," he shrugged, tongue darting. "It was a dumb idea I had once."

"Once?" Mud laughed. "For sixteen years? Sounds more like a dumb idea you *keep* having."

"What idea?" scoffed Red.

Egg shrugged again and pointed to the house they just left behind.

"You remember way back before you killed Gray, when it was common knowledge Gray Wendler had the best five horses in the state? No one could ever steal those horses of his 'cause, even though he only got around to building half a fence, he didn't need any security at all. Well, it's these trees right here, the only ones in town. That's his security. Back when these trees were alive like us, riding these woods was as hard as trying to ride a horse underwater. So . . . "

"So what?" snarled Red.

"So I weakened 'em. Right in front of everyone. I've been walking around, putting my initials on everything for a long time now. I figure one day if I can't ride the sheriff's best horses out through trees that thick, maybe I could ride those horses out *through* 'em instead."

"Ain't no sheriff in this town," Red muttered. "Never was and never is again . . . "

Red trailed off as a horse stepped from the other side of the tree line, dried blood around its muzzle, flies around the hole below its ear where Red had plugged it.

"Ha!" Red coughed. "Look at that goddamn thing. Bullet through its head, but nobody told it."

He ran up and grabbed the bridle, and the horse followed him with yellow eyes angled back toward the gang. Suddenly, Red stopped and stared at the trees. Jackass stood next to him, uncorking another bottle of whiskey, drinking and knowing he shouldn't.

"What is it, boss?"

Red mounted the horse in silence.

"Uh, you don't wanna' do that," Mud said, catching on. "Let's just go around."

"Any of you see a boy in those trees?" Red asked, strangely thoughtful.

"Who?"

"Got a dumb idea," Red said as he pointed to the horse's dripping head, then heeled it hard and galloped past the men, heading fast for the first tree.

The horse galloped hard, yellow eyes flashing with life. It lowered its nose and crashed into the first trunk, splintering it like a giant wishbone. The gang ran to follow. The horse hit a second tree, its body curling and shivering as it buried its head into the wood. The second tree fell, crackling like a bonfire.

Blood and spittle ran down the horse's snout, and Red turned the horse again, kicking its flanks harder, thundering through the dead woods faster and faster. They headed for a third tree, the last tree, a huge oak with green still speckling its branches, not a single initial or heart carved into its trunk. Alive.

Red and his dead horse plowed into the last tree like a steam engine folding up against a cliff wall. Both shuddered, the horse's ribs buckling like an accordion. Then the horse dropped to a knee, black blood foaming, hole in its skull boiling, then it was falling, falling. Red jumped off at the final thud, stepped back, and stood over the animal, hat tipped in respect, boot nudging its leg in disgust.

"Dead again."

"That was probably the last one," slurred Jackass, running up, out of breath.

"Nope," Mud said. "Wendler's wife is hiding horses. I heard them in her barn when you fools were looking under beds for money."

"What?" Red said through his teeth.

"I *heard* 'em back there," he insisted.

Soon they were all trotting back toward the barn. Then running.

"At *least* five horses. And if she's got horses, she's got to have water . . . "

"Ain't none left," Red said, running now, too.

"I'm telling ya', there's . . . "

"Ain't," Red said again louder. "And if there is, there still ain't."

"But I heard . . . " Mud started before Red elbowed him in the jaw and put a boot on his throat where he fell.

"Listen to what I'm telling you," Red told the thing squirming under his foot. "There is no law here. No horses neither. And if there's still horses in this town, in about five seconds, there *ain't* gonna' be no horses in this town. Get it?"

Red lifted his boot to let him up.

"That's the problem around here," he told them as he walked on. "A town still thinks it's a town just because it's got horses."

***

Agua Fría burned. A dead undertaker was grinning in the coffin he built, propped against a smoking porch. The last man on Main Street took a long drink and played with the undertaker's jawbone.

"Hey!" the Last Man mocked out the side of his mouth. "If I'm dead, then who put me in the suit!"

The second to last man on Main Street laughed at this, then a third man reached in, too, and the bottom half of the undertaker's skull tore free like overcooked turkey meat.

None of them saw the Preacher walk up, all black except for chipped teeth and the silver flash of a gun stuck in a belt pulled tight to its last notch. The gun was the only thing keeping his pants up.

The men stopped laughing when he spoke, his voice rattling around his throat like coins.

"Why didn't you leave when the water ran out?" the Preacher asked.

"Plenty to drink," said the Second-To-Last Man, looking for his whiskey.

"And what's it to you?" asked a Third Man as the Preacher stepped closer.

"Oh, I'm sorry, boys," the Preacher sighed. "I guess you didn't recognize me without my collar."

"What collar?"

"It's gone black from the smoke."

The men twitched uneasily as the Preacher walked past them, tipping up a huge wide-brimmed hat and rubbing red eyes caked with ash from the burning storefronts on each side of the street. Then they went back to their bottles. They stared at each other until the Last Man tried to clear his throat, hacking a spider of black mucus onto the top of his fist instead.

"Heard Red came by to see you, too," the Last Man said. "Looking for Holy Water to drink."

"Well, I suspect anybody left around here is about as dry as summer amadou," the Preacher said. "And so full of alcohol a match and a bit of wind would be enough."

"I heard there's really only three ways to die," said the Last Man.

"If you don't count lack of water," said the Third Man.

"More like a hundred and five," said the Preacher, pulling out a wooden match and striking it on the undertaker's coffin. All three men moved toward their guns at the snap and hiss. They were so drunk and dehydrated they couldn't stop laughing.

"You wouldn't light a Christian on fire, would ya?" the Last Man snickered.

The Preacher turned and flicked the match. It thumped against the Last Man's chest, and the other two held their breaths, expecting the detonation. There was a quick tongue of smoke and flame, then nothing. They giggled. Then a high-pitched crack and a hole in their friend's chest where the match was snuffed. He dropped.

The last two men on Main Street turned to face a Preacher who was now aiming his gun as if Preachers had always done this. They were momentarily distracted by the Preacher's pants sliding off the knobs of his hip bones, so the Preacher quickly fired one, two, three more shots, blowing off teeth, chins, ears, smirks. Heads erupted in black blood and dust, all three men crumpling like money in a fist. One slumped into a rocking chair on the porch.

His fire climbed the highest.

The Preacher pulled his smoking hat down to shield his eyes, then picked up three more guns to tuck into his belt. Now they held his pants up just fine.

***

Red stopped at the double doors on McKenna's barn and ripped the lock off its hinges with one bloody, thorn-covered hand. Flinging them open, he stepped inside as his gang ran past him to stand in the doorway, eyes smiling.

Five healthy horses snorted and stomped, damp buckets and troughs of feed lining each pen. Jackass, Egg, and Mud shoved each other to fight over the buckets, shaking and licking the last drips of moisture. Then the buckets fell from their hands when Red walked up to the nearest horse and drew his pistol. The gunshot inside the barn ruptured three eardrums.

The horse kicked a hole in the wall behind it, then collapsed. The rest of the animals screamed in panic as Red's gang ducked down and huddled against the walls in a panic.

Red moved to the next horse. Another shot echoed. It fell.

"Boss, don't!" Jackass said, arms wide. "We need 'em. It's two weeks of desert in either direction."

Another shot, and another horse crashed to the dirt, neck whiplashing in denial.

"See 'em drop?!" Red yelled. "That's what's supposed to happen when you shoot something in the goddamn head!"

Boom.

The fourth horse executed, he clicked on an empty chamber while aiming at the eye of the fifth. As he reloaded, Egg cautiously crept closer.

"Wait, wait," he said. "Please."

Red looked to Mud.

"Kill it," Mud said. "Why not?"

"Damn right," Red laughed. "Hell, I wish there was a goddamn unicorn in here so I could shoot that, too."

"A what?" asked Mud.

"Those ones with the wings," whispered Jackass. "He'd do it, too. Then barbecue the wings."

Red stepped forward to ruffle Mud's hair. About a third of it came out in his hand, fluttering to the ground like tinder. Then he cocked his pistol and moved it back to the fifth horse's eye.

He hesitated, taking a long look at the animal for the first time.

"Hey, is that . . . "

"That's the horse the Ranger rode in on," Egg said. "Black Mustang. Saw it from a distance."

"Well, fuck him, too."

"But both him and that deputy had Mustangs, boss."

"No," Mud pouted, worried the animal wouldn't get shot. "This ain't it. That Mustang was barely broke. And more blue than black. I saw it buck him off. This one's *more* than broke. Shit, it looks like it's holding its breath."

"Wouldn't you?" Red asked Mud, staring at it another ten, twenty, thirty seconds. Then he lowered his gun and stroked it, his thorny hand getting tangled in its mane. The horse was calm, eye locked on Red. It snorted mucus onto Red's chest, making him smile. He whispered in its ear as he led it out.

Mud took a bucket and walked over to position it under one of the dead horses' heads. Thick blood trickled from the wound, drips popping like hammer strikes through the barn and his ruined ears.

Outside, Red pulled the Mustang out and swung himself up onto its back. Mud climbed on and sat behind him, head resting lovingly on his shoulder, the bucket of blood rattling in his hand. Egg climbed on, too, squeezing behind Mud, almost hanging over the tail. The horse tolerated the weight and turned to look down at Jackass. Jackass just smiled and patted the horse's neck.

"Thanks, but I think I'll walk."

Right then, a lone gunshot in the distance.

"The hell was that?"

"Nothing," Red insisted, wrapping the reins around his fists. "Ain't nothing left around here to kill."

The horse trotted while Mud tipped the bucket back to drink. Coughing and gasping after a long draw of blood, Mud flashed a red-stained smile down at Jackass.

"Want some?" he asked.

"Got some," Jackass slurred, uncorking another bottle of whiskey.

Their third day without water, Red's gang turned to face the sun with no hope of catching it.

Behind them, the Preacher leaned against a dead tree covered in hearts to watch the strange, four-headed shadow on the horizon. He saw the wobbly shape of Jackass stumbling beside it. Jackass tipped his bottle high, then drunkenly wove his way further and further away from the sun and the horse.

Three more tips of the bottle and he was walking alone.

***

The Ranger stood in the doorway while McKenna restrained Bobby with an arm tight around his chest, struggling to keep him from going inside.

"How many?" McKenna asked, teary-eyed.

"Four," the Ranger sighed. "But mine's missing. Of all the damn horses to save . . . "

"You can't still hate that horse when it's the last one in the world."

"Sure can."

"But what about the man you came with?" McKenna pleaded, then to Bobby, "Stop it! You aren't going in there!"

"We can't wait for Tom," the Ranger said. "And we gotta' *ride* outta' here. You don't walk into a desert and back out."

"But we don't need to go anywhere," McKenna said. "Gray just filled those wells with sand. It was a trick to make people leave. We still got plenty of . . . "

They all turned to the tree line. It was Tom's horse, nose streaked with ribbons of red and black, walking slowly from the woods. And in spite of splinters in its muzzle, a beam of sunlight shining straight through Red's bullet hole in its skull like the ear of a gecko, and one eye glued by scabs, the Mustang seemed more alive than ever. The Ranger put out a hand, and it nuzzled him, nose rooting in the salt of his sweat.

"I've never seen that," McKenna said. "From either you or a horse."

They all climbed up. The dead horse barely noticed.

***

Three miles away, Red and his gang rode the second-to-last horse in the world in the opposite direction, passing a bucket of blood and thorns like it was a bottle of whiskey. An hour later, all three were dead before the Mustang stopped to take its first piss.

It shook them off like flies.

***

Night.

The Ranger, McKenna and Bobby were riding in silence, working through some brush. They came to a clearing, and the horse snorted as Jackass suddenly yanked himself free from a shrub and lurched into view. He walked out in front of them, weaving like a cattail in the breeze. The orange glow of the burning town filled the sky behind them.

"Does he hear us?" McKenna whispered.

"Does he *see* us?" Bobby whispered back.

An empty bottle slipped from the drunken man's hand, and he swerved to keep from tripping. Then he pulled two more bottles from his coat and worked on uncorking one with his last tooth.

"Doubt it," Jackass answered them over the cork.

The Ranger pulled his gun and lined it up with the back of Jackass's head. He cocked the hammer, then changed his mind, lowering it. He holstered his gun and looked around, noticing a nearby tangle of chicken wire next to a collapsed fence.

"Stay here," he told every living soul left in Agua Fría.

The Ranger dismounted, then took Jackass's gun before he could react, flinging it into the dark. He clapped him hard on the back, dust exploding like a bomb.

"Who the hell are you?" Jackass mumbled.

"The law," the Ranger said, pulling him close by the collar.

The word meant nothing to the man.

"You seen my deputy? Or his horse?"

"Did it have wings?" Jackass wondered quite sincerely.

"Been drinking?"

"Maybe."

"You know it's dangerous to drink and ride, right?"

"But I ain't on no horse."

"Yes, you are!" the Ranger barked. "Now step down off your animal and follow me."

"Okay," he swung a leg as if dismounting, tripped and fell.

The Ranger stepped back to scratch a long line in the dirt with his boot.

"If you ain't drunk, then walk that line."

"What?"

"Heel to toe. All the way."

Jackass looked down, then carefully planted his right foot. Then his left. He took one step, got tangled, and then he was back on the ground wondering how he got there.

"Who the hell are you?"

"Told you already," the Ranger said, pulling him up by the collar, gun under his chin. He led him to the chicken wire and shoved his face into the dirt. Then he dragged the wire until it formed a half-circle around them.

"You're gonna spend the night in jail. Sober up."

Jackass jumped back to his feet, hesitating at the edge of the makeshift chicken coop. In spite of the wire only reaching his knees, he was convinced he was locked inside some kind of cell, and he sat down again, slumped.

"You can't keep me in here. I'll be dead by yesterday!"

"It's the thirst. Makes him see things that ain't there," the Ranger explained, climbing back on his dead horse. They rode past Jackass still screaming in his chicken coop.

"Let me out, goddamnit!"

Jackass kept yelling until the dead horse disappeared in the dark, then he put his spinning head between his knees. About an hour later, he heard twigs snap and turned to face a shape approaching in the dark. He tried to stretch a grin across his teeth to seem friendly.

"Hey, did you bring a key?"

Jackass stopped grinning when the shadow got close

and its smile cracked to reveal more teeth than Jackass thought possible. The shadow got down on all fours and crept towards him like an animal that wanted to play, then it climbed in to share his invisible walls.

Jackass's expression twisted like a snake under a boot as recognition flooded his face. In his drunken daze, he saw a dog, snarling, steadying for a lunge. Then the dog ripped his scream out into the dust while it was still in his throat. It spoke.

"Sorry," it said. "I guess you didn't recognize me."

***

The Ranger, McKenna, and Bobby rode, the boy hanging over the tail, weak from the hammer of the desert sun. He strained to pull himself up as he noticed a dead animal in the wagon tracks behind them.

"What is it?" McKenna asked weakly.

"Nothing anymore," the Ranger said. "Things are gonna' have to learn to stay off our trails. Gonna' be more and more wheels every day."

"That'll be hard," McKenna muttered. "Animals usually want to take the same paths as men."

"One day, you'll see something like this every fifty feet," the Ranger nodded, then turned to tell Bobby without conviction, "Don't worry, boy, we're close. I swear."

"We're going in circles," Bobby said, staring at the skeleton, wondering how anyone could restrain a dog with only the collar of a priest.

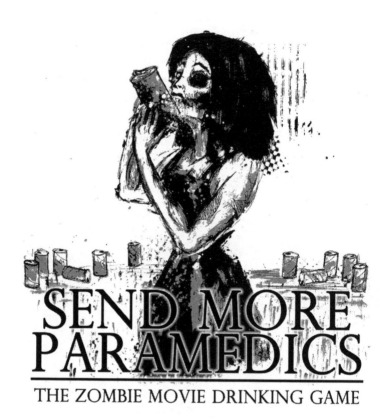

SEND MORE PARAMEDICS

THE ZOMBIE MOVIE DRINKING GAME

Stick in your favorite Zombie Movie and play along!

GAME A—THE LIVING DRINK . . .

- when the city of Pittsburgh, its streets, or any of its three rivers are referenced by name.
- when a newspaper, radio, internet, or television transmission reports on a zombie event.
- when a zombie is mistaken for a non-zombie human character or animal.
- when a paramedic, doctor, or other medical professional appears for the first time.
- when a character says 'zombie' or any other assigned designation for a zombie.
- when a farmhouse, mall, pub, or other normally innocuous structure is fortified against a zombie invasion.
- when a non-zombie character enters a basement, underground garage, sewer, tunnel, or cave.
- when a priest, rabbi, occult leader, or other religious practitioner appears for the first time.
- when a way to de-animate a zombie is theorized, explained, or revealed.
- when a character experiences a memory, hallucination, or dream.
- when a security guard, police officer, soldier, or other armed authority figure appears for the first time.
- when a sporting-goods store, armory, or personal firearms collection is raided for weapons.
- when a non-weapon item or homemade explosive is used is used to attack a zombie.
- when a character intentionally mimics, lures, distracts, or otherwise deceives a zombie.

- when a lone ethnic minority character appears for the first time.
- when a weapon malfunctions, lacks ammunition, or is otherwise inoperative.
- when an armed stand-off between non-zombie characters occurs.
- when a grocery store, vending machine, or trash bin is scavenged for food or drink.
- when a non-zombie character or animal kills another non-zombie character or animal.
- when any type of music or musical instrument is played for or by a zombie.
- when a non-zombie character must decide whether or not to de-animate a zombie companion.
- when a mentally or physically handicapped non-zombie character appears for the first time.
- when a character performs an amputation, autopsy, or other surgical procedure.
- when a diagram, scale model, or other replica of a brain appears for the first time.
- when a character demonstrates uncharacteristic cowardice or courage.
- when a bodily fluid drips, sprays, or splashes onto a non-zombie character.
- when a character is immune from or cured of the contagious effects of zombification.
- when a personal or transit vehicle is augmented with armor or weaponry.
- when an aircraft of watercraft is used as a means of escape.
- when a non-zombie character inhabits an island, desert, or other isolated natural environment.
- when the film's credits reveal the actual location as anything other than Pittsburgh, Pennsylvania.

GAME B—THE DEAD DRINK . . .

- when a zombie speaks any intelligible word for the first time or says 'brains' repeatedly.
- when a zombie escapes from a grave, tomb, or other internment location.
- when any biological, chemical, or radioactive waste is released into the environment.
- when the country of Haiti or its Vodou tradition is referenced by name.
- when a character enters a cemetery, crypt, mortuary, morgue, or place of worship
- when a zombie, revenant, or other animated corpse appears for the first time.
- when a prayer, séance, exorcism, or other spiritual communication occurs.
- when any hazardous-material-protection equipment is worn for the first time.
- when a priest, rabbi, occult leader, or other religious practitioner dies.
- when the origin of a zombie or group of zombies is theorized, explained, or revealed.
- when a zombie eats the brains or bowels of a character or animal.
- when a paramedic, doctor, or other medical professional dies.
- when a zombie breaks through a window, door, ceiling, floor, or Fourth Wall.
- when a zombie emerges from fog, water, or soil.
- when a character hides a zombie attack wound or zombie from another character.
- when a zombie's head is shot, stabbed, bludgeoned, or separated from the body.
- when a lone ethnic character is the first or last to die.

- when a zombie is burned, frozen, electrocuted, submerged, crushed, or obliterated.
- when a security guard, police officer, soldier, or other armed authority figure dies.
- when a zombie's disembodied head, limb, or organs is independently animate.
- when a mentally or physically handicapped non-zombie character dies.
- when a zombie wearing any civilian or military uniform appears for the first time.
- when a non-zombie character befriends, loves, kisses, or performs any sex act with a zombie.
- when a zombie performs a specific non-zombie recreation or profession.
- when any apocalyptic statement such as 'The end is nigh' is proclaimed or displayed.
- when a character commits suicide rather than being killed by or becoming a zombie.
- when child zombie or animal zombie appears for the first time.
- when a zombie demonstrates the ability to hear, smell, taste, dream, reason, or dance.
- when a human body is cannibalized or otherwise utilized for nutritional supplement by a zombie or non-zombie character.
- when a zombie engages in a conflict with a plant, animal, or other zombie.
- when a nuclear device is detonated or a wide-scale containment protocol is enacted.

GAME C—THE UNDEAD
TO PLAY GAME C, COMBINE BOTH
GAMES A AND B*

(*DO NOT EVER DO THIS)

BONUS ROUND!

- stick your finger down your throat if, during any life-threatening situation, a non-zombie character begins to walk or a zombie begins to run.

Original brainstorm (brainstorm? delicious!)
copyright © Nathan Lamoreau (recreational drinker, prospector, skull collector, apocalypse connoisseur), 2011

*send more paramedics if the game lasts longer than the movie

WELL, SIR, IT WOULD BE GOOD NEWS
EXCEPT THAT THE EGGS HAVE HATCHED.
—COLONEL GLOVER
5:01 A.M. EASTERN DAYLIGHT TIME

ACKNOWLEDGEMENTS

Thanks to the original Team Zee Bee & Bee, the first proprietors of our doomed zombie bed & breakfast before it all burned down; Nathan Lamoreau, David Tallerman, D.W. Stripp, and Cheryl Mullenax. Special thanks to Nate and his ever-evolving Drinking Game, which he modifies at least once a year when he crawls up from his spider hole. Thanks to Stephen Graham Jones for his *History of Zombies in Ten Minutes* (you can find it on YouTube), George Cotronis and Dyer Wilk, for their beautiful art, and Max and Lori, for all their hard work on this book. And finally, thanks as always to my wife, Amy, the inventor of Zingo and the only person to order steaks bloodier than myself, who I met in Pittsburgh, the zombie capital of the world, and who is also the one person I've vowed to devour if she dies before I do. This is way less threatening than it sounds. Oh, and a shout to all the horrorphiles out there weathering the current storm of zombie scorn and over-saturation, confident the true undead will easily outlast all the milquetoast, mainstream bullshit.

IF YOU ENJOYED *STEALING PROPELLER HATS FROM THE DEAD*, DON'T PASS UP ON THESE OTHER TITLES FROM PERPETUAL MOTION MACHINE . . .

VAMPIRE STRIPPERS FROM SATURN
BY VINCENZO BILOF

ISBN: 978-0-9860594-8-3

Page count: 210

$12.95

Time is infinite, and so are strippers.

The beautiful and sultry Rene leads her trio of vampire strippers from (around) Saturn to destroy Earth. Their demonic foes-the plots-have hunted them across time; Earth is the last remaining planet with sentient life in this version of the universe. Rene's love affair with a man who is half-horse, half-boy in a future version of Earth threatens her desire to inspire the apocalypse; if the vampire strippers fail to destroy the world now, men will be nearly extinct, and women will be hunted for sport by the surviving males.

True love, time travel, bad music, shapeshifting plots, and a brooding supernatural detective named Will decide the fate of Earth in more than two realities. Can Rene prevent an apathetic future while allowing Earth to survive?

Time travel, it turns out, really isn't all that complicated, and neither are women.

DEAD MEN
LIBROS DE INFERNO: BOOK 1
BY JOHN C. FOSTER
ISBN: 978-0-9860594-7-6
Page count: 372
$14.95

Roaring south in a black Cadillac, John Smith is on the road trip from Hell through a nightmarish version of Americana, a place of rotting hollows and dusty crossroads, slaughterhouses and haunted trains. He doesn't know how he woke up after sitting down in the electric chair, where he got the black suit with the slit up the back or even the cigarettes in his pocket. All he knows is that there is a woman guarding a great secret and he's supposed to kill her.

"Frankly, I haven't been this impressed with an authorial debut since Clive Barker's Books of Blood. And no, that isn't hyperbole. John C. Foster really is that good."—Joe McKinney, Bram Stoker Award Winning Author of Dead City

SIRENS
BY KURT REICHENBAUGH

ISBN: 978-0-9887488-3-5

Page count: 286

$14.95

Just another Saturday night, sometime in the middle of that decade we call the 70s, when Disco was queen and shows like Charlie's Angels and Happy Days reigned on television. But there are no angels, happy days or dancing queens for four bored friends, Kevin, Brad, Nick and Otto, who go looking for action on a sweltering Saturday night and instead get themselves involved in murder. A murder that spins them into a twisted web of vengeful rednecks, psychotic cheerleaders, a missing flying saucer, a hybrid creature on four legs, a sadistic ghoul or two, and one lethal bad-ass babe in a leopard-skin bikini who just might give our friends more action then they'd ever dreamed of. Take a sweltering mix of swamp noir, drive-in grind house, sex and rock n' roll seventies style, and you've got what SIRENS is all about.

The Perpetual Motion Machine Catalog

Another Happy Ending | E.E. King | Story Collection
Page count: 310 | Paperback: $14.95
ISBN: 978-0-9887488-9-7

Bleed | Various Authors | Anthology
Page count: 286 | Paperback: $16.95
ISBN: 978-0-9887488-8-0

Cruel | Eli Wilde | Novel
Page count: 192 | Paperback: $9.95
ISBN: 978-0-9887488-0-4

Dead Men | John Foster | Novel
Page Count: 360 | Paperback: $14.95
ISBN: 978-0-9860594-7-6

Four Days | Eli Wilde & 'Anna DeVine | Novel
Page count: 198 | Paperback: $9.95
ISBN: 978-0-9887488-5-9

Gory Hole | Craig Wallwork | Story Collection (Full-Color Illustrations)
Page count: 48 | Paperback: $12.95
ISBN: 978-0-9860594-3-8

The Green Kangaroos | Jessica McHugh | Novel
Page count: 184 | Paperback $12.95
ISBN: 978-0-9860594-6-9

Last Dance in Phoenix | Kurt Reichenbaugh | Novel
Page count: 268 | Paperback: $12.95 |
ISBN: 978-0-9860594-9-0

Long Distance Drunks: a Tribute to Charles Bukowski
    Various Authors | Anthology
    Page count: 182 | Paperback: $12.95
    ISBN: 978-0-9860594-4-5

The Perpetual Motion Club | Sue Lange | Novel
    Page count: 208 | Paperback $14.95
    ISBN: 978-0-9887488-6-6

The Ritalin Orgy | Matthew Dexter | Novel
    Page count: 206 | Paperback $12.95
    ISBN: 978-0-9887488-1-1

Sirens | Kurt Reichenbaugh | Novel
    Page count: 286 | Paperback: $14.95
    ISBN: 978-0-9887488-3-5

So it Goes: a Tribute to Kurt Vonnegut | Various Authors
    Anthology
    Page count: 282 | Paperback $14.95
    ISBN: 978-0-9887488-2-8

Tales from the Holy Land | Rafael Alvarez | Story Collection
    Page count: 226 | Paperback $12.95
    ISBN: 978-0-9860594-0-7

The Tears of Isis | James Dorr | Story Collection
    Page count: 206 | Paperback: $12.95
    ISBN: 978-0-9887488-4-2

Time Eaters | Jay Wilburn | Novel
    Page count: 218 | Paperback: $12.95
    ISBN: 978-0-9887488-7-3

Vampire Strippers from Saturn | Vincenzo Bilof | Novel
    Page count: 210 | Paperback: $12.95
    ISBN: 978-0-9860594-8-3

Forthcoming Titles:

Website:
www.PerpetualPublishing.com

Facebook:
www.facebook.com/PerpetualPublishing

Twitter:
@PMMPublishing

Newsletter:
www.PMMPNews.com

Email Us:
Contact@PerpetualPublishing.com

Made in the USA
Middletown, DE
19 November 2015